# Under the Shadow of a Steeple

# Under the Shadow of a Steeple

**A Novel**
**By Carol Kinsey**

## Under the Shadow of a steeple

Published by Breautumnwood Publishing

This is a work of fiction. Names, character, places, and incidents either are the product of the author's imagination or are used fictitiously. Any resemblance to actual persons, either living or dead, events, or locales is entirely coincidental.

First Printing – June 2013

ISBN-13: 978-1490454283
ISBN-10: 1490454284

Cover created by Carol Kinsey
Special thanks to Lacey, Kendra, Bryce and Ashton Cromwell

Edited by Rachael Woodall

Coming Soon
from author Carol Kinsey

Two new books:

*Special Ops and the Grace of God*

*Until Proven Innocent*

# Dedication

To Von, Autumn and Breanna. Thank you for believing in me.
I love you.

To my Lord Jesus Christ. May You be glorified.

Thank you, Meghan, for inspiring me to start publishing my books.

"Whatever you do, do your work heartily, as for the Lord rather than for men, knowing that from the Lord you will receive the reward of the inheritance. It is the Lord Christ Whom you serve."

Colossians 3:23-24

# Chapter 1

*Something's got to change.*

It was with a mixture of anger and gloom that Hailey Goodman sat at the top of the dirty, carpeted stairs listening to her foster parents scold her little brother, Grant.

She brushed a long brown hair behind her ear and closed her eyes to ward off a stress headache.

*Don't cry over spilled milk.* She could still hear her grandmother say years ago while the dear old woman was still alive. *But that's not the policy in this house.*

Hailey wished she could just run and hide. Pretend none of this was real. Pretend her grandma was still alive and that she and her two younger brothers weren't part of the foster care system. But she couldn't… and the terrible truth was in three years she'd be eighteen and most likely lose what little control she had in the lives of her brothers. She would be out of the system and her brothers would still be in.

"You're an idiot!" Keith Prescott yelled in a tone that must have reached at least three houses up the road. "If you're too stupid to use a regular cup then you need to start using a Sippy cup like a two year old." Hailey heard her foster parent storm off to another room.

"Hailey!"

She knew what was about to follow. It would be her responsibility to clean up whatever mess her brother made.

Without a word, Hailey pulled her slender form to her feet and walked slowly down the stairs, ready to meet her brother's sad, withdrawn blue eyes that never seemed to shed tears, and Tara's biting tongue which was sure to thrust more insults upon Grant and twice as many on herself.

Keith and Tara Prescott weren't Hailey's first foster parents. But they were by far the worst.

"You need to clean up this mess," Tara spat as soon as Hailey appeared in the doorway to the kitchen. "This is the second time in the past week that your little brother knocked over his cup. This has to stop. I'm not paying for food for you kids if you're going to turn around and waste it!"

Wordlessly, Hailey found the kitchen sponge and began mopping up her brother's spill. Good thing it was milk this time. Milk was a lot easier to clean up than fruit punch.

She glanced up at Grant who was still standing in the middle of the kitchen holding his empty cup. His face was red and in his blue eyes she could read the sorrow of a thousand hurtful words, but his face was dry.

*He's the bravest seven-year-old I've ever seen.*

Hailey tried to give him a sympathetic smile, but Grant's eyes were somewhere else. Maybe at Grandma's house... But could he remember Grandma? He was only three when she died.

"Make sure you get under the table real good," Tara micromanaged Hailey's work. "I don't want nothing sticky under the table. Keith said we need to get that child a Sippy cup." Tara moved one of the chairs so Hailey could get under the table. "Between Grant's clumsiness and Hayden wetting his bed every night, you kids are like having a family of toddlers."

Hailey wanted to tell Tara that maybe she and Keith should just send them away if she felt that way, but Hailey was too afraid of the hostile woman's biting tongue. Tara had a way of making Hailey feel small, both physically and emotionally.

A moment later, Hailey saw her brother Hayden standing in the doorway, his face as red as his hair. He'd heard Tara's insults and was seething.

Tara's insensitivity to Hayden's bedwetting problem was more than the ten-year-old boy could take. Hailey knew Hayden tried not to wet his bed, and in spite of Tara's cruel words, he didn't wet every night. But it hurt him that he wet at all and hurt even more that Tara made an issue of it.

"And don't you come in here giving me an attitude!" Tara shot down any idea Hayden had of defending himself. "Get your brother cleaned up."

"But I still want a drink," Grant's soft voice squeaked out and he held up his empty cup.

"Well you can wait until tomorrow morning then, because your drink is all over the floor."

Hayden grabbed his brother's hand and led him around the wet floor to the stairs. "Come on. Let's go."

"You boys just get into your pajamas now," Tara called to them. "It's almost bed time and I've had about all of you that I can handle for the night. Don't forget your diaper, Hayden."

Tara's last words stung the most. Hailey wanted to throw the wet sponge at the insensitive woman's face. Hayden hated when Tara called his night pants 'diapers.'

*Why does she even do foster care if she hates children this much?*

Hailey cleaned up the mess without another word and slipped quietly from the kitchen to her brothers' bedroom on the second floor. Both Hayden and Grant were already in bed but neither of them were asleep.

"Did you boys brush your teeth?" She sat at the edge of Grant's bed and smoothed a stray golden hair from his eyes.

Grant nodded, still doing his best to hold his emotions inside.

Hailey kissed the top of his curly, blonde head and placed a gentle hand on his face. "You're not stupid, Grant."

The hurting child lowered his eyes.

"But Tara is," Hayden spat.

Hayden never used to be so full of anger. He used to be a laid back, happy-go-lucky, middle child. It saddened Hailey to see her little brother so full of hostility.

"Did you boys pray?" Hailey didn't have enough energy to correct her brother at that moment.

"What good is praying?" Hayden pulled a ragged gray blanket over his head and mumbled a few words Hailey couldn't understand.

Hailey slipped over to Hayden's bed and pulled the blanket away from his face. "Don't give up praying, Hayden." She tried to keep her emotions in check. "Grandma always said when we don't feel like praying that's usually when we need to pray the most."

"Fine, then you pray!" Hayden kicked his blankets off. "I'm done with God."

*Done with God?* Hailey lowered her soft brown eyes and wondered how to deal with this. Her grandma always told Hailey that if she and her brothers never learned anything else in life she wanted them to learn to love God. What would Grandma think now?

"Please don't blame God," Hailey tried to fix her brother's blankets. "We've got to keep praying. We promised Grandma."

"You promised Grandma!" Hayden spat. "I hardly remember her."

Hayden rolled over and pulled the pillow over his head. Hailey thought he was fighting tears.

"I'll pray with you," Grant said in his sweet little boy voice.

Hailey knelt beside Grant's bed and asked God to bless each one of them.

"And please help Tara and Keith be nice," Grant added before Hailey said amen.

Hailey tussled the hair on his head and kissed him goodnight. It would be all the tucking in her brothers would receive. Tara never came upstairs at night. She and Keith stayed in their master bedroom on the first floor watching television from eight o'clock until eleven every evening.

"Goodnight, Hayden," she whispered to her brother before turning out the light.

Hayden didn't answer.

*** 

"I think I'd have to agree with your brother."

Hailey closed her bedroom door and glanced toward the top bunk. The foster child Hailey shared a room with sat on the bunk with a scowl.

Twelve-year-old Kyra Washington was a spunky little African American girl who Hailey met when they moved into the Prescott's' house almost a year ago. It was Kyra's unfortunate lot

4

in life to have lived with the Prescott's for over two years and she'd learned to keep away from the sharp-tongued foster parents whose only service to her was a roof over her head and something that resembled food.

Kyra set down the homework she'd been doing and let out a heavy sigh. "If there is a God, then I'm not sure I ever want to talk to Him anyway."

Hailey kicked off her shoes and pulled a pair of pajama pants out of her drawer. How could she explain it? Her grandma used to tell Hailey that God didn't want bad things to happen, but Hailey herself didn't really understand why He let them.

"We can't blame God for how mean Tara and Keith are." Hailey did her best to stick up for God.

"Well then why don't you ask God to smash them like a couple of big fat flies and we'll all be better off." Kyra pulled a sheet of notebook paper out of her folder. "Did you get your homework done?" She changed the subject.

Hailey glanced at the clock and let out a heavy sigh. "No. Great way to start out a new year, isn't it?" She pulled her backpack onto the bed and dug through it to see what all she had to have done for the morning.

This was her freshman year and Hailey knew she couldn't afford to let herself fall behind. But Tara and Keith seemed more concerned with how quiet and trouble free the children were than with how well they were doing in school.

"I'm supposed to have read the first two chapters of *The Scarlet Letter* for tomorrow," Hailey leaned back in her bed and shoved her long brown hair away from her face. "Mr. Adams is giving us a quiz."

Kyra lay on her stomach and looked over the bunk bed at Hailey. "Did you read it?"

"I don't even have the book," Hailey rolled her eyes and shook her head while a moan escaped her lips.

Kyra raised her eyebrows and climbed down from the bed.

Their room was small and extremely cluttered, which went against everything Hailey wanted in her life. But with only two small dressers, and a bunk bed, the girls hardly had enough furniture to keep their lives organized.

"What are you looking for?" Hailey watched Kyra crawl into their messy closet and dig through a box underneath their shoe rack.

"This." Kyra held up a little red paperback triumphantly.

"*The Scarlet Letter?*" Hailey's eyes grew wide and she reached for the book. "Where did you get this?"

Kyra did a sassy little dance and climbed back into her bed. "I got it at a yard sale this summer."

"Did you read it?"

"Of course I read it!" Kyra said offended. She leaned back over the bed. "If you need any help, just ask."

Hailey knew that Kyra was a "brain" but it amazed her that this little seventh grader polished off a ninth grade English required reading just for leisure.

"How was it?" Hailey asked.

Kyra shrugged. "It was okay. They all talk in old English, but it's a pretty clever story."

Hailey smiled endearingly at Kyra. "Thanks. You may have just totally saved my high school career."

"The fate of a gorgeous high school freshman girl lies in the hands of a scrawny little seventh grader…" Kyra tried to sound creepy.

"Oh stop," Hailey reached up and grabbed one of Kyra's thick little black braids. "And I'm not gorgeous."

"Whatever." Kyra sat up in her bed and giggled.

Hailey leaned back with her book and crossed her legs on the bed. "But thanks."

# Chapter 2

Wednesday morning met Hailey with a thunderstorm, both inside and out. She'd stayed up half the night reading her two chapters and fell asleep with the light on. It seemed her fate that morning that Tara would decide to come upstairs to make sure the windows were all closed only to find the light on and Hailey asleep.

"So your brother wastes milk and you waste electricity," Tara pulled Hailey's blanket off of her and practically yanked her out of bed. "Did you have this light on all night?"

Hailey did her best to blink off the fog of early morning and form her reply. "I… I was doing my homework."

"You call this homework?" Tara snatched the book off Hailey's bed and flung it carelessly across the floor. "Reading little romance novels?"

Kyra sat up and tried to see if her garage sale treasure was damaged in flight.

"It's for my English Lit class… I'm so sorry. I…"

"Just get out of this bed and go wash your brother's sheets." Tara didn't let Hailey finish. "His room smells like pee again. I told him to wear his diaper."

Hailey heard a shoe hit the wall from the other room and knew her brother heard Tara's remark.

"Don't you go tearing up that bedroom!" Tara stormed out of Hailey's room and into the boys' room. "If you don't stop peeing in that bed I'm going to start making you sleep in the bathtub! Now you get up and don't you go throwing shoes at the wall you stupid little bedwetter!"

Kyra glanced at Hailey and shook her head. "That lady is psycho," she whispered.

Hailey went to her brother's room and helped Hayden strip his bed while Tara went downstairs still ranting about the smell of pee and how Hayden would be paying for a new mattress.

"I wore my stupid diaper," Hayden spat. "It just leaked that's all… cause she only buys the cheap ones."

Hailey tossed the wet sheets carelessly on the floor. "Hayden," she placed her hands lovingly on her brother's shoulders.

"Don't touch me," Hayden shrugged her away.

Hailey swallowed back the lump in her throat and carried her brother's bedding to the washing machine. *What a way to start a day.*

\*\*\*

By the time Hailey got the wash started and her brothers both up and dressed, she knew she'd never get a shower and make it in time for the bus. With a quick brush of her hair and only a second to look in the mirror, Hailey headed out into the rain to meet the rest of her day. She hoped her brothers would be okay as they went off to the elementary school after such a traumatic wake up.

Since Hailey's stop was one of the first and everyone was half asleep in the morning, it was quiet on the bus. Hailey leaned her head against the cold window and watched the rain hit the wet sidewalk. It was still pretty warm for October in Cleveland, but Hailey was too preoccupied to care about the weather. Something had to change.

Tara's constant yelling, her daily insults and belittling of the boys and even Hailey, was more than the fifteen year old could take. Every day the children walked on eggshells, uncertain if they were going to upset their foster parents or walk into an argument between the quarreling couple.

Hailey sighed and watched as the bus drew closer to the school.

The hallways of Central High School were alive with students and Hailey made her way through the crowd with her head bent low. Even though Hailey began attending Central School district when she first moved in with the Prescott's a year ago, she still felt like an outsider.

Hailey was an introvert. At least that's what the school psychologist told her last year. He said that being an introvert wasn't a bad thing. Some of the greatest discoveries, most famous novels, and profound works of art were done at the hand of introverts.

It suited Hailey fine to finally have a name for why she preferred small groups to large crowds and why she saw no point in trying to run after the 'in' people. Until that school psychologist helped her understand herself a little bit better, Hailey believed Tara's cruel assessment that she was shy and backwards.

"Introverts aren't shy," Hailey remembered Mr. Roberts saying. "They're just simply content with their own thoughts."

Hailey liked Mr. Roberts. She wished he were the high school counselor too.

"Just remember," he told her. "Introverts make the very best kind of friends. They are deep and thoughtful and when a person is lucky enough to gain the trust and respect of an introvert, that person has made a loyal friend for life."

Hailey grinned to herself as she relived his words. Somehow Mr. Roberts helped Hailey see her quiet personality as something special and unique; something that others could only hope for.

*But if only I could meet one of those kind of people… someone who could be a friend for life.*

Hailey closed her locker and carried her worn out, overstuffed backpack to her first class of the day, praying she'd remember the details of those first two chapters of *The Scarlet Letter.*

\*\*\*

"That child is sleeping in the tub tonight." Tara met Hailey at the door and thrust her brother's clean bedding into her arms before she could set her book bag down. "Keith already took Hayden's mattress to the dumpster, I'm tired of this house smelling like a urinal."

9

Hailey attempted to gather her composure. Surely, Tara was overreacting. Hailey set down her backpack and got a better grip on her brother's sheets and blankets. "Do you need me to make his bed?"

"I told you, Keith took the mattress to the dumpster. It smelled like a sewer." Tara moved Hailey's backpack to the stairs. "When we took you all in no one told us that brother of yours was a bed wetter."

"It was never this bad before," Hailey tried to explain.

"Well it needs to stop or I'll be seeing about finding another placement for him."

Hailey narrowed her eyes. What did Tara mean? She wouldn't try to separate their family, would she?

"Don't get yourself all in a hissy," Tara turned and started to walk to the kitchen. "Keith said we'd buy an air mattress and cover it with a plastic sheet. But tonight I want to teach him a lesson." She stopped and turned to Hailey. "He's sleeping in the bathtub."

Hailey just stared. Was Tara serious? What did she hope to accomplish? Hayden was already full of anger and rage – what would this kind of humiliation do to him?

"Go take his sheets up there. I'm getting dinner ready."

There was no way Hailey was going to make up a bed for her brother in the bathtub. She grabbed her backpack and did her best to carry everything upstairs.

Sitting on the edge of her bed, Hailey buried her face in her hands. *What am I going to do?*

\*\*\*

Hayden and Grant's talking pulled Hailey from her studying. She saw them walk past her bedroom door to their own room and heard them both grow silent.

"Keith threw out your mattress," Hailey said. She stood behind her brothers and looked at the old metal bedframe where Hayden's mattress once lay.

"Where am I going to sleep?"

"You can sleep with me tonight," Hailey leaned against the doorframe. "Or with Grant."

10

Hayden threw his books on the floor and sat on the edge of the frame. Hailey could tell he was struggling with his emotions.

A few minutes later, Tara called the children to the kitchen for dinner.

"Where is Kyra?" Tara set plates on the table for Hailey to arrange.

Hailey wasn't sure. She figured Kyra must have stayed after school for something but believed Tara would have known that.

Keith sat down and put a scoop of mashed potatoes on his plate. "You mean she's not home yet?"

"No." Tara scooped a spoonful of potatoes out for both boys and motioned for Hailey to take some.

Hailey wished there was a way to decline. It was no secret that Tara made her mashed potatoes from a box and Hailey could think of nothing worse just then.

The front door opened and Kyra burst through excitedly. "I made it! I got the part!" she exclaimed before anyone could ask where she was. There was a sparkle in her huge dark eyes and her face glowed with enthusiasm. "I got the part!"

The beam on Kyra's face was enough to make a rational person happy, but Tara's eyes flashed with something beyond hostile and Hailey wished there were some way to warn Kyra before whatever excited dream she was about to share was pulverized before their eyes.

"Where have you been, young lady?" Tara grabbed Kyra by the arm and shook her.

Kyra's excitement waned and her excited expression changed to concern. "Today was auditions for the play. I told you last week…"

"You go to your room this instant!" Tara turned Kyra around and shoved her toward the hallway. "There will be no play for you! It's after five o'clock. You should have gotten our permission to stay after school."

"But I told you…" Kyra did her best to explain.

"You don't *tell* me anything. You *ask*! And I'm saying, 'No!'" Tara glanced at Keith for his support.

"We don't have time in our schedules to go adding a school play into the mix." Keith added. "You're grounded. You can go to bed without your supper tonight."

Kyra's dark eyes filled up with pools of tears. Hailey had to look away to keep herself from crying. Whatever this play was, it obviously meant something to Kyra. How could they do this to her?

"But I got the lead part! I've been practicing for this all last week. You can't do this to me!"

Keith rose to his full height of six foot two and glared down on Kyra's slim dark form. "Don't you sass me, you little brat. There will be no play."

Kyra threw her backpack across the kitchen floor and ran to her bedroom.

Hayden and Grant quietly ate their dinners, obviously hoping to slip away unscathed from Tara and Keith's wrath.

Tara's eyes shifted from the backpack to her husband as if uncertain what to do about Kyra's outburst.

"After dinner you can take Kyra her backpack," Keith said to Hailey. "And tell her that her little tantrum has only made things worse. She needs to clean up the dishes tonight as well."

Hailey picked through the flakes in her potatoes and the clumps of meat in her meatloaf wishing there was some way to escape. This was no way to live.

*** 

Kyra lay in her bed crying bitter tears when Hailey walked into their room. How could she tell this hurting girl that she had to go do the dishes for the dinner she didn't eat, for the foster parents who weren't going to let her be in the play? This was insanity.

Hailey placed a gentle hand on Kyra's smooth brown arm. Kyra was so pretty. Hailey felt a kind of sympathy for the younger girl tonight that she'd not felt for her before. "Keith said you have to do the dishes," Hailey said.

Kyra responded with some choice words that Hailey hoped her little brothers didn't hear.

"I'm sorry," Hailey touched Kyra's head. "I wish there was a way I could do the dishes for you, but Tara and Keith…"

"I hate them!" Kyra sat up and stared at the dark window. "I'll break every dish they own just to show them how horrible they are."

It sounded reasonable, but Hailey knew it would be wrong. "You can't do that, Kyra. They'll make it even worse for you then."

"There is nothing worse. They're taking away the one thing I wanted most this year." She turned her tearstained face toward Hailey. "I got the part," her voice was soft.

"I'm not surprised." Hailey climbed up onto Kyra's bed next to her and let her feet hang down. "You're very talented."

Kyra sat staring at the window.

"Look. You go do the dishes tonight," Hailey suggested. "Be on your best behavior and I will do everything I can to talk Tara into letting you be in the play. Even if that means cleaning up her messy kitchen every night for a month."

"You'd do that for me?" Kyra studied Hailey's face for a moment.

Hailey smiled. "Hey, you saved me from failing English Lit. I aced that test by the way."

Impulsively, Kyra reached her arms around Hailey and hugged her. It was the first time Kyra ever hugged her. Hailey returned the hug and wondered if this was what it felt like to have a sister.

***

Hailey breathed a sigh of relief when Kyra returned to their bedroom forty-five minutes later to announce that the dishes were done and without any eruptions.

The house had quieted down and Hailey hoped the rest of the night would be incident free.

After a quick shower, Hailey got her brothers ready for bed and was about to tuck them both into Grant's bed when she heard Tara's footsteps climbing the stairs.

"No, absolutely not," Tara said tersely. "This is not going to work. I'll not have that boy ruin another bed in my house. I told you, he's sleeping in the bathtub tonight."

Hayden's eyes flashed angrily. "I'm not sleeping in the bathtub."

"Oh yes you are," Tara marched into the room and grabbed Hayden's arm. "Then you can just pee all night long and let it go down the drain."

Hayden attempted to pull his arm free.

Tara glared at Hailey. "I told you to take his blankets to the bathroom. Why did you disobey me?"

"Tara," Hailey said. "I don't think the bathtub is a good idea."

"This is not your decision."

Keith appeared in the doorway moments later and ordered Hayden to the bathroom.

"No!" Hayden ran to the corner and clutched the side of his brother's bed. "I won't pee! I promise!" His pleading cry was so pathetic that Hailey wanted to run to him and hold him.

Tara had no sympathy. "You've ruined a mattress! I've never had any foster kid ruin a mattress. You're sleeping in the tub tonight so I can burn it into your mind that your bedwetting has to stop!"

Keith grabbed Hayden's arm and began dragging him down the hallway kicking and screaming.

"Don't let them hurt Hayden." Grant ran into Hailey's arms. His eyes were wide with fear, but no tears came.

"Grant, you get into your bed!" Tara scolded.

Still clutching Hailey, Grant's whole body trembled. "I want to sleep with Hailey."

Tara stopped in front of Hailey. "I hold you responsible for this tirade. You were told what to do when you got home. If you'd have gotten his bed ready and told him he'd be sleeping in there tonight he wouldn't be acting like this."

Hailey's own blood was beginning to boil. Hayden's screaming and yelling could be heard down the hall. Grant was terrified. This was unbelievable. "You're wrong! Hayden doesn't mean to wet his bed. I'm calling our social worker and telling her that you're trying to make Hayden sleep in the bathtub!" Hailey knew her words would be a challenge to Tara.

Tara stormed into the hallway and brought Hailey the cordless phone. "You go right ahead. Maybe they'll find another home for that little bed wetter. But mark my words – it's not everyone who's going to keep you three together."

Clutching the phone angrily in her hands, Hailey wanted to scream. Never before had a foster parent driven her to such anger. Tara turned to walk away and Hailey raised the phone to throw it at her.

Tara turned around just as the phone was in flight and it hit her square in the cheekbone.

Before Tara could even scream, Hailey was by her side apologizing.

"You hit me!" Tara's eye's flashed angrily.

"I didn't mean to… I'm so sorry…"

Keith's heavy footsteps marched down the hall. "What did she do to you?" He moved his wife's hand away from her face to see the red welt appearing below her eye.

Hailey trembled with fear. "I'm so sorry…"

"We'll be the ones calling the social worker," Tara spat. "There is no place for a violent foster kid in this house."

Keith picked the phone up from the floor. The back had broken off and the battery was hanging out. "She broke the phone on your face."

"I told you we should never have gotten a kid this old." Tara ran her fingers over the welt. "She needs to be in a juvenile detention center."

Fear crept down Hailey's spine. *Not juvie…* "I didn't mean to. I was just upset."

"You're nothing but rebellious trash! Go to your room." Keith stood glaring down at her. He pulled Grant from her side and motioned for the young boy to go to his own room. "I don't want to see your face the rest of this night."

Trembling, Hailey threw herself on her bed and heard the door slam behind her.

\*\*\*

Hailey had a terrible night. Even Kyra's comforting hand on her back didn't take away any of the pain.

They wanted to separate her family. *Oh, God… why is this happening?* She lifted up a quiet prayer.

15

Sleep wouldn't come. In the wee hours of the night, Hailey sat on the floor by her bed and tried to clear her head of this craziness.

It was never like this when they lived with Grandma. She wouldn't have tried to make Hayden sleep in a bathtub. She wouldn't have called him a bed wetter and told him to put on his diaper. Grandma was sweet and kind. *Why did Grandma have to die?*

Hailey stood up and walked to her window. The rain had stopped, but the storm inside hadn't. She watched the streetlight flicker outside and wondered when the weather was finally going to grow cold.

*Are they really going to send me away? Are they really going to try to find another home for Hayden?* Hailey couldn't imagine what it would do to Grant if his brother and sister were suddenly stripped away from him. What would it do to any of them?

Hayden acted like he was too tough to care, but Hailey knew he did.

*Grandma wanted us to be together.* Something had to change… quickly. Hailey sat back down on her bed and began to plan.

\*\*\*

At five a.m. Hailey woke Kyra. "I need to talk."

Kyra tried to open one eye and saw how dark it was outside. "What time is it?"

"Five."

"Go back to sleep." Kyra pulled her blanket over her head and started to roll over.

"No. I need to talk." Hailey pulled Kyra's blanket away. "It's important."

Because Hailey was not in the habit of waking Kyra at five a.m., Hailey hoped Kyra would understand this was serious.

Kyra rubbed her eyes and climbed down from her bunk, taking a seat next to Hailey on the lower bunk. "Okay. What?"

"We're running away."

Kyra blinked a few times and stared curiously at Hailey. "Say that again because I thought you just said you're running away."

"That's what I said. I'm taking the boys." Hailey licked her lips. "But I want you to come too."

A heavy sigh escaped Kyra's lips. "Do you know how much trouble we'd get into if we ran away?"

"For me it wouldn't be any worse." Tara's words about the juvenile detention center stuck in her head. "But I guess it could be for you…"

Kyra smoothed her thick black hair and adjusted one of her braids. "There's not much worse than this place."

Hailey nodded. "I really think my plan could work." Her eyes pleaded. She really wanted Kyra to go with them.

"Tell me the plan," Kyra glanced up quickly, scanning the room as if she suspected Tara to be eavesdropping somewhere.

"I know the perfect place." Light from the streetlamp outside glistened in Hailey's eyes. "My grandma's old church."

"Church people aren't going to hide us… they'll turn us in just like…"

"Not the people." Hailey interrupted. "The place. It's perfect. We were there every Sunday morning and evening, every Wednesday night, and then a couple other days a week for my grandma's Bible study and other activities she was in. I know every inch of the place."

Kyra didn't look convinced. "A building doesn't help us much when we're hungry."

"That's just it. This place has everything!" Hailey turned excited eyes onto Kyra. "There's a full kitchen and it's always loaded with food. The church serves dinner on Wednesday's for Family Night. I remember because my grandma helped make the meals. There was always stuff left over and people nibbled on it throughout the week."

The sounds of someone walking around downstairs made them both soften their voices.

"But best of all, it has the coolest hiding place in the world right under the stage in the sanctuary. I was thinking we could hide under the stage during the day and sleep or do schoolwork, or whatever."

17

"School?" Kyra interrupted. "How would we do schoolwork?"

"We'll be home schooled… or church schooled really." A grin spread across Hailey's lips. "You and I can teach the boys and we'll just work really hard on our own education to make sure we're still learning."

Hailey figured Kyra could help motivate them all to learn. She loved learning more than anyone Hailey knew.

"Then in the evenings," Hailey continued. "We can come out of hiding. If the church has activities, we'll attend them. If not, we'll have full reign of the whole building all night long!"

"What if someone recognizes you?" Kyra whispered. "I mean… you used to go there."

"I was ten the last time I was there… I don't look anything like I did back then."

Kyra chewed on her lip. "How would we get there?"

"I've thought it all through," Hailey said. "Today's Thursday, I'll skip school and go buy bus tickets, stash a few of our things in a locker at the bus station and come on home. I'll clean the house for Tara so when she gets home from work and finds out I skipped school, so she won't have a hissy." Hailey hoped Kyra was following the plan.

"Then tomorrow, I'll leave for school at the normal time and wait for you down behind Parker's warehouse. The boys walk to school, so they'll be easy. We'll meet them along their normal route and then head to the bus station."

"So when the news gets out that three white kids and a black girl have run away we'll just stick out like a sore thumb." Kyra shook her head.

Hailey nodded. Kyra had a point.

"What if I went in and bought three tickets today and then tomorrow I'll buy another one right before we leave?" A grin passed over her lips. "That way it won't look as suspicious. We can act like strangers at the bus station."

Kyra grinned. "That's pretty smart. Where is this place?"

"It's way out in the country… Warsaw."

"So we'd be hiding out with a bunch of hicks?" Kyra leaned back in the bed and pulled her legs up close to her chest. "Don't you think I'd stand out a little bit? I'm black…"

"There are other African Americans there. Anyway, once we're away from here we can figure out the rest later."

Kyra glanced at the digital clock across the room. The alarm was about to go off. "Do busses even go to places like that?"

"I'll have to find the closest stop. We may have to walk a little… or a lot. But I really don't see any other option. I won't let them separate my family." Hailey studied Kyra for a moment. The two of them were rarely vulnerable with each other, however Hailey wanted to be honest. "And… I don't want to leave you either."

Streams of golden sunrise brought a hint of morning light into their room. Kyra's eyes glistened with what Hailey thought were tears.

"You really don't want to leave me?" Kyra barely choked out the words.

Hailey shook her head. "No. You're… you're kind of like my little sister, you know?"

"I've never had a sister." Kyra lowered her face.

"Me neither," Hailey reached out and took Kyra's hand.

Impulsively, Kyra threw her arms around Hailey and hugged her, almost as tight as Grant did when he was really scared.

"I'll go. I'll run away with you guys…"

# Chapter 3

Hailey packed her backpack with necessities; clean underwear for all four of them, a few clean shirts, her straightener and the few special things she had from her grandmother. She hid her books under the bed and made herself look ready for school.

Downstairs, Keith was finishing his cup of coffee while Tara made sandwiches for their lunches. She turned around when she heard Hailey enter the kitchen.

Hailey couldn't miss the small bruise under Tara's eye. "I'm sorry about last night," Hailey said.

Tara didn't answer.

Coffee sounded good. Hailey poured herself a cup and searched the refrigerator for milk. Half coffee and half milk was the only way she liked it.

"I put in a call to your social worker." Tara's icy words sent shivers down Hailey's spine. "I expect you'll be getting a visit from her today."

Keith got up and left for work. Hailey glanced at the clock. She needed to leave soon to make it out the door before the bus. What if her social worker showed up at school today and Hailey wasn't there?

"Don't forget your lunch," Tara said.

Hailey thanked Tara and accepted the brown paper bag. This might come in handy on the long bus ride tomorrow.

With her backpack over her shoulder and her purse stuffed with every bit of money she had, Hailey headed out the door, hoping her plan would work.

\*\*\*

Hailey pulled her red and black plaid coat close around her neck and shivered as she took the three-mile walk to the bus

20

station. *Of course it's cold today... we have abnormally warm weather all month and today it's in the 40's.*

Walking past a police car, Hailey swallowed hard, hoping she could pass as a young adult. She'd purposely put on makeup this morning and worn her most sophisticated sweater, hoping to add a few years to her appearance. Boldly, she smiled at the policeman and he nodded back.

*Look confident and people will believe you are.*

The two women behind the counter in the bus station were carrying on a deep conversation when Hailey walked in. With her shoulders back and a smile plastered on her face, Hailey greeted the women in a tone that wasn't natural for her.

"I need one adult and two children's tickets for Zanesville, Ohio," she said.

A middle-aged woman with short blonde hair and bright red lipstick began typing into her computer. Her long painted nails made a tapping sound as they hit the keys. "When did you want to leave?"

"Tomorrow morning if possible."

"We have a bus going out at ten and one that leaves at twelve-twenty." The woman only gave one quick glance at Hailey and chewed her gum indifferently.

"Ten." Hailey pulled out her wallet. "Can you tell me if there are any stops?"

"You'll be switching busses in Columbus and taking the east bound bus to Zanesville."

Hailey nodded. She hoped she didn't mess this thing up.

The woman told Hailey the amount for the tickets and Hailey's heart almost skipped a beat. Counting out her money, it was clear that she wouldn't have enough to pay for Kyra's ticket. She tried not to show her concern.

"What time should we be here?"

"No later than 9:45." The woman handed Hailey the tickets and turned around to finish talking to her co-worker.

Hailey found a locker in the bus station and deposited a few coins. She shoved her book bag into the locker and took note of the number. Everything that was special to her was in that bag. Her hands shook as she walked from the station. How was she going to get the money for Kyra's ticket?

Hailey's next stop was the public library. Smiling confidently at the librarian, Hailey slipped into one of the computer cubicles and began searching Google maps for Warsaw Chapel. Hailey knew that Zanesville was the closest town, but she had no idea how far away Zanesville was from the little country community of Warsaw.

Much to her disappointment, Hailey found that it was thirty miles from Zanesville to the church. She printed out a map of the area. Her next plan was to find a Wal-Mart. She knew they would all need sleeping bags for staying in the church. She remembered the underneath side of the church stage as being carpeted, but it would not be a comfortable place to sleep.

Zanesville had two Wal-Mart stores. Hailey figured out which one was en route to the church and printed out the map. She then deleted her history from the computer and slipped away undetected.

The house was empty when Hailey arrived home shortly before lunch. She wasn't hungry, but decided to make herself a quick bite to eat before tackling the messy house.

Tara didn't usually get home from work until three so Hailey figured she could get a lot done in those three hours.

Beginning with the kitchen, Hailey washed the dishes, scrubbed the dirty counter, mopped the floor and used lemon oil on the drab wooden cabinets.

She vacuumed the living room, stairs, and bedrooms. Tara hardly ever vacuumed and the floors were matted with cat hair and trash.

Finding a dust rag, Hailey decided to tackle the furniture in the downstairs. The living room was easy. The only furniture to dust was the television stand, coffee table and two end tables. After piling all the newspapers into one neat pile and throwing away the empty soda cans, Hailey decided to dust Keith and Tara's room.

Hailey couldn't remember the last time she'd walked into Keith and Tara's bedroom. The couple was strict about the kids staying out. But Hailey figured even Tara couldn't resist clean sheets, a made bed and clean dressers.

It only took a few minutes to strip the bed and find a clean set of sheets in Tara's closet where Hailey was met by the nasty hiss of Tara's fat orange tabby. *Her cat is as mean as she is.*

Hailey did her best to make the room look nice. She folded a few pairs of clean socks and stuffed them into Keith's drawer. It was then she noticed a wad of bills in the corner of the drawer.

Hailey's heartbeat quickened. She pulled out the money and counted it. There was over four hundred dollars in cash. *Thou shalt not steal.* Hailey sat on the bed and stared at the money, agonizing over what to do. This money could pay for Kyra's bus ticket... but she could still hear her grandmother reading through the Ten Commandments as if it was yesterday.

*What if I borrow it?* Hailey chewed nervously on her lower lip. She counted out enough to cover the cost of one more bus ticket and four sleeping bags and returned the rest to the drawer.

Hurrying to the kitchen, Hailey wrote a quick note, telling Keith that she would return the money as soon as she could. She would leave the note on her bed before she left in the morning.

*God, I promise I'll pay him back.* She prayed as she tucked the bills safely into her purse.

*** 

It was almost three when Hailey finally wound up the cord on the vacuum cleaner. The house looked cleaner than Hailey ever remembered seeing it. She'd worked hard cleaning all the bathrooms and even swept off the front porch. She just sat down when Tara walked in with Hailey's social worker behind her.

Hailey shot to her feet. Her eyes shifted from one angry face to the other.

"You skipped school?" Tara set her purse on the table and crossed her arms.

Ms. Cooper shook her head with obvious disappointment. "Where have you been today, Hailey?"

Hailey stared at her social worker nervously. "I was here... I cleaned the house." Surely Tara would attest to that.

Tara's eyes narrowed angrily. "What? You mean you finally put away that load of laundry I hounded you about?"

A confused expression crossed Hailey's face. "What laundry?"

Tara shook her head. "Then what exactly did you do?"

Hailey stared at Tara. What was she saying? "I cleaned the whole house!"

Tara let her eyes roam the room. "Show me one thing you did?"

Hailey's mouth dropped open. Was she serious?

Ms. Cooper cleared her throat. "Can we please sit down?"

Tara motioned toward the kitchen table and sat across from the social worker.

"Hailey," Ms. Cooper began. "Tara called this morning and told me that you became violent with her last night."

"It was an accident," Hailey sat at the other end of the table. "I didn't mean for the phone to hit her."

Ms. Cooper folded her hands on the table. "Hailey, I can see the bruise. Whether you acted impulsively or not, it's obvious that you intended on hurting Tara."

"Did she tell you what she was doing? Did she tell you she made Hayden sleep in the bathtub?"

Tara glanced knowingly at Ms. Cooper. "This is the kind of thing I told you about."

Ms. Cooper let out a heavy sigh. "Hailey, don't lie to me to try to make this thing better."

"Lie?" Hailey turned her eyes to Tara. "You know it's true… you told him he had to sleep in the tub to teach him a lesson about his bedwetting."

"Sometimes she tells her stories so well I think she actually believes them," Tara explained to Ms. Cooper. "But what concerns us most is that her lies put me and Keith in a questionable light."

"It's not a lie!" Hailey stood up. "Ask Hayden and Grant! They'll tell you…"

"Of course they'll tell you," Tara said. "Hailey can get those brothers of hers to go along with anything she wants them to."

"Sit down, Hailey." Ms. Cooper ordered. "Tara," she turned to the other woman. "I need to know if you believe Hailey's behavior is putting the other children in danger."

Hailey could hardly believe her ears.

"It does concern me," Tara turned her face toward Hailey and looked right into her eyes. "Hayden's bedwetting has gotten worse and I've wondered if Hailey's hostile behavior might be contributing to it."

"You're lying!"

"This is going to merit further investigation." Ms. Cooper pulled out her organizer and made a few quick notes. "Hailey, I have to admit I'm surprised to see this kind of behavior from you: skipping school, throwing things, threatening Tara and making up these stories…"

Hailey's mouth went dry. Tara was lying! "I'm not making up stories, Ms. Cooper. Keith and Tara are terrible foster parents! Ask Kyra, she'll tell you. She heard the whole thing last night."

"Stop, Hailey. This is serious!" Ms. Cooper said. "When Tara phoned this morning she was ready to press charges against you. It's only out of the goodness of her heart that she's willing to give you a second chance." She leaned forward in her seat and pointed a long, plump finger at Hailey. "And if I hear you've skipped school again, I'm going to come down on you even harder."

Hailey glanced at Tara, whose eyes narrowed into two dark slits. Tara meant to win this war, even if she had to lie. The challenge was on.

Ms. Cooper glanced at her watch. "I've got a four o'clock appointment." She rose to her feet. "I've been looking for you since one."

Hailey held her tongue.

"I've spoken with your principal. You are to check in with him in the morning and he will call me to let me know you're there. You will be there."

"Thank you for your help, Ms. Cooper," Tara said politely. "Me and my husband have been beside ourselves with how to help these kids."

*Sure you have…* Hailey listened to the honey drip from Tara's lips.

"Call me if you have any more problems."

Tara walked Ms. Cooper to the door and Hailey escaped to her bedroom where she could unleash a torrent of angry tears.

***

Hailey was thankful she'd eaten lunch. It made it easier to skip dinner. After Tara's outright lies, Hailey had no desire to face that woman.

Why would Ms. Cooper simply believe Tara and not give Hailey the chance to tell her side of the story? Hailey hated the look of disapproval Ms. Cooper gave this afternoon. *Tara's lies made me look like the monster.*

Hailey pulled a piece of notebook paper out of her closet and sat on the floor, using her Geography book as a desk.

She'd let Ms. Cooper know what really happened. She would write a letter explaining her side of the story. *That way if I'm ever caught I at least have this…*

*Dear Ms. Cooper,*

*I felt it was only right that I give you some explanation as to why I had no choice but to take things into my own hands and run away with Kyra and my brothers.*

*In the year that I have been living with the Prescotts, Tara and her husband have done nothing but ridicule and insult us. They continually hound Hayden for his bedwetting, blaming him as if it is something he can help. Poor Grant barely talks anymore because they continually insult him for every mistake he makes.*

*Tara continually threatens to separate my brothers and I, telling me that no one else will take a family with three children. I did not mean to hurt Tara with the phone. I admit I was wrong to throw it at her. I was about to call you to tell you that she was going to make Hayden sleep in the tub when she started taunting me. I acted in anger. But after doing so, she threatened to send me to juvie.*

*I love my brothers. I don't want to be separated from them. I used to think you were there to protect me, to help keep my family together. But after today, I can see that you believe Tara's lies rather than me.*

*I want you to know that I borrowed $300.00 from Keith Prescott. I left them a note promising to return the money just as soon as I can. I will send the money to you to give to them.*

*The four of us are tired of being hurt. Since we can see that the foster care system is no longer willing to help us, we have chosen to leave the foster care system. It is my intention that you will never find us.*

*I would like to recommend that before you give Keith and Tara any more children to foster, you investigate their behavior.*

*Sincerely,*
*Hailey Goodman*

Hailey read through her letter. There were so many details she could have given, things that Tara said to her and her brothers, arguments between Tara and Keith that involved cruel words about the foster children. But what good would it do? Ms. Cooper chose her side, and Hailey knew that arguing didn't change minds.

Kyra and the boys ate dinner with Tara and Keith and then made their way upstairs to escape the tension still hanging in the air like a long, dark veil.

"What got into Tara today?" Kyra closed the door and sat across from Hailey on her bed.

"What do you mean?" Hailey folded her letter and waited for Kyra's explanation.

Kyra waved her hands around the air. "The house. I've never seen it look this nice."

Hailey shook her head and let her eyes rest on the window. "I cleaned the house before she got home today."

"You did this?" Kyra's eyes were wide. "But Keith just complemented Tara on the house and she thanked him."

"I'm not surprised," Hailey said. She shared with Kyra the details of her day, omitting the money she'd borrowed from Keith. It would be best if Kyra didn't know anything about that.

"When should we tell the boys?" Kyra asked.

Hailey sighed. "I'm not sure. I mean, that's an awfully big secret to expect them to keep. They might accidentally give it all away to Tara." Hailey leaned against her headboard and fidgeted with the edge of her faded, pink comforter.

Kyra got up. "What should I pack?" she whispered.

Hailey glanced around the room. "Not too much, we don't want it to be obvious."

"Can I bring my school books?"

Hailey blew out a heavy sigh. If they wanted to continue their education they would need their textbooks. But their textbooks belonged to the school. Could they borrow them too? "You've only got a backpack... what is most important to you?"

Kyra shrugged. "I guess I can learn history and literature through a lot of sources... but I need my math book."

That made sense. "Make sure you have pencils and paper too."

Kyra nodded and Hailey slipped out of the room to tuck in her brothers.

\*\*\*

Hayden's new blow up mattress sat on the floor of the boy's bedroom covered with a plastic sheet. Hailey could see from Hayden's expression that he wasn't pleased.

"At least it's not the bathtub," he sniffed.

Hailey closed the door to her brother's room and sat on the floor. "Are you boys all ready for bed?"

Grant nodded and Hayden shrugged.

"I still need to brush my teeth." Hayden let out a sigh.

Hailey considered this for a moment. She hadn't packed toothbrushes. She wondered if Tara still had a stash of new toothbrushes in the hall closet. Tara always watched for things like that to go on sale and stocked up on them. There should be a stash of shampoo, conditioner and deodorant in the closet too. She would check on that after she got the boys in bed and pack them in the sports bag she planned to take with her tomorrow.

"Why don't we pray," Hailey motioned for Grant to sit next to her.

Grant sat down but Hayden stood standing.

"Dear God," Hailey prayed. "Thank You that You love us. Please help us in the things we are doing... give us safety and guidance..."

Grant added a few more words to her prayer and closed with amen.

Hailey kissed him goodnight and reached to give Hayden a hug, but Hayden stepped away. Hailey lowered her eyes. *God, why is Hayden's heart so hard?*

***

Hailey woke up extra early Friday morning and hoped she could work quiet enough to go undetected. It was common for Hailey to bring her gym bag to school so she felt confident that Tara wouldn't question her if she left the house with it this morning. Working by the light of the streetlamp, she packed her gym bag with extra toothbrushes and toiletries. She added a few textbooks, her tennis shoes and her grandma's Bible.

She ran her fingers tenderly over the well-worn leather Book. Grandma's Bible was her most precious possession. Inside it were her grandma's scribbled notes in almost every margin and colored highlights, showing verses her grandmother must have loved.

Sneaking quietly into the boy's room, Hailey found Grant's favorite stuffed animal, Fuzzy Puppy, snuggled up next to Grant. Carefully pulling it away from him, she carried it out of the room, praying he wouldn't miss it in the morning.

With a heavy sigh, Hailey zipped up the gym bag and prayed that God would help them pull this off.

When her alarm went off at six, Hailey turned on her bedroom light and woke up Kyra. Kyra practically jumped out of her skin at Hailey's touch.

"What's wrong?" Kyra's startled wake up frightened Hailey almost as much.

Kyra blew out a shaky breath. "I could hardly sleep last night and when I finally did go to sleep I think I must have dreamed all night long. Just now I dreamed we were all about to get on the bus when a police officer grabbed my arm.

"Right when I touched you?" Hailey thought she understood.

"Yes!" Kyra hopped down from her bed. "Did you get everything packed?"

"Everything I can pack." Hailey blew out an unsteady breath. "Wear your favorite clothes and your most comfortable shoes."

Kyra nodded.

"I'm taking a shower and plan to leave in a hurry so Tara doesn't question me about where my backpack is." Hailey turned and studied Kyra's face. "Do you think we can pull this off?"

"I hope so," Kyra whispered.

*** 

Everything was going to have to run smoothly for this thing to work. Hailey reminded Kyra to make sure the boys had good shoes on before they left for school.

She grabbed the lunch bag Tara had sitting out for her and said a quick good-bye to the boys.

Walking outside into the cool October morning, Hailey began praying, as she never had before. The sky was gray and overcast and Hailey buttoned her coat as she hurried to the old warehouse where she would meet Kyra.

The old brick structure stood like a memorial to the thriving businesses that once made this part of Cleveland a successful city. Now the building was abandoned and sprayed with large painted letters, symbolic of the gangs she knew ran through this part of the city.

In spite of the city's attempt to board up the broken windows, teenagers and other wanderers pulled boards away over the years, leaving Hailey several possibilities for entering. She glanced quickly up and down the street hoping that no one was paying attention to her. Waiting for a car to turn the corner, Hailey climbed through one of the large windows and searched for a place to hide herself while she waited for Kyra.

All kinds of what-ifs ran through her mind. *What if it starts to rain and Tara drives the boys to school? What if Grant notices that Fuzzy Puppy is missing? What if the principal calls Ms. Cooper when he realizes I'm not at school today and Ms. Cooper begins looking for me before we can get out of town? What if the police see us walking to the bus station and we get caught?*

*Stop this Hailey!* She scolded herself. She held her head high and tried to steady her breath. She glanced quickly at her grandmother's watch, which she was wearing for the first time in her life. Kyra would be leaving in about a half hour. *God please help this all work out.*

***

Hailey sat on an old empty paint can inside the deserted warehouse waiting for Kyra. Broken bottles and cigarette butts lay scattered across the dirty floor and she pulled her thin coat closer around herself as the eeriness of the vacant warehouse sent shivers down her spine.

"Hailey?" She heard Kyra's trembling voice whisper into the dark, dingy building.

"I'm right here." Hailey breathed a sigh of relief. "Was everything okay this morning?"

"Yeah," Kyra seemed edgy. "Except Ms. Cooper called a few minutes before I left."

Hailey's stomached dropped.

"I picked up the phone, but I only caught a little bit of the conversation. Tara started pitching a fit when Ms. Cooper told her you weren't at school today."

Hailey blew out her breath. "So she knows already…"

"Yeah."

"How were the boys?" Hailey tried to stop the trembling in her hands. Her heart was beating so fast, she thought it might just burst through her chest.

"They were good. They were eating breakfast when I left."

Hailey started pacing the floor. "Was I crazy for trying to do this?"

"No." Kyra sat on a pile of boards. "They're the ones who are crazy and leaving their house was the most sane thing we could do."

The sound of a garbage truck outside interrupted their conversation and they both froze.

"I don't know when I've ever been this afraid," Hailey whispered.

The truck moved on and Kyra blew out a heavy breath. "What time do we have to meet the boys?"

"They take Straight Street to Main." Hailey glanced over the notebook where she'd written her plan. "The boys have to be at school by 8:20. So in order to meet them before they reach the school we should be at that intersection by 8:05 at the latest."

"So we'll have to kind of hang out there 'til they come?" The tone in Kyra's voice betrayed concern.

"Pretty much. There's no place to hide on their route." Hailey checked her grandmother's watch and chewed on her lip. "I don't want to get too close to the school." She glanced up at Kyra. "It's ten till eight."

Kyra pulled her backpack onto her shoulders. "We should probably head to the corner then."

Hailey stood up straight and faced Kyra. "Look confident." She brushed one of Kyra's braids behind her shoulder. "If you look like you haven't done anything wrong people won't assume you have."

Kyra nodded. "I can do that."

The two girls slipped quietly out of the abandoned building and walked with their shoulders back and forced confidence on their faces.

\*\*\*

Waiting at the corner for her brothers, Hailey's imagination went wild. *What if Tara already drove them to school? What if a police car pulls up and asks why we are loitering?* After letting her mind live through just about every scenario there was, Hailey breathed a sigh of relief to see her brothers walking straight toward them.

"Hailey!" Grant ran to his sister the minute he spotted her.

Suddenly relieved, Hailey knelt down and caught her little brother in her trembling arms. *Thank You, God...*

"Why are you guys here?" Hayden seemed torn between rebuking them and being pleased.

"We've got a surprise." Hailey rose to her full height and winked. "But we have to hurry. She grabbed Grant's hand and motioned for Hayden to follow. "We're not going to school today."

Hayden stopped mid step and clenched his hands into fists. "No way!" He shook his head. "You're not getting me in more trouble. Tara about blew her top this morning when she found out you weren't at school. She said the police are out looking for you."

A car drove slowly past the congregated children and Hailey licked her dry lips. "Hayden," she spoke softly. "That's

32

why we need to go… we're running away."

Hayden's eyes grew wide. "Really?" He sounded hopeful.

"Yes. But we've got to get downtown to the bus station and it's at least a half hour walk."

"Well, let's go!" Hayden turned his course and started up the sidewalk in the direction of downtown.

"But I can't." Grant's eyes grew sorrowful and he kept his feet planted on the sidewalk.

Hailey knelt down to her little brother's level. "Grant, we have to go…"

Grant shook his head. "Mrs. Williams has been reading us *The Boxcar Children* and today we find out the end. I can't go. I won't know what happens to them."

"Grant, I'll find that book for you, we can read it together," Hailey said.

"But Mrs. Williams does voices," Grant protested.

"I can do voices." Hailey was willing to try.

"And so can I." Kyra grinned at Grant.

Grant still seemed uncertain.

Hailey watched a few cars drive slowly passed and hoped none of them were looking for her. "We all have to make some sacrifices for this to work," she explained. "Kyra is giving up the school play. Think about that."

Kyra blew out a heavy breath.

"Come on, Grant!" Hayden stormed back over to his brother. "We need to follow Hailey's plan before we get caught. If we get caught because you had to be a baby about a stupid old book, I'll…"

"That's enough, Hayden," Hailey interrupted her brother. "Let's go Grant. I promise we'll find that book for you."

Grant sniffed and nodded, allowing his sister to take his hand.

As the four children walked, Hailey explained the plan. "I have to purchase Kyra's ticket when we get there. We didn't want to purchase all four at the same time because we didn't want raise any suspicions that might lead the police to us.

Hailey quickly stopped at a mailbox and dropped in her letter to Ms. Cooper. Her social worker should get the letter by Monday

The boys seemed to understand the plan and Hailey hoped it would work.

*** 

"The 10:00 to Zanesville is sold out," the woman behind the counter explained to Hailey.

Sweat formed on Hailey's forehead. She hadn't counted on this complication.

"What do you have for Zanesville?" Hailey tried not to show her concern.

"We have openings on the 12:40. Do you want that?"

Hailey nodded numbly and counted out the cash.

The others were waiting near the lockers and Hailey motioned for them to follow her to a quiet place in the bus station where they could talk. "There were no more spots on the 10:00 bus…"

Kyra's eyes grew wide with concern.

"I purchased the 12:40 which means that one of us will have to travel alone," Hailey explained.

"It should be me." Kyra reached for the ticket. "You three match. It won't seem strange for me to be traveling alone, but it may draw attention to see me traveling with the boys."

Hailey knew Kyra was right. She also figured Grant would be too scared to get on the bus without his sister, but what about Kyra? Could she travel alone?

"Are you sure? I mean… you'll have to wait almost two and a half hours by yourself…"

"I'll be fine," Kyra promised. "I brought some books and that yummy lunch Tara packed for me." Kyra's face spoke volumes. "I'll come up with a good story in case anyone asks me why I'm here. Don't worry, I'll be fine."

Hailey tried to feel hopeful. "I have no idea what the Zanesville bus station looks like," she said to Kyra. "But we'll watch for your bus to arrive. They told me the bus arrives in Zanesville at 4:10."

Kyra nodded.

"Just don't miss that bus."

# Chapter 4

It was difficult for Hailey to leave Kyra standing alone in the bus station. She felt responsible for her. Hailey prayed the younger girl wouldn't run into any problems getting onto that later bus.

She studied the younger girl for a moment. Kyra's second hand jacket was noticeably out of style and her worn out blue jeans hung loosely on her slender legs. Kyra never complained about her clothes, but Hailey wondered if Kyra got teased in school for her lack of fashion.

Before boarding, Hailey placed her grandmother's watch in Kyra's hand. "This was my grandmother's. Put it on and keep an eye on the time."

Kyra's eyes grew wide. "I can't hold on to this... what if I lose it? What if we get separated?"

"You won't lose it and you can give it back to me in Zanesville." Hailey picked up her bag to walk away. She tried to hide the fear she felt.

She and her brothers boarded quietly and took seats toward the back.

Hailey could see Kyra's little dark head bent over the watch. Hailey hoped the girl would be careful with it. But since neither of them had a cell phone, and Kyra needed a way to keep her eyes on the time, it made sense to let her hold on to it. Maybe it would help Kyra feel a little more connected to her. Hailey knew the younger girl was taking a huge risk running away with them.

What if Kyra backed out? What if she told the police where they were going? All kinds of fearful thoughts flooded Hailey's mind.

The feeling of her youngest brother's hand reaching for hers pulled Hailey from her fears. He snuggled close to her on the large bus seat and rested his head against her.

Hayden was across the aisle, looking out the window. He was ready for adventure. Maybe this would pull him out of his anger.

*\*\**

The bus route from Cleveland to Columbus took them down interstate 71. Once there, the children boarded the eastbound bus taking the 70 to Zanesville.

The Zanesville bus station wasn't very busy. Hailey wished it were. She wanted to blend into the background. A tall, hefty, janitor smiled at them as he walked past with a mop bucket. Hailey nodded and walked her brothers to a series of blue, vinyl-covered chairs lined up against one of the windows. She encouraged them to eat their lunches and reminded them that this would be the last time they'd have to eat something Tara made for them.

Hayden pulled his bologna sandwich out of its baggie and stuck his tongue out at it. "I never want to eat bologna again."

Hailey sighed. She understood. She'd made it known to Tara a long time ago that she didn't like bologna. Her foster mother told Hailey that she didn't live in a made-to-order restaurant and continued to make bologna sandwiches for lunch. Hailey wondered if it gave Tara some kind of satisfaction to make something she knew Hailey didn't like.

Hailey pulled her sandwich out of the bag and removed the slimy slice of bologna and tossed it into the trash. She'd eat her sandwich the way she usually did… bread and cheese.

"What will we eat when we move to grandma's old church?" Hayden asked through his bites of food.

"There used to be a food pantry at the church for people in need," Hailey said. "Hopefully they still have it. I figure we would count as people in need…"

"So the food is free?" Grant asked.

"Yes." Hailey hoped this was entirely true. "I don't know exactly what to expect until we get there," she continued. It suddenly occurred to Hailey that it had been several years since she'd been to grandma's church. What if things changed? What if the church wasn't even there anymore? Hailey tried not to let those thoughts consume her.

36

The janitor walked past again dragging his mop and bucket along. Hailey gave him another quick smile and wished Kyra's bus would hurry. More "what ifs" ran through her mind as she considered what would happen if Kyra missed that bus.

The hours ticked away slowly and Hailey tried to distract her brothers from their boredom by reading to them from one of the magazines sitting on the table in the waiting room. The selection of magazines was reflective of the fact that they were now in a more rural community. Hayden seemed to appreciate hearing stories about hunting and fishing in Ohio.

"Do you think I'll get to go hunting?" Hayden asked.

"Maybe some day." Hailey sighed. It seemed unlikely that he would have an opportunity to hunt while they were in hiding, but she didn't want to discourage him.

"Dad used to hunt." Hayden surprised her by saying.

"You remember?" Hailey asked. Their dad died while their mother was still pregnant with Grant. Hayden was only three.

"Kind of. I remember that picture Grandma had of Dad with that huge buck."

Pictures have a way of retaining memories. "She said it was a twelve point buck." Hailey remembered it too. "I wonder what happened to that picture."

After their grandmother went to stay in assisted living, things just seemed to have disappeared.

Hailey closed her eyes for a moment and tried to picture what memories she still had of her mother and father before they passed away. She didn't those memories to disappear.

Her father was a truck driver. He was gone a lot. But the memories Hailey had of him were good. He'd died in an accident while driving his truck through Pennsylvania during a bad snowstorm. Her mom, pregnant with Grant, never recovered from the depression and shock. She died shortly after Grant was born, leaving the three-orphaned children in the care of their elderly grandmother.

Hailey wondered what ever happened to all of her grandmother's old photo albums and picture frames. She knew that her mother's younger brother took some of the things that belonged to their grandmother. But he didn't want the children.

With a simple refusal of custody, he thrust his niece and nephews into the foster care system and disappeared.

Hailey glanced at the large clock over the bus station entrance. It was after four and Kyra's bus should be here any moment.

"You boys stay here. I'll go meet Kyra." Hailey glanced at Hayden to make sure he heard.

"We'll be right here."

Trying to shrug off her suddenly somber mood, Hailey went to meet Kyra's bus.

***

"There's my sister," Hailey heard Kyra's voice before she saw the girl. "Thank you so much for sitting by me on the bus. It was so nice having someone to talk to." Kyra used her free hand to steady an elderly African American woman as she walked down the bus steps.

The woman glanced at Hailey curiously. "You're this young lady's sister?"

Hailey grinned and let out a relieved sigh that Kyra was okay.

"I'm adopted," Kyra explained. "But I love my dear, white sister." Her eyes twinkled.

Hailey tried not to let it bother her that Kyra was lying to this unsuspecting senior citizen.

"Well, you girls have a good time at your grandmother's farm." The woman waved as she walked away.

Hailey resisted her desire to pull Kyra into her arms for a hug. "I'm so glad you're okay." Her blue eyes showed her relief.

Kyra watched the older lady disappear into the crowd. "So am I. It was pretty scary hanging out in the bus station by myself."

"Were you spotted?" Hailey asked.

Kyra grinned. "After you left I felt like everyone was staring at me. Then I found Mrs. Wells. I heard her telling someone she was going to Zanesville too, so I made a point of sitting beside her and talking to her. I figured anyone who might be curious about me would just assume I was traveling with my grandmother."

"That's pretty creative," Hailey said.

"I even carried her bag onto the bus." Kyra was obviously proud of herself.

"She seemed like a sweet lady. I hope you didn't lie to her too much." Hailey knew Kyra did not share her same convictions about honesty.

Kyra shrugged. She took off Hailey's watch and handed it to her. "Thanks for trusting me with this."

Hailey smiled. She wanted to tell Kyra that she was happier to see her than the watch.

The girls made their way to the boys.

"So this is Zanesville, Ohio." Kyra blinked a few times as the sunshine hit her face.

"According to my map, we're just two blocks away from Zanesville's famous Y bridge," Hailey said.

"What's a Y bridge?" Grant asked.

"It's actually part of the U.S. National Register of Historic Places," Hailey explained. "It was built in the 1800's and spans the place where the Licking and Muskingum rivers come together. The bridge is actually shaped in a Y."

"Can we go see it?" Grant jumped up and down a few times with enthusiasm.

Kyra's eyes twinkled. "You said we were going to be homeschooled. I guess this would be like a field trip."

"It does seem educational." Hailey took her younger brother's hand and began to walk down Main Street towards the bridge.

"Are we allowed to walk on it?" Hayden asked.

The children walked in a small group toward the bridge, careful not to get in the way of traffic. Hailey thought Hayden actually seemed excited.

They all walked slowly, enjoying the novelty of the historical bridge. Hailey watched the water pour over the nearby dam and spillway. The sound of traffic drowned out the sounds of the water, but Hailey found it peaceful anyway.

"How are we getting to your grandmother's church?" Kyra stood next to Hailey, staring out at the water.

"I guess we're going to have to walk." Hailey turned towards Kyra and shrugged. "But I wanted to stop at Wal-Mart first. I thought it would be good to get four sleeping bags. Once we get to Warsaw Chapel, there aren't any stores around."

"Do we have enough money?" Kyra asked.

Hailey nodded. She still felt guilty about the money she'd taken from Keith's night table. She was sure they knew it was missing by now, sure that they told her social worker that Hailey stole money from Keith and probably even made up false stories about how they suspected her of stealing other times. *I will pay him back...*

"How far away is this church?" Kyra interrupted Hailey's thoughts.

"About thirty miles," Hailey said softly. "We won't make it there tonight."

"Where are we going to sleep tonight?" Hayden had obviously been listening and interjected.

"I thought we'd camp." Hailey smiled.

The boys both showed enthusiasm and Kyra sniffed.

"Where are we going to camp?" Kyra's dark eyes bore into Hailey's. "You never mentioned camping. You said we'd be staying at some nice new church building with free food and nice clean carpets..."

Hailey placed a comforting hand on Kyra's arm. "There are lots of nice barns on the way to Warsaw Chapel."

"Barns?" Kyra seemed even more unimpressed. "We'll be sleeping in a barn?" She shook her head. "No way, not me." She started walking away.

Hailey took her youngest brother's hand and motioned for Hayden to follow. "Kyra... It will be fine. Trust me."

Kyra did not look convinced.

"We'll have our nice new sleeping bags and it will be an adventure. You can use it in a book when you become a famous author some day." Hailey knew Kyra aspired to becoming an author and hoped this might pique the other girl's interest. "You can talk about the smell of hay mingled with..."

"The smell of fresh cow manure. Yeah, I'll be using that in my best selling novels," Kyra said sarcastically. "I can say, 'the lovely princess trampled through the fresh piles of cow manure into the arms of her strong, red neck farmer prince.'"

40

Hailey raised her eyebrows. "Are you making some kind of rude statement about country boys, Miss Washington?"

Kyra ignored the question. "Let's just go. I don't want to be hiking all across farm country forever."

The children followed Hailey's lead down the busy city sidewalk toward the closest Wal-Mart, passing a variety of restaurants, shopping centers and other businesses on the way.

Once at Wal-Mart, Hailey let everyone pick out the sleeping bag they liked best. "Remember, we have to carry these," she said.

Hailey also purchased a few other necessities and food that they could take with them as they walked, careful not to buy more than they could carry.

They kept their sleeping bags in the Wal-Mart bags and left the store to grab a quick bite to eat before hitting the road in earnest.

It wasn't far to the edge of town and the children stayed off the main road, hoping to keep themselves from view. The sun began to set quickly and Hailey hoped the children could find a barn or other abandoned building to hunker down for the night.

*\*\**

It was more difficult to find an abandoned barn than Hailey hoped. Hailey was surprised when she glanced at her watch and found that it was almost nine.

"How are you guys holding up?" Hailey asked.

Hayden switched hands that he was carrying his sleeping bag and tried to adjust his backpack on his shoulders. "I'm getting tired."

Hailey nodded. She knew Grant was tired. She carried his sleeping bag because the tuckered seven-year-old was dragging his feet. "I was thinking about the Israelites and how they wondered around in the wilderness for forty years," she said.

"The who and how they what?" Kyra clutched her Wal-Mart bag tightly.

"In the Bible. God called Moses to lead His people, the Israelites, out of Egypt where they had been living as slaves. God promised the Israelites a new place to live, the Promised Land. But

41

before they got there, the people wandered through the wilderness for forty years."

"So are you like Moses then?" Kyra's dark eyes twinkled. "You're leading us out of Tara's bondage to a place you've promised will be better."

Hailey chuckled. "I hadn't thought of that part of it. I was thinking more about us wandering around trusting God to provide for us."

"Isn't that a barn?" Hayden pointed to the horizon.

On a low, dark hill, the children could see the silhouette of a big barn not far in the distance. Hailey became hopeful.

Quietly, the children picked up their pace, slipped through a barbed wire fence and made their way across a large, treeless pasture toward the barn. Finding the door, Hailey led the others inside with her new flashlight and pointed toward the hayloft.

"How's that for accommodations?"

The boys showed their excitement.

The spacious barn was obviously in use. Inside was a tall hay elevator leading to a high hayloft. From one of the inside doors, Hailey saw a drop off that lead to the bottom level of the barn where the farmer obviously dropped hay to feed the cows. She could hear the animals below. Their soft moos and chewing noises were the only things breaking the silence of the old barn.

"Are there snakes up there?" Kyra asked as the children climbed the ladder to the hayloft.

Hailey opted to ignore the question. Once up the ladder, she spotted two shining eyes reflecting the light of her flashlight and almost dropped it. It was a cat. Hailey breathed a sigh of relief.

It didn't take much convincing to get the others to roll out their sleeping bags and crawl inside. The night air had become cool and everyone was tired.

"Why don't we thank God for getting us this far," Hailey suggested.

"I'll pray!" Grant offered.

"You really think God helped us get away from Tara?" Kyra narrowed her eyes in the dimly lit loft. "Doesn't that mean He aided four criminals?" She chuckled.

Hailey snuggled down in her comfortable new sleeping bag and considered Kyra's question. Did God help them escape? Was it morally right for her to help her brothers and Kyra break the law and leave? Suddenly, Hailey felt the weight of what she'd just done.

Her brother's soft voice carried itself through the night air as he thanked God for each person there and asked for God's help as they made their way to the church. But Hailey struggled. *Please forgive me, God...*

***

Hailey woke early. The sweet smell of hay and the sound of cows moving around on the lower level of the barn reminded her that at any moment a farmer could come walking into the barn to feed his cows.

"Kyra, Hayden, Grant," Hailey called their names softly. "We've got to get out of here before the farmer comes. The sudden realization that she'd forgotten to have Hayden put on a night pant caused her another moment of panic.

"Hayden?" she whispered his name again.

Hayden smiled when he opened his eyes. "I dreamed I was a dairy farmer. I was drinking a glass of warm milk."

"Did you stay dry last night?" Hailey hoped the milk from his dream was still undigested.

Hayden's brown eyes lit up. "I did!" He felt around his sleeping bag. "That's cool."

Kyra got to work rolling her sleeping bag immediately. "Can I eat one of those granola bars you bought last night?"

"Of course. But let's get out of here first." Hailey glanced quickly at her watch. It was almost seven. "I'm not sure what time this farmer feeds his cows, but I don't want to get caught."

The children were packed up and ready to walk outside the barn when they heard a truck pull up outside.

"That can't be good," Kyra whispered.

Hailey scanned the barn for a safe, dark corner. A large stack of drying lumber on the far side of the barn seemed like their best option. She motioned toward it quickly and helped Grant crouch down beside her.

The soft sound of whistling broke the silence and the cows responded with loud mooing.

"All right, all right," the farmer talked to the hungry animals. "You'll get your food." He climbed the hayloft where only moments ago the children had scrambled down.

Hailey hoped none of them left anything up there.

The farmer tossed down four bales of hay and climbed back down the ladder. "You ladies are going to need to finish what's in the pasture before winter comes along you know," he talked to his cows. One by one he unbound the hay bales and tossed them to the cows below. "Out of the way Bessie or you're going to be wearing that bale," he chuckled.

New sounds of loud munching replaced the mooing and the farmer returned to the song he'd been whistling when he arrived.

Hailey held Grant's hand and tried to keep her breathing soft. Hayden was lying down behind the sweet smelling lumber and Kyra crouched just beside Hayden's head. They all sensed the seriousness of this situation.

The farmer coughed a few times and closed the door to the cows. The children remained quiet while he exited the barn.

*Drive away... just drive away...* Hailey waited to hear the sounds of the man's truck. He seemed to be doing something right outside the barn door.

Hailey heard him talking. He must have a cell phone.

"Alright, I'll see if I can pick that up this afternoon. Yeah?" The man chuckled at something the other person said. "Alright then..." his voice faded and the distinct sound of a truck door closing helped Hailey relax.

The truck drove away and the children waited just long enough to feel they were safe leaving.

"That was so cool!" Hayden opened the barn door and glanced outside at the bright blue autumn sky. "We were like spies!"

"That was scary." Hailey waited until everyone was out the door and closed it. "But I'm impressed. That's the kind of quiet we might need to be at times when we're hiding at the church. It was good practice for us."

"Kind of like a fire drill," Kyra joked.

"That was our people drill," Hayden offered.

The children made their way quickly across the field back to the road and continued their journey. A quick glance at the road signs compared to the location of the church on her map convinced Hailey that they might need to sleep another night in a barn. Hopefully they could find another one.

*** 

"It's like a picnic," Grant said.

The four children sat on an outcropping of rocks just far enough from the road to not be noticed. They ate the cheese and crackers they'd purchased the day before and enjoyed a rest from their walking.

They had been walking for hours and seemed to be making progress. Hailey hoped they could keep up their momentum but she was worried.

"Tomorrow is Sunday. If we can arrange it so we arrive at the church by morning we can hide our stuff in the woods behind the church and then slip in during the service."

"Won't we have to see people then?" Kyra asked.

"Yes. That's the idea. We'll be one of them. New members of Warsaw Chapel." Hailey grinned.

"But we haven't showered in two days and we've been sleeping outside." Kyra almost sounded disgusted.

"If we slip in when they first open the building we can head to the bathrooms and get cleaned up." Hailey knew her hair probably didn't look as nice as she'd like it to but what else could they do?

"We don't have churchy clothes," Kyra glanced down at her blue jeans.

"That's okay. I remember some people at my grandma's church dressing more casual."

"What about wearing the same clothes every Sunday?" Kyra raised her eyebrows.

Hailey considered this for a moment. They'd packed very few outfits. "We'll just have to pace our clothes well. We can wash our clothes in the church sink during the week. I brought laundry soap." She wondered if Tara noticed that missing yet. "And just rotate the few things we have so we look like we have more clothes than we do."

Hayden rose to his feet and put his backpack on over his shoulders. "Come on you guys, we need to get hiking if we want to get closer to that church by tonight."

Hailey appreciated how excited Hayden seemed about this new adventure. She hoped it wouldn't disappoint him.

# Chapter 5

The children watched curiously as an Amish buggy drove past them with a lantern hanging from its side. The steady sound of horse hooves clip clopping echoed on the dirt road.

"That was about the freakiest thing I've ever seen," Kyra whispered into the cool night air.

Hailey smiled. "We're not far. There are several Amish living around the church. I remember seeing them when I was a child."

"What are Amish?" Grant asked.

"The Amish are people who live without any of the modern conveniences that we use. They don't drive cars, they don't use electricity, and they all wear old-fashioned looking clothes."

"Why do they do that?" Hayden wanted to know.

"It's part of their religion. They don't want to be worldly." Hailey remembered her grandmother explaining the Amish to her when she was younger.

"I'm hungry." Grant interrupted Hailey. "And I want to go to bed."

*Poor Grant.* Hailey knew she'd pushed her little brother today. But she was eager to get close to Warsaw Chapel to ensure they could get in Sunday morning. *He'll be so tired tomorrow he won't want to go to church.*

"Look," Hailey attempted to get the other children to gain perspective. "We're almost there. I think we should find a nice cozy Amish barn to settle down for the night."

"An Amish barn?" Hayden sounded intrigued. "Is an Amish barn any different from the barn we stayed in last night?"

Hailey considered his question and chuckled. "I guess not. I suppose it wont have a light inside. That's all."

The children crossed a main road and followed another dirt road in the direction of the church. In the dark of night it was difficult to see where a good place to sleep might be. Clouds overhead blocked the moon and gave the road an eerie, lonely feeling.

A house with an Amish buggy parked out front got their attention. They quickly found the barn and made their way quietly inside.

This barn was laid out differently. There was no hay elevator and there were no cows inside. The children found a secluded place in the barn and unrolled their sleeping bags.

The soft sound of rolling thunder in the distance interrupted Grant's nighttime prayer and he scooted closer to Hailey before saying amen.

Hailey wrapped an arm around Grant and let him snuggle close to her. She leaned back in her sleeping bag and closed her eyes.

Two days. They'd been gone for two days. How strange. Hailey wondered what kind of consequences would meet her if she were to get caught now. Juvie, for sure.

The rain started outside and Hailey listened to the soft tinkling sound of water drops hitting the metal roof. A roll of thunder echoed through the barn and Hailey felt Hayden move his sleeping bag closer.

She hoped it wouldn't rain in the morning. They'd need to get to the church in dry clothes. They would also need a dry place to store their belongings until they could sneak everything inside. Hailey hoped it all would all work out.

*** 

"They could be anywhere." Dahlia Cooper leaned back in her desk chair and blew out a heavy sigh. She'd spent the last two days working with the police to locate the Goodman children and Kyra Washington, but they still had no leads. It was late and she knew she should go home, but her heart was heavy with concern.

Dahlia rubbed her temples and tried to think. The police investigated all the abandoned buildings near the Prescott's house, but there was no sign of the children.

The next step was to question any known family members. Dahlia needed to do a little research to find the Goodman's biological uncle, but doubted she would learn anything from him.

48

The man seemed to hold no connection to his niece and nephews. Kyra's family seemed even more unlikely, but Dahlia was going to leave no stone unturned.

Why would they run away? Dahlia couldn't understand it. In all her years of social work she could usually spot the children who would cause problems in the system. The Prescotts and Kyra were not on her potential delinquent list.

She'd searched Hailey and Kyra's belongings, hoping to find some kind of lead, but there was nothing. The children seemed to take very little, although Tara and Keith were quick to tell her that Hailey had stolen several hundred dollars from Keith's sock drawer.

"She was told to stay out of our bedroom," Tara had fumed. "That little thief searched our drawers for money and stole from us!"

It just didn't match what Dahlia knew about Hailey. She'd never been reported as steeling from anyone.

Dahlia's stomach growled and she glanced at the clock. It was well past her dinner time. This was not how she'd planned to spend the weekend.

She wished the children had left a note - something to give her a reason. All she could do was keep searching and hope that the children were safe.

*** 

The sound of a rooster pulled Hailey from sleep. The sun was just beginning to touch the horizon and the sky appeared to be clear. She was relieved. After the thunderstorm the night before, Hailey wasn't sure what to expect. She woke up the others and hurried to get everyone ready for church.

"What is there to eat?" Hayden asked.

Hailey pulled a granola bar out of her bag and handed it to him.

Hayden glanced at it blankly. "Another granola bar?"

Hailey knew her brother wanted a real meal. They all did. But there was nothing she could do. Not yet.

The children got their things packed and did their best to look tidy. Hailey would have been much happier with a hot shower, but at least her hair didn't get oily easily. She knew some girls whose hair looked oily after one day.

The children hurried out of the barn and onto the road leading to the church. They only had a few miles to go this morning, but Hailey wanted to make sure they got their early enough to hide their belongings. She wasn't sure what time church started and didn't know what to expect once they got there.

It was a lovely autumn morning. The trees were alive with color and the roads were covered with leaves from the storm the night before. The children kicked through the leaves and breathed in the smells of fall.

"I've never seen so many leaves," Grant said.

The leaves crunched beneath their feet, releasing their spicy fragrance. Hailey loved the mixed smell of the cool morning air and fallen leaves filled with last night's rain. It was so peaceful.

Grant's only real memories of fall were of Cleveland where there were nowhere near as many trees. When the leaves did begin to fall, Tara was outside with her leaf blower getting them off her small, green lawn. She never let the children play in the leaves, not that there was ever a large enough pile to make it fun. But Hailey determined that Grant would have the chance to jump in the leaves some day.

Hayden was the first one to notice the church. "Is that Warsaw Chapel?" He pointed at the large pole barn style structure next to a smaller, old wooden chapel with a tall, white steeple.

"Yes!" Hailey's eyes lit up. It was just as she remembered it.

Warsaw Chapel had been around for many years. The original building was put up in the mid 1800's. When Hailey and her brothers went to live with their grandmother, the church built the new building. It was a nice, clean structure with a large sanctuary, kitchen and several offices and classrooms. They still used the old building for Sunday school classes and other church activities, but the main hub was the new building.

"I'm surprised there'd be such a big church in the middle of nowhere," Kyra said.

Hailey agreed. But she remembered there always being a good number of people at the church. "There must be something drawing the people here."

The children found a secluded place in the woods behind the church to hide their belongings and watched for the first person to arrive and unlock the building. Hailey still hoped to get cleaned up before having to meet people.

*** 

A man and woman drove up to the church at 8:30 and Hailey watched from the woods as they unlocked the church and slipped inside. While the children waited a few more cars drove up and Hailey glanced at the others. "Should we go in now? I know where the restrooms are. We can head straight there and get ready."

Kyra nodded but then grabbed Hailey's arm. "What if this doesn't work? What if we're on the news and someone identifies us?"

"We won't be on the news, Kyra," Hailey reassured the younger girl. She hoped she was right.

The doors to the church were unlocked and Hailey led the children quietly to the bathrooms. They all appreciated a place with running water and mirrors. When they finally stepped out into the hallway, they felt better.

"The sign said that Sunday school starts at 9:30," Hailey explained. She smoothed one of Hayden's red hairs and grinned when he took a step away from her hand. "That's in about twenty minutes."

"We're really going to go to Sunday school?" Grant sounded excited.

"Yes." She placed a hand on Grant's shoulder. "I'll probably come with you to your class for this first time just to make sure no one asks you anything about us that is difficult to answer."

"Yeah. Don't mess this up," Hayden shot.

"That goes for all of us." Hailey gave her brother a stern glare. "Remember what we talked about."

"I know… we're new in town and we are visiting the church." Hayden's tone was sarcastic.

"Yes. And what will you say if they ask for your name?"

"Hayden Evans."

"Why can't we say Goodman?" Grant asked.

"Because we don't want to be found. If anyone finds out we are the Goodman children who ran away, then we're caught. You've got to be very careful about that." Hailey hoped her brothers would remember their new name.

"And I'm Kyra Evans." Kyra's eyes twinkled. "No more Washington for me."

Hailey nodded. Was this insanity? Trying to pull off new names and hide out in a church? Was it right to even ask for God's help in this deception?

Their plan was about to be put to the test. A tall, slender man, who Hailey guessed to be in his early forties, walked toward them, wearing a warm smile.

"Good morning," he greeted the children and reached to shake Hayden's hand. "I'm Pastor Lane Evans."

Hailey's eyes almost bugged out of her head; how in the world did she pick the same last name as the pastor?

"I'm Hayden." Her brother accepted the handshake like a man. "Our last name is Evans, too."

Hailey wished he hadn't just said that but forced a smile. "I'm Hailey," she greeted the man. This was not the same pastor she remembered when she was a child.

Grant and Kyra both introduced themselves.

Lane's wife rounded the corner and smiled at her husband and the children. "Well hello," she greeted them with the same warmth her husband exhibited. "I'm Kate Evans."

Kate was a tall slender woman in her late thirties. She had short brown hair and dark brown eyes that drew you in with their warmth.

Lane introduced his wife to the children. Hailey was impressed that he remembered all their names.

"Are your parents here?" Kate asked.

Hailey was glad for the chance to show the younger children how to do this. "No. They don't attend church."

"Oh, okay."

Hailey could tell Kate was trying to hide her embarrassment.

"Well I'm glad you are visiting," Kate said. "Do you know which Sunday school classes you will be in?"

"No, Ma'am." Hailey did her best to sound polite.

Kate asked each child their age and told them which room they would be in. "Hailey, the high school Sunday school class meets upstairs in the youth room. We have a really nice senior high youth room. Senior high youth group is on Sunday nights and junior high meets on Wednesday nights. You'll love it I'm sure."

Hailey nodded. "I'll probably just stay with Grant this morning if you think that's okay."

"No problem at all," Lane said. "I think you'll like Mrs. Robins. She's a wonderful teacher." The pastor smiled warmly at Grant.

The children thanked the couple and left to find their classrooms. Hailey wondered if they'd passed the test.

***

Mrs. Robins was a nice, older woman who was as round as she was tall. She smiled sweetly to the children and offered them all a homemade donut before she began the lesson. Hailey figured Grant appreciated the freshly made baked good more than the teacher could ever imagine.

Grant loved Sunday school. Hailey was impressed how much her younger brother actually knew of the Bible story their teacher was discussing. In spite of Hailey's own limited spiritual direction, she did her best to teach her little brothers what she could.

"You seem to know quite a bit about Daniel and his encounter with the lions," Mrs. Robins said to Grant after he answered another of her questions.

"My sister reads the Bible to me sometimes," Grant explained.

The teacher turned her twinkling gray eyes toward Hailey. "What a wonderful sister you have."

Hailey blushed. A few of the other children in the class glanced curiously at Hailey and one of the little girls whispered that she thought Hailey had pretty hair.

The teacher continued the lesson and challenged the children to remember the message. "King Darius did not want to have to put Daniel in the lions' den, but I love what he said to

Daniel. 'Your God Whom you serve continually, He will deliver you.' And God did! God delivered Daniel."

Grant listened intently.

"What are the lions' dens in your lives?" the teacher asked the children. "Are there any lions you have to face? Maybe a kid at school who picks on you… maybe it's a subject that you have a difficult time learning?"

Hailey glanced compassionately at her little brother. Was he thinking about Tara and Keith? If there were ever lions in their lives it was Tara and Keith.

"Just remember," Mrs. Robins continued. "The God Who we serve can and will deliver you. All you need to do is ask."

Grant glanced at Hailey and smiled.

Mrs. Robins led the class in a simple prayer, asking God to help them with whatever things they were facing and thanked God for their new guests. When she closed the prayer, Grant and Hailey rose to go.

"Thank you so much for bringing your brother this morning," Mrs. Robins stopped Hailey to say. "I hope you will be able to come back next week," she said to Grant.

"Me too." Grant's big blue eyes showed how much he enjoyed Mrs. Robins' class. "Will you have donuts next week too?"

"Well, next week I was thinking of making blueberry muffins."

"I love blueberry muffins!" Grant beamed.

Hailey knew Grant would be talking about Mrs. Robins all week.

Hayden and Kyra were in the hallway when Hailey and Grant found them. Hayden's arms were crossed and he wore an impatient scowl.

New faces glanced curiously at the children, some of them stopping to say hi, as they made their way back to the main building where the worship service was going to be held.

Hailey decided not to ask Hayden how Sunday school was and helped her siblings make their way to a cozy spot near the back of the sanctuary. An elderly couple greeted them warmly and Hailey returned their friendliness.

Hailey also noticed several teenagers scattered throughout the church. She wondered what these teens were like. Would any of them be friendly to her?

As the sanctuary filled up, Hailey did her best to relax and enjoy herself. This was the first time she'd been in a church since her grandmother's funeral. Her grandmother was buried in Cleveland, near their grandfather's grave, and the funeral was held at a church there. Before that, Warsaw Chapel was the last church Hailey had been to.

She glanced around the sanctuary. It had been a long time since she'd been here. It felt good to be back.

There were a few familiar faces scattered through the congregation, but Hailey didn't know who they were. She hoped no one knew her either.

The service started with a few announcements and a worship song. Hailey glanced over at Hayden and saw his scowl deepen. She did her best to ignore it and followed the song on the overhead.

Pastor Evans led the service beautifully. The congregation sang a few more songs and the pastor presented a sermon from the book of 1 Peter.

One of the verses he quoted stuck out in Hailey's mind. It was 1 Peter 5:7, "Casting all your anxiety on Him because He cares for you."

Hailey had a lot of anxiety she needed to take to God. It seemed difficult for her to imagine that the God of the universe would care about her simple little life. She remembered her grandmother always telling her to take everything to Jesus, the big things and the small things. No matter what it was, Jesus wanted to help her through it. He wanted to be her friend. Pastor Evans sounded a lot like her grandmother.

\*\*\*

After the service, Hailey drew the other children aside and explained the game plan.

"We need to one by one slip into the choir room before the church gets too empty. There is a little hidden door beside the piano. I checked this morning to make sure nothing was blocking

55

it. Just open the door and climb in. It leads to the underneath side of the stage. We'll need to be totally quiet until everyone leaves the church. Then we can go get our stuff."

Hayden nodded. "I'll go first."

Hailey glanced around to see if anyone would notice her brother slipping into the choir room. She smiled when he successfully made it in. Grant went next. Hailey and Kyra pretended to be gathering their belongings while they watched Grant disappear.

"You go next," Hailey instructed Kyra. "I'll be right behind you."

Kyra hurried away and Hailey ran a nervous hand through her long dark hair. *Don't get caught... don't get caught...*

"Hailey," she heard her voice just as Kyra disappeared into the room.

"Hi, Mrs. Evans," Hailey smiled nervously at the pastor's wife.

"Oh, please call me Kate." She glanced around as if looking for the rest of Hailey's clan. "Where are your brothers and sister?"

"Oh, they probably already left. They're hungry for lunch." Hailey knew that was true. She was starving.

"Did you see in your bulletin that we have youth group tonight?" Kate asked. "I was hoping to catch you before you left to introduce you to the youth pastor and his wife, but I'm afraid they've already gone home. We have a wonderful senior high youth group. I'm sure you'd enjoy it. You might actually know some of the teens. Do you go to West High?"

Hailey shoved her hands nervously into her pockets. "No. We're homeschooled." It felt funny saying it.

"Oh. That's wonderful. My sister and her husband homeschool their children. They have a daughter in the youth group. She's fifteen... didn't you say you were fifteen?"

Hailey nodded.

"You two should meet," Kate continued. "She is so sweet. I'm sure you will hit it off."

Hailey wasn't sure how to respond. She would have to be careful not to get too close to any of these teens. Hailey couldn't tell them the truth about herself… what kind of friend could she ever really be to any of them?

Much of the congregation had already left the building and Hailey knew Kate was expecting her to walk toward the doors to leave. How could she get to the choir room now?

"Youth group starts at 6:00. They serve dinner before youth group. Usually pizza." Kate started walking with Hailey. "Do you think you might be able to come?"

Hailey cleared her throat. "I help Kyra watch our brothers on Sunday nights. I'm not sure how I can make it work."

"Just bring them with you. They can have pizza too and hang out in the sanctuary while you're upstairs in the youth room."

Hailey glanced at the choir room door as she walked passed with the pastor's wife. Hailey was going to have to leave the building to keep Kate from becoming suspicious. How was she going to let her brothers and Kyra know to let her back in?

"We're so glad you came today," Kate placed a kind hand on Hailey's arm.

As they approached the pastor he greeted Hailey too. "I didn't see your siblings slip out."

"They must have gone out a different door," Hailey answered honestly. "It was nice meeting you." She shook his hand.

"We hope to see you Wednesday. We have family night on Wednesdays. We serve dinner at 5:30 and activities begin at 6:30.

"We will be sure to check it out," Hailey promised. *Free dinners twice a week… that's a good start.*

She walked outside and slipped away into the woods where the children had hidden their belongings. Hailey crouched down and watched for the pastor and his wife to leave. She remembered the car they arrived in and scanned the parking lot for it from her hiding place.

A few more people left the building and Hailey waited nervously. She hoped the others would keep quiet and not worry about her while the pastor and his wife left.

Time seemed to take forever while Hailey waited. Would Grant be scared? Would Kyra know how to keep her brothers quiet? Hailey's stomach growled and she wrapped her arms around her waist, wishing Pastor and Mrs. Evans would hurry up and leave.

Hailey knocked on the window to the choir room after the pastor and his wife drove away. It took a few minutes for the children to hear her. Hailey breathed a sigh of relief when she saw Kyra open the small stage door and walk toward the window.

"What happened to you?" Kyra asked as she opened the window.

Hailey wasn't sure if the younger girl was scolding her or sounded relieved. Maybe both. Hailey tossed their sleeping bags inside.

"The pastor's wife stopped me to tell me about youth group. It would have looked really strange if I lingered around the sanctuary when everyone else was leaving." Hailey hurried back up the hill to gather the rest of their belongings. The window was actually a great entrance. Because it was at the back of the church no one from the road could see them. Hailey wondered if there was a way to keep the window unlocked at all times so they could just use it to get in and out.

Hailey handed the rest of the stuff to Kyra through the window and climbed inside.

"When is youth group?" Kyra asked.

"Senior high is tonight. Junior high is Wednesday night. But Kate said I could bring you guys and that you could hang out in the sanctuary while youth group is going on. They're serving pizza and you can all have some."

"I want pizza!" Grant hurried out from his hiding spot.

"That's tonight," Hailey hugged her little brother.

Hayden came crawling out of their place still wearing a scowl. "I'm hungry now."

"We'll get something together. First let's put our stuff under the stage." Hailey carried her bags to the small hidden door and glanced inside. There was a light switch on the wall just inside the door and she turned it on to get a better idea of what their new home looked like. It had been a long time since she'd been under the sanctuary stage.

The floor was all carpeted, but they had to crawl to get around. Hailey could sit on the floor and still had a few inches above her head. There was enough light from the few bulbs to light up a good portion of the area. There were a few boxes labeled Christmas near the front of the door, and Hailey figured this meant they'd need to keep themselves to the farthest part of the stage so as not to be discovered.

"What do you guys think?" she asked as the others dragged their stuff to the far end of their hidden cavern.

"I like it!" Grant's enthusiasm warmed Hailey's heart.

"I kind of like it too," Kyra confessed. "It's cozy and clean. I like that there are little corners and walls under here. It gives us privacy."

"I think we should all sleep near the back so our stuff won't be discovered. It looks like they do use this place to store Christmas boxes." Hailey unrolled her sleeping bag and spread it out on the clean, carpeted floor.

"And since Christmas is just a couple months away they will probably be getting in here pretty soon," Kyra said.

Hailey agreed.

"How long will we be living here?" Hayden finally spoke up still scowling.

Hailey sighed. "I'm not sure." She studied Hayden curiously. He'd been in a sour mood since the morning. Was it only because he'd had a bad night's sleep in the Amish barn? The storm kept her awake for several hours. Maybe it kept Hayden up as well.

"Can we live here forever?" Grant continued inspecting.

Hailey wasn't sure how to answer. How long could they conceivably hide in the church? "We'll just have to take it one day at a time."

"Do we have to keep going to Sunday school?" Hayden spread out his sleeping bag and crossed his arms.

"What's gotten into you, Hayden?" Hailey asked. "Did you have a bad experience in Sunday school?"

Hayden sealed his lips together and his scowl grew even more severe.

"Man, Hayden," Kyra finally joined in. "You look like you just sucked all the juice from a lemon and topped it off with an onion."

"What on earth happened?" Hailey drew herself closer to her brother.

"All those stupid kids think they're so cool because they know where to find all those Bible places." Hayden kept his gaze off his sister to hide his emotions. "But I don't care. I told them I knew how to start a car without the keys."

"You do not!" Hailey rebuked her little brother.

Hayden shrugged indifferently. "They don't know that and I could tell a couple of them were impressed but Mrs. Whoever She Was told me that hot wiring a car was not something to brag about."

"Do I need to remind you that we're supposed to live here at this church? We don't need to start trouble."

"So."

"Why don't you learn how to find the books of the Bible?" Hailey suggested. "Show them that you're just as quick at it as they are. That would impress the kids and Mrs. Whoever She Was."

Hayden shrugged. Hailey wasn't sure what he was going to do. But she knew her brother well enough to know he was usually up for a challenge. Maybe learning the books of the Bible in order to show up the other kids wasn't the best motivation, but Hailey figured it wouldn't hurt him to learn them.

Grant finally said what everyone was thinking. "Let's go find our lunch."

# Chapter 6

True to Hailey's memory, the church refrigerator was thoroughly stocked. The children found eggs, maple syrup, and butter. Some digging through the cabinets led to a box of pancake mix.

"I remember hearing one of the kids in my Sunday school class talking about a pancake breakfast fundraiser," Kyra said. "This must be left over from that. Can we make pancakes for lunch?"

Pancakes sounded great to everyone.

Hailey couldn't remember the last time she'd had so much fun with her brothers. Hailey noticed that even Hayden seemed to be having fun.

They explored the kitchen and found everything they needed to make their lunch.

Warsaw Chapel had a nicer kitchen than Tara and most definitely cleaner.

Grant found an opened bag of chocolate chips and Hailey added them to a few of the pancakes.

"I can't remember the last time I've had pancakes," Kyra sat at the edge of the counter with a spatula in her hand.

"So how was your Sunday school class?" Hailey asked Kyra.

"I liked it." Kyra flipped a pancake and set the spatula down. "The teacher was really nice and no one laughed at me when I told them I'd never been to church before."

"Is this really your first time coming to church?" Hailey tried not to sound too surprised, but she was.

Kyra nodded. "None of the families who I lived with ever went to church."

Hailey wanted to ask Kyra how long she'd been in the foster care system, but wasn't sure if she would mind answering something that personal. In the time they'd lived with Tara and Keith, the two girls never talked about personal things. It was almost surprising that Kyra trusted Hailey enough to actually run away with her.

Once the pancakes were done, Hailey served them to the children on plates she'd found in one of the kitchen cabinets and they sat around a table like a real family.

"We really need to thank God for this meal." She stopped Hayden from touching his pancakes.

Kyra nodded. "Its funny, I never thought about the fact that God provides our food before. But sitting here in a church it's obvious."

"I'll pray," Grant volunteered.

Hailey nodded and peeked at Hayden to see if her other brother was showing any signs of acknowledging God's provision. Hayden's head was bowed but Hailey couldn't read his expression.

***

After lunch, the children cleaned up their mess and Hailey hurried to wash her hair. Using the shampoo and conditioner she'd packed, she washed her hair in the bathroom sink and did her best to dry it using the towel she'd packed. When she was done, the children roamed the church. There was a lot to discover. The pastor's office and the front office were both locked. Hailey figured that's where the computers were.

Much to Hailey's excitement the church had a clothing closet. She never remembered it having one when she was a child. She was amazed at all the clothes people from Warsaw Chapel donated to the needy. The sign on the door said the clothes were free.

"Maybe we won't have to wear the same clothes every week." Kyra held a gently used pink hoodie up to herself and smiled. "This is absolutely adorable. Do you really think it's okay to take it?"

Hailey nodded. "That's what they're here for."

Both girls spent a fun half an hour exploring the racks of clothes and trying things on while the boys played hide and seek from each other in the racks.

"It's like having a really big closet full of clothes at our disposal!" Kyra giggled.

A sound in the foyer quieted their playful chatter. Grant and Hayden stopped cold and looked to Hailey for what to do.

"Hello?" A man's voice called out.

Instinctively Hailey turned off the light and motioned for everyone to take cover behind the clothes.

From her place on the floor, Hailey saw a man walk past. She buried herself deeper into the clothing rack and tried to still her breathing. She could hear his footsteps echo through the quiet church.

"Hello?" The man called out again. He walked back down the hall and into view. In his hands he carried a set of keys. Hailey watched him as he stopped across from the clothing closet at the office door. He glanced around, almost nervously before unlocking the door.

Hailey studied him intently. She wished she could become invisible and follow him into the office. Something at the pit of her stomach told her that he was being as sneaky as they were.

He was only in the office for a few minutes but Hailey noticed him putting something into his coat pocket before closing the door. Was that money?

The children remained in their quiet hiding place until they heard the church door close.

Kyra was the first to speak. "What was that about?" She stepped out from behind a clothing rack and stared at Hailey curiously.

"I have no idea. Could you see him?"

Kyra nodded. "He was being all sneaky like."

"I thought the same thing." Hailey crawled out of her hiding place and picked up the shirt she'd dropped when the man interrupted them.

"I didn't see him," Hayden said disappointedly. "Was it the pastor?"

"No. I didn't recognize him. But there are so many people at this church I'm not sure I would have paid attention to him if I had seen him this morning."

"What did he look like?" Grant asked.

"He was a big guy. I thought he was bald, but I couldn't see his face," Kyra offered.

"I guess that means one thing though." Hailey glanced at the clock. "Even though youth group doesn't start until six, we're still going to need to be careful on Sunday afternoons."

***

As it drew closer to 6:00 the children knew they would need to be scarce.

"Why don't we just all go outside and walk around for a while until six. Then we can show up when the others do." Kyra glanced out the choir room window.

Hailey nodded. "That's a great idea."

She'd already made adjustments to the window to keep it permanently unlocked. The four children climbed out the window and began their walk down the road just before five thirty. It gave them a chance to get some fresh air and explore the area.

At quarter 'til six they noticed cars pulling up in front of the church.

Hailey wasn't sure why but there was a little part of her that was afraid to go to youth group. What if the other teens didn't like her? What if they asked too many questions and figured out that she was a runaway? She'd never had to be so cautious before. Was their disappearance on the news? Hailey had no way of knowing.

"Well, Big Sis." Kyra put an arm through Hailey's and glanced toward the church. "Are you ready?"

Hailey took a deep, steadying breath and nodded. She figured once they got into the swing of things it wouldn't feel so scary.

***

The youth room was full of teenagers. Kyra, Hayden and Grant stayed downstairs with the few other younger siblings whose parents brought them while they waited for the high school youth group to be over.

Hailey brought them each a couple slices of pizza and warned them to behave. She hoped they would be okay.

64

Because she'd been in her little brother's Sunday school class with him in the morning, the faces in the youth room were all new to her.

Hailey glanced around and felt alone. Little groups of friends chatted happily as the teens filled the room.

The youth room was spacious and up to date. It was definitely designed for teens. The walls were painted in what reminded Hailey of coffee shop colors. Two walls were leathery brown, one was a muted green and the other was burnt orange. A couple of Bible verses were scripted across the wall in lighter paint with a few added swirls to the writing. It was creative and fun.

Several matching sofas, brown beanbag chairs and pillows filled one side of the huge room, while a Ping-Pong table and corn hole game took up the other side. Teens stood around talking, listing to contemporary Christian music on the youth group stereo system.

"You must be, Hailey," the youth pastor greeted Hailey with a grin. "I'm Chad. Kate told me you might be coming."

Hailey was impressed that the pastor's wife remembered her. "Will she be here?" For some reason Hailey liked Kate.

"She might," Chad said. "Kate helps out with the youth group quite a bit."

Hailey was glad to hear it.

"Kate said you're new in town." Chad waved at one of the youth group boys who greeted him upon arrival. "Where do you go to school?"

"I'm homeschooled," Hailey answered confidently. It was one of the few things she didn't mind saying since in her mind it was now true.

"That's cool. Have you met Janie? She's about your age I bet. She's homeschooled too." Chad glanced around the room looking for the girl he wanted to introduce to Hailey. "Hey, Janie," he called to a petite blonde who just walked in with a couple young men. "Come here, there's someone I want you to meet."

Hailey fidgeted nervously with the edge of her sweater and attempted to smile at this new girl.

"Hi," Janie greeted Hailey warmly. "I'm Janie." Her smile was so friendly it lit up her face. It reminded Hailey of Kate's smile. Hailey noticed a scattering of freckles and two adorable dimples on the lovely girl's face.

Hailey did her best to return Janie's smile. "Hi." Meeting new people was never easy for Hailey.

"Hailey is homeschooled, too." Chad offered to Janie as a conversation starter before he slipped away to prevent two boys from opening a soda can over someone's head after just shaking it.

"You're homeschooled?" Janie continued. "That's great. Have you always been homeschooled?"

Hailey shook her head. "No. Only since we moved. How about you?" Hailey was careful to turn the conversation right back on Janie.

"Always. My brother, Paul is homeschooled, too." Janie called to her brother and the two teens Janie arrived with came toward her. "This is Hailey," Janie introduced. "This is my brother Paul and his best friend, Wade."

"Hi," Paul said, followed by a smile very similar to Janie's. Even his blonde hair matched Janie's.

"She's homeschooled," Janie went on to share.

"Oh, cool." Paul nodded. "What year are you?"

"A freshman."

"So am I!" Janie seemed happy to meet another freshman. "Paul and Wade are sophomores."

"I'm Wade." The other young man finally spoke up.

Hailey tried not to let her eyes linger too long on Wade's attractive blue eyes shining out from beneath curly dark brown hair. "Nice to meet you." She did her best to sound confident. "Are you homeschooled, too?"

"No." Wade shook his head. "I go to West High."

The teens talked for a few minutes longer when Chad motioned for Wade to come up front.

"Gotta go." He grinned.

Hailey watched as Wade picked up a guitar and did a quick tuning job while Chad called all the teens together to open in prayer.

Janie invited Hailey to sit beside her and quickly introduced Hailey to another girl as everyone settled down.

A tall slender girl with a warm, friendly smile passed out a book of worship songs and Hailey flipped through it curiously. It

66

was interesting to watch the evening unfold. This was unlike anything Hailey had ever experienced.

Wade led the youth group in three worship songs and Hailey was impressed to see this group of about thirty-five settle down and focus on singing songs to God. She'd never seen anything like it.

After the singing, Wade returned his guitar to its case and sat down beside Paul and Janie.

Paul gave his friend a quick fist bump. "Good playing."

Chad began making announcements of upcoming youth group events and Hailey sat back on the sofa and took it all in.

"We do have two visitors tonight." Chad glanced at Hailey and winked. "This is Hailey, and over here, Sarah brought her cousin, Amy."

Everyone's eyes were on her for just that moment and Hailey hid her nervousness as best she could.

After the introductions, Chad went into the lesson. Hailey breathed a sigh of relief and listened as he began the talk.

Hailey didn't notice Kate slip into the room during Chad's message.

Chad spoke from the book of 1 Timothy. "Someone read 1 Timothy 4:12," Chad began.

Hailey was impressed with the number of teens who raised their hands to read the Bible. She was also impressed with how many of them brought their Bibles and eagerly turned to the right page.

"Let no one look down on your youthfulness, but rather in speech, conduct, love, faith and purity, show yourself an example of those who believe,'" a young man read.

"Thank you, Ben," Chad said. "Okay, so let's talk about that verse. God tells us not to let anyone despise, or in other translations it will read 'look down upon, your youth'. But instead, we are to be an example of the believers in our conversation, charity, spirit, faith and purity."

Hailey listened as Chad talked to the teens about what it means to be an example to others for the sake of Christ. He hit on each thing mentioned, bringing up the things people talk about, their language, how they treat others, their walk with the Lord and how they behave in dating relationships.

With the exception of a few giggly girls who were slightly distracted by something on one of their cell phones, everyone listened.

Chad took a few moments to focus on what it meant to be a follower of Jesus Christ and encouraged anyone who did not understand what it meant to be a Christian to talk to him or Kate. Then he closed in prayer and the teens lingered around talking and playing games.

"What did you think?" Janie asked.

"It was really nice." Hailey wasn't sure how to express all she was feeling. It was like she'd been very hungry for a long time and was suddenly given a huge meal. How long had it been since Hailey had been drawn into God's word that way?

"Chad is a great teacher," Janie said. "His wife is really sweet too. She just had a baby so she's been staying home on Sunday nights for a while. I'm sure you'll like her too."

"Do you think you'll come back?" Wade interrupted their conversation.

Hailey nodded. "Absolutely."

"How close do you live to the church?" he asked.

"Very." *You have no idea just how close...*

"Hailey," Kate approached. "I'm so glad you came."

"Hi Aunt Kate." Janie put her arm around Kate's back and gave her a friendly hug.

*No wonder Janie's smile reminded me of Kate.* Their coloring was different: Kate's hair was brown and her skin more olive, but Hailey could see a family resemblance.

"I'd hoped you two would meet." Kate glanced from Hailey to Janie. "Remember me telling you I had a niece in the youth group?"

Hailey nodded. What would it be like to have this nice woman be her aunt?

"I saw your brothers and sister downstairs."

"Are they okay?" Hailey felt a moment of panic.

"They're doing great. They were playing a couple games with a few other children who are waiting for activities to finish up. My husband has a men's prayer group on Sunday nights during youth group and one of the men brought his children tonight. I think your brothers are having a good time with his boys."

Chad joined in the conversation and asked Hailey if she could fill out a sheet with her name and contact information. Hailey glanced at the paper nervously and carried it to a small table where she could fill it out.

*Hailey Evans. Homeschooled. Age 15. Phone number... no phone. Address...* Hailey sighed. *I can't write 'none'.* She left it blank, carried the paper back to Chad and acted casual.

"Well, I should probably get my brothers and sister." Hailey was glad for an excuse to disappear. She noticed Chad glancing over the information sheet.

"You guys don't have a phone?"

"No. But I'll be around... you can let me know of upcoming things that way."

Janie joined Hailey as she walked down the stairs to meet her siblings. "I wanted to tell you, since you homeschool," she began, "on Thursdays at the church there's a ladies Bible study and my mom attends. During that time a bunch of us who are homeschooled hang out in the church library. We do school together and kind of hang out. You'd be welcome to come if you'd like."

"But my mom's not in the Bible study."

"That doesn't matter. You'd still be welcome." The smile on Janie's face said that she really wanted Hailey to come.

"We'll come."

Janie gave Hailey all the details as they walked into the sanctuary to find Hailey's brothers and Kyra.

\*\*\*

Hailey, Kyra and the boys walked from the building and slipped off into the woods to wait for the church to be empty. Hailey hoped no one checked the window and locked it.

From the woods, the children could see the various cars drive away and waited as the pastor and his wife turned out all the lights and walked to their car. They talked softly to one another and Hailey noticed the pastor opened the door for Kate. It was sweet.

Once the coast was clear, the children hurried to the window and slipped back into the church.

"Well." Hailey let out a huge sigh of relief. "We did it!"

"That was just day one," Kyra reminded her.

"How was it?" Hailey wanted to know what they all thought. Was it unrealistic to think they could actually live in Warsaw Chapel for an extended period of time? Hailey tried not to think too far into the future. Three years… in three years she'd be eighteen. Then she could take care of Kyra and her brothers on her own. Couldn't she?

"I liked it," Kyra confessed.

"We haven't seen Tara in three days!" Grant's eyes sparkled.

"Yeah. I haven't been called a bed wetter the past two nights." Hayden's tone revealed the resentment he felt.

Hailey was pretty sure her little brother stayed dry the past two nights, but she didn't want to embarrass him by asking. There was a lot of hurt buried in Hayden's heart and Hailey ached for him.

The children got their sleeping bags ready in their cozy little cove underneath the stage. The carpet under the stage was new, but could have used a vacuum cleaner for the dust. Hailey reflected that it was far cleaner than the carpet in the Prescott's house.

Hailey wanted to keep everyone up just a little later than normal so they'd all sleep late. The church office was opened from 9:00 am until 1:00pm. She wasn't sure how long the pastor and youth pastor were in the building. Hailey figured if she and the other kids slept late it would mean less time that they would need to be quiet while they were awake. She suggested that Kyra tell them a story.

"I would love to tell a story," Kyra was honored that Hailey would ask. "Do you want a mystery or a drama?"

"You decide."

"Okay, then how about the story of the Church Mice Kids." Kyra's eyes sparkled as her imagination began to whirl.

"Is that like the Box Car Children?" Grant asked excitedly.

"Yes. Only these kids live in a church!"

Hailey listened quietly, impressed at the younger girl's creativity, as she took their very story and turned it into an adventure even more thrilling than the one they were experiencing.

# Chapter 7

In spite of going to sleep late, Hailey woke up early. She could hear voices in the sanctuary and hoped it wouldn't wake Kyra and her brothers.

As quietly as she could, Hailey sat up and put together the lesson plans for her brothers. She planned to make them each do math, read, practice handwriting, and spelling. She hoped to find books they could use for science and history in the church library.

Kyra woke up and asked Hailey what they were going to do for personal needs while there were people in the church.

Hailey had already thought of that and had a bucket and toilet paper stationed at the other end of their secret hiding place behind a wall.

"You really did think of everything, didn't you?" Kyra grinned.

"That was a great story last night by the way." Hailey took a moment to encourage Kyra. "I had no idea you were so creative."

Kyra's dark eyes lit up and a smile crossed her lips. "Thank you."

The two girls worked on their own schooling while the boys slept. It was close to noon before the boys woke up.

Hailey had peanut butter and crackers stashed away for their breakfast and reminded them that they needed to be very quiet. "Until we know how everything works here through the week we need to be extra careful."

Hayden handed Hailey a church bulletin he'd gotten the day before and folded it to the weekly calendar. "Did you look at this, Einstein?"

Hailey knew he was only teasing her but she gave him a rebuking glare. She accepted the calendar and nodded her approval. "This is good. Way to be on top of things, Hayden." She showed Kyra. "According to this, Mondays, Tuesdays and Wednesdays, there is nothing going on during the day. But

Thursday is the women's Bible study that Janie told me about. Fridays it looks like the church office is closed. That's a good thing. We've also got Wednesday night church and youth programs, Sunday morning and Sunday night church and youth group."

"And this Upward Basketball thing is about to start up soon," Hayden pointed out on the bulletin.

Hailey smiled at her brother. "Would you like to do that?"

Hayden shrugged. "I guess."

At least it was something. Hailey hoped Hayden's attitude would get better now that they weren't living with Tara.

Hailey also noticed a note at the bottom of the page saying that the church was looking for someone to do light cleaning in the church until the janitor was back from his trip out west. "Look at this," she pointed to the announcement. "Do you think we could do it?" She glanced at the three others. "It would give us an opportunity to be here and earn a little extra money."

"I'd do it," Kyra volunteered.

Hailey glanced at her mother's watch. "Its almost one. The church office closes at one. Why don't we slip outside and come back to the front doors, go in and apply for the job?"

They all liked the idea.

Very quietly all four children climbed out the window and approached the church as if they'd just walked there from home.

\*\*\*

"Pastor Evans knows we're homeschooled so he shouldn't question us being out in the middle of the afternoon." Hailey said as she straightened her sweater before opening the large church doors.

The four children walked back inside as if they'd just arrived and approached the church office nervously.

"Good afternoon," a little round woman with soft white hair and a welcoming smile greeted the children when they peaked into the office. "Can I help you?"

"Hi." Hailey was the official spokesperson for the group. "I'm Hailey... Evans and this is my sister, Kyra, and brothers Hayden and Grant."

"I'm Ruby Blackaby, the church secretary," the older woman motioned for them to come into the office. "How can I help you?"

"We wanted to see about your need for someone to help with the cleaning until the janitor gets back." Hailey held out the bulletin. "We'd like the job."

"Don't you have school?" Ruby glanced at the clock across the room.

"We're homeschooled," Hailey explained. "So we do school at all kinds of weird times."

Ruby studied them curiously. "Let me talk to Pastor Evans." She lifted up the phone and called his office. "Pastor, there's a small posse of children in here who'd like to help with the cleaning until Ned gets back in town." She paused for a moment while the pastor spoke. "That's fine, I'll tell them."

Ruby hung up the phone and smiled. "He'll be here in a moment." She studied Hailey for another moment, fixing her gray eyes on the girl as if she was trying to figure something out. "You look familiar to me. Have you gone to church here very long?"

Hailey shook her head and shifted nervously. There was something familiar about Ruby, painfully familiar. Without a doubt, Hailey recognized this woman from her childhood. But she'd have to play it off. "We just moved here."

"Well if it isn't the Evans'," Lane greeted them warmly.

Hailey was thankful for the interruption.

"Ruby, these are the four children I told you about this morning."

Ruby's eyes lit up. "Oh," she chuckled. "Of course. Well aren't you an adorable bunch? I bet I saw you Sunday morning – that's why you look so familiar."

Hailey glanced at her brothers and Kyra, wondering how they were feeling right now.

"So you'd like to help with the cleaning until Ned returns?" Lane leaned against one of the tables in the room and studied the children curiously.

"Yes, sir." Hailey stood to her full height and kept her shoulders back. "We're good at cleaning and thought it was something we could all do to earn a little extra money."

Ruby was about to say something but Lane interrupted. "It doesn't pay much."

"That's okay. Anything is more than we earn," Kyra spoke up.

The pastor glanced at Ruby for her reaction. Ruby gave a willing shrug. "They look like a capable crew."

"Are your parents okay with it?"

"Oh yes. They don't mind at all." Hailey shifted her feet nervously. "As long as we get our school work done."

"Well then, we'd be happy to have your help." He reached into a cabinet and pulled out a key. "We keep the vacuum and cleaning supplies in a closet just outside the foyer. We need someone to vacuum, clean the bathrooms, and dust the furniture. Do you think you can do all that?"

"No problem." Cleaning this place would be a breeze after cleaning Tara's house.

"There are also rooms in the lower building. We have another vacuum cleaner for that carpeting and there are two more bathrooms. I'll give you a key." He paused as if to consider the responsibility he was about to give them. "You can't lose this. It's the key to both buildings of the church."

"I won't lose it," Hailey promised. "I'm very responsible, sir."

Lane smiled at the word 'sir' and handed her the key.

"When do you want us to start?" Hailey could hardly believe it. She was holding the key to the church. This was almost too good to be true.

"Monday and Thursday are Ned's big cleaning days," Lane explained. "The church usually gets the messiest on Sundays and Wednesdays. But you can work at your own pace."

Hailey nodded. "Thank you."

"How did you like youth group last night?" Lane asked. "Kate told me you were there."

"I liked it a lot." Hailey brushed a long dark hair out of her eyes. "I met your niece and nephew."

"That's what Kate said." Lane smiled. "Janie and Paul are great kids."

"Well." Hailey took a nervous step backwards toward the door. She didn't want the pastor asking any personal questions.

"We should probably find the closets and see if we can get a start on the cleaning."

Lane nodded. "I'll show you where they are."

"So glad you children will be helping out," the church secretary waved.

***

Lane walked the children to the closet off the foyer and showed them where everything was. "Ned should be back from California in about a month. He and his wife went out there to visit their daughter and son-in-law and their new baby."

"That's nice."

"I wish I could go to California," Hayden spoke up for the first time.

"California is beautiful. Kate and I lived there for a few years." Lane pulled out the vacuum cleaner and showed Hailey where the hoses attached.

"Did you ever surf?"

"A little bit."

A slight smile formed on Hayden's lips. "But you're a pastor." His tone said that somehow pastors weren't cool enough to surf.

"What does that have to do with it?" Lane grinned at Hayden.

"I don't know." Hayden shrugged. "Surfing seems pretty cool."

Lane put his hands on his hips and looked at Hayden. "And pastors don't do cool?"

"I don't know. The only pastor I remember was a really old guy at my grandma's church. But I was pretty young. He probably didn't even know what a surf board was."

Hailey glanced at her brother nervously. *This is Grandma's church... they just have a new pastor.* She hoped her brother wouldn't offer any more information about grandma's church.

"So you haven't gone to church in a while," Lane clarified.

"No." Hailey decided to take the conversation back over.

"Yesterday was my first time ever being in a church," Kyra interjected.

Hailey wished they'd have stayed under the stage.

The pastor's eyes grew tender. "Well I'm certainly glad you all started coming here." He studied each of the children curiously. "Are you guys hungry? Ruby brought in an amazing coffee cake this morning. We could all go into the kitchen and have a piece. I'm kind of hungry."

"Me too!" Grant spoke up.

Lane led the way to the kitchen and they all followed. Hailey hoped this wasn't going to turn into an interrogation. She wasn't sure the others could keep up their story – it was still so new.

Lane cut five hearty slices of the coffee cake and offered them all a glass of milk. "I love milk with my coffee cake, that's why Ruby brought it in. This is fresh cow's milk; Ruby's husband keeps a couple cows."

The children welcomed the milk and coffee cake and sat around the table with the pastor.

"Since yesterday was your first time here, I'm curious what you all thought." Lane took a bite of his coffee cake and waited for their reply.

"I love it here," Grant was the first to speak up. "We talked about Daniel in my Sunday school class and I knew almost all the answers Mrs. Robins asked us."

"Very nice," Lane said. "Where did you learn about Daniel?"

"From Hailey. She teaches me things from the Bible all the time. Next Sunday, Mrs. Robins said we are going to talk about Shadrach, Meshach and Abednego and I can't wait because I know the story really, really good. Hailey told me that Jesus was in the furnace with them and He protected them just like He goes through hard times with us and protects us."

Lane gave Hailey an approving smile. "It sounds like Hailey knows her Bible."

There was something in Lane's approval that made Hailey feel good.

Grant nodded. "She reads her Bible all the time. That's why Tara calls her a fanatic." Hayden kicked Grant under the table. "Ouch!" Grant narrowed his eyes on his brother.

Hailey gave her brothers a silencing glare and hoped Lane missed the interchange.

"Where did you get your Bible knowledge, Hailey?" the pastor turned his eyes to her.

"My grandmother." Hailey lowered her eyes. She really didn't like how personal this conversation was getting. Grant came frighteningly close to telling the pastor about their foster mom. Did the pastor miss the comment or choose to ignore it?

"Do you know Jesus personally, Hailey?" Lane asked her directly.

Hailey nodded shyly. "Yes."

"That's wonderful." Lane studied her quiet expression for a moment. "How about the rest of you?" He turned his attention to her siblings.

"I know Jesus," Grant spoke up again. "Last Christmas Hailey told me that Jesus gave me His life by dying on the cross for my sins and that the best gift I could give to Jesus was my heart so I gave it to Him."

Lane reached his hand across the table and patted Grant's arm warmly. "You're sister is right and I'm so glad to hear it." Lane glanced at Hayden. "How about you?"

Hayden shook his head. "No." He stuffed the last bite of coffee cake into his mouth. It was obvious he didn't wish to talk about it.

Lane glanced at Kyra for her response.

Kyra sucked in a deep breath and sighed. "It's all pretty new to me. I mean… I've heard Hailey talk about it some at home and stuff, but I don't know much about God."

"Would you like to learn more?"

"Yes." Kyra pushed the crumbs around on her plate. "I would. I do plan to come Wednesday night to the junior high youth group."

"You'll really enjoy it, I'm sure. Kate said you met our niece, Angela, last night while the high school youth group was going on."

Kyra nodded. "Yes. She seems really nice. I met her in the Sunday school class actually. But we played games together last night."

Hailey watched Lane's interaction with the others curiously. He was so gentle and seemed genuinely interested in them. He was very different from Keith who never seemed to talk to any of them unless he was scolding them for something.

What about her father? Hailey tried to remember what her dad was like. She was eight when he died. Because he was a truck driver, her dad wasn't around very much. But when he was home, Hailey remembered him being a good dad. He loved her. She remembered crawling up in his lap and him calling her his little princess. A smile crossed Hailey's lips as the memory flashed through her mind.

Hayden finished his milk and got up from his seat. "Can I go start cleaning?" he asked.

Hailey knew her brother didn't like these spiritual conversations. She wished his heart would soften towards the Lord.

"Sure." Lane stood up and carried his plate to the sink where he quickly washed it and put it away.

The children followed his example and Lane wiped the crumbs off the table. "I'm so glad we got to have this little snack together." He walked with the children toward the closet where the cleaning supplies were stored. "If you need anything, just let me know."

Hailey nodded shyly and thanked him.

"Kate and I just live about a mile down the road in that little white farm house with the green metal roof." He helped Hailey pull out the vacuum cleaner. "Where do you guys live?"

Hailey hoped this question would not come up. She took the vacuum cleaner and began unwinding the cord. "Not far."

The kids hurried to get busy cleaning. They all knew they needed to avoid that question.

\*\*\*

Dahlia Cooper's eyes grew wide when the office secretary handed her a letter post marked Hailey Goodman. She hurriedly tore open the envelope and began reading the letter.

A letter from Hailey was the last thing the social worker

expected after spending the weekend with the authorities searching for the three Goodman children and Kyra.

She'd struggled with what would cause the four kids to run away from their foster home. It seemed strange that Kyra would join them if Hailey was truly as bad as Tara made her sound. Kyra had been with the Prescotts for over two years.

A talk with Kyra's school teachers revealed that Kyra had gotten the lead part in her school play but told the director she was not allowed to be in in the play the very next day. Her teacher said that a very distraught Kyra explained that her foster parents would not let her be in the play.

Why would the Prescotts not allow Kyra to be in the play?

The letter said that Hailey borrowed money from the Prescotts. Dahlia tried to put things together. Tara Prescott told Dahlia about the money but never mentioned a note. Dahlia reread Hailey's letter.

*If Hailey left Tara some kind of note, Tara needed to tell me that.* Every *bit of evidence helps.*

Dahlia thought long and hard about Hailey Goodman. The fifteen-year-old was one of the sweetest foster children she'd ever worked with. The way Hailey took care of her two brothers was priceless.

But Hailey never complained about Tara and Keith during the meetings she had with her social worker. Why wouldn't Hailey have told Dahlia these things before? *Unless she was truly afraid of being separated from her brothers.*

Dahlia was going to have to handle this case carefully. There may be more to this than simply a rebellious girl who didn't like her foster family.

The social worker called her manager and decided to further her investigation into the Prescotts.

# Chapter 8

Lane asked the Lord's blessing on their meal and smiled when his wife passed him the sweet potato casserole. "You made my favorite."

Kate's eyes twinkled and she carried a small baked chicken to the table. "And there should be enough for you to have leftovers for the next couple days."

Lane was used to leftovers. It was difficult to cook meals without leftovers in a family of two.

"How was work today?" Kate asked her husband.

Lane took a bite of his sweet potatoes and savored it for a moment. "It was a good day. I visited Mr. Kraft in the hospital this afternoon."

"How is he doing?"

"Much better. They think he'll be coming home tomorrow." Lane poured cream in his coffee and gave it a quick stir. "And I had something unusual happen today." He grinned. "Those four children who visited yesterday came in and asked about the church cleaning job."

Kate furrowed her eyebrows curiously. "Did they think it was a paid position?"

Lane took another bite and nodded. "They did."

"What did you tell them?"

"I hired them. I figured I'd just pay them out of my pocket. It will be a great opportunity to interact with the kids. They're an interesting little group. The oldest girl, Hailey, seems to understand what it means to be a follower of Jesus Christ and she's led her little brother Grant to the Lord."

"That's encouraging."

"Hayden and Kyra don't appear to know Him though."

"Anne said her children enjoyed meeting them yesterday," Kate said. "They seem like very sweet children. How precious that they would come to church, even without their parents."

Lane nodded. "We'll pray that God will work on their parents."

"Can you visit them?"

"Not yet. I asked Hailey where they lived and she didn't give me a very clear answer. They all kind of acted strange about it, actually."

"Well, I'm just glad they're visiting. Let's pray that God will work in their hearts and that we can be a blessing to them."

\*\*\*

After scraping together a quick dinner using a box of macaroni and cheese from the food pantry and the milk Lane left in the refrigerator, Hailey and the children curled up on the sofas in the youth room and finished their school work. Hailey was determined that they were not going to fall behind in their education.

She pulled the key out of her pocket and turned it over in her hand. "You do realize that having this key opens all kinds of possibilities for us," she said to Kyra.

"And a lot of doors," Kyra teased.

Hailey laughed. "There is a shower in the basement of the lower building and now that we have a key we can get in and out of that building without any trouble."

"What about bath towels? We only have a couple."

Hailey shrugged. There's an old washing machine and dryer in the basement of that building as well. We'll just have to keep them clean."

"Why would a church have a washer and dryer?"

"Probably so they can wash their table linens. They have weddings and other special events here."

"This place really is nice." Kyra glanced around the youth room and let out a contented sigh. "I could get used to it."

Once again, Hailey kept the children up late so they would sleep in. Kyra continued making up her story about the Church Mice Children and they tidied up the youth room before heading downstairs to their secret hiding place.

\*\*\*

Tuesday was much like Monday. Hailey kept the children quiet until afternoon and they snuck out the window just before one o'clock to arrive for cleaning.

The pastor was in a meeting with someone in his office and Ruby was preparing to leave when Hailey walked into her office with the vacuum cleaner.

"Would you like me to clean in here, too?" Hailey asked.

"That's fine." Ruby stood up and pushed her chair in. "I'm about to leave. I need to run to the bank."

"Pastor Evans gave us some of your coffee cake yesterday. It was amazing." Hailey plugged in the vacuum and got ready to begin.

Ruby smiled. "Well, I'll have to make some more. I'm glad you liked it."

The secretary left and Hailey quickly vacuumed the office. She noticed a few cobwebs in the corners and used a broom to knock them down. Lane walked into the office just as she finished up.

"Wow! Look at this." He leaned on the door. "I'm not sure when Ned dusted the corners last. You're doing a great job."

Hailey tried to hide her smile at his complement.

"Hi, Hailey." The youth pastor walked in behind the pastor. "Lane told me you guys were going to be helping out around here until Ned gets back in town."

"Yeah," Hailey nodded. It seemed strange to be so warmly welcomed. Tara and Keith were never this kind to her.

"How'd you like youth group?"

"It was great." Hailey shifted nervously.

Kyra and the boys could be heard chatting down the hallway and greeted Chad and Lane when they reached the door.

"Well, we should probably get this stuff put away." Hailey wound up the vacuum cleaner cord and waved to the pastors as she slipped out of the office with the other kids.

\*\*\*

Wednesday night at the church was family night. A hot meal was offered to everyone who attended. There was a suggested donation, and Hailey made a mental note that once they started getting paid for cleaning the church she would pay for their meals.

The food was served lunchroom style in the kitchen and could be taken to one of the many tables in what was fondly called the fireside room. The smell of pine burning in the large stone fireplace drew Hailey's attention away from the food. A large grate guarded the front to prevent children from getting too close to the fire, but the warmth of the crackling logs filled the room.

Grant and Hayden hurried to sit with the boys they'd played with on Sunday night leaving Kyra and Hailey to find a place to sit by them selves.

"Homemade fried chicken." Kyra took a long breath to savor the smell. "This is amazing. I remember one of the foster families I stayed with for a couple years, they ate like this." She took a bite of her potatoes and closed her eyes to relish the flavor. "These are real mashed potatoes, not from a box."

Hailey enjoyed the meal as well. They'd been living on food pantry items since Sunday so this was a treat.

"Hi you guys," Janie greeted Hailey and Kyra with a smile.

Angela asked if the seat next to Kyra was open.

"You can sit here." Kyra moved her chair over slightly to make room for her new friend.

"Our parents are both here tonight." Janie's eyes traveled to the kitchen door to see if they were coming. "Do you mind if they sit with us too?"

"Not at all."

Anne and Chuck Duncan walked into the fireside room carrying their plates of food and sat down by their daughters.

"This is Hailey and Kyra," Janie introduced the two girls. "These are our parents."

Anne and Chuck greeted the girls warmly and asked a few simple questions about how long they'd been attending and how they were enjoying the church.

Paul and Wade sat with Wade's family after greeting Hailey and Kyra.

"So where did you children move from?" Chuck asked curiously.

"Northern Ohio," Hailey gave as honest an answer as she could.

Kate stopped by her sister's table and greeted Hailey.

Hailey thought that Kate and Anne looked a lot alike. Both of them were tall and slender and had very similar eyes, although Kate had brown hair and Anne was blonde.

Kate pulled up a chair close to Hailey and asked how they were doing.

"We're good." Hailey appreciated Kate's friendliness. There was something about Kate that made Hailey feel welcome.

"Lane told me that you guys are helping keep the church clean until Ned returns."

Hailey nodded.

"I'm so glad you're doing that. Lane and Ruby have been doing their best to keep it up, but they are both so busy with their other church responsibilities it was hard for them to have to clean the church."

"I don't mind it at all. I'm glad to help."

Kate smiled. Hailey noticed that when Kate smiled her whole face showed her happiness. *I hope I'm as pretty as Kate when I'm an adult.*

The girls sat and talked with Kate and the Duncans until it was time for the various church activities to begin. Kyra attended the junior high youth group in the youth room and Hailey went with Grant and Hayden to the other building while they got settled into the children's program. Janie volunteered with the children's program, as did several other high school teens, so Hailey didn't feel out of place.

The entire evening ran smoothly and Hailey started to believe that everything was falling into place. Grant and Hayden were making new friends, she and Kyra were growing closer, and they were both making friends of their own.

\*\*\*

During ladies' Bible study Hailey, Kyra and the boys joined the other homeschooled children in the library to do their school.

The comfortably sized library had several well-stocked bookshelves lining the walls. Two large wooden tables in the center of the room provided the students with an inviting place to do their schoolwork and be together.

Janie explained that a lifelong member of the church left it in her will, several years ago, for the church to have an updated library. "These two tables were hand crafted by one of the church members," she said. "He used walnut from his own farm."

Hailey ran her hand over the smoothly planed wood. It was lovely.

The chairs were also walnut, but Janie told her that they had been purchased with the money from the will.

Being that this was only their first week of being homeschooled, Hailey paid close attention to the others to see how they did it.

Several of the younger children had workbooks. Hailey wished she had workbooks for her brothers. They were working from home made lesson plans that she and Kyra put together. Hailey was sure Grant would have much more fun with a colorful page full of pretty pictures while he did his lessons.

Hailey asked Janie what she was reading for literature. Hailey had finished *The Scarlett Letter* and was ready to start another book.

Janie made several suggestions and helped Hailey find a couple of them on the library shelves.

In spite of her search, Hailey couldn't find the Box Car Children in the church library but promised Grant they would find it some day.

Hayden worked quietly and only stopped when some of the other boys finished their work and invited him to play a game.

*I think I like being homeschooled.* Hailey opened her physical science book and began to read.

\*\*\*

"I think this might actually work," Hailey said to Kyra on Saturday after the boys went to sleep. They'd all taken showers in the basement of the other building and had their clothes picked out for church the next day.

"I can't believe it's only been a week." Kyra snuggled down into her sleeping bag. "Do you think Tara and Keith even miss us?"

Hailey tried not to think about Tara and Keith. "I'm sure there is probably a search going on for us, although I'm not sure Tara and Keith really care that much about our actual well-being." She laid her head back on the pillow she'd made out of a clean towel. "Did I tell you that I sent a letter to our social worker telling her why we ran away?"

"No." Kyra turned onto her stomach and propped herself up on her elbows to better see Hailey. "Did you tell her how mean Tara and Keith were?"

"I didn't go into detail. But hopefully she'll at least investigate them."

"Hailey," Kyra said softly. "I'm really glad we left."

"Me too."

\*\*\*

Sunday morning ran smoothly. Hailey took Grant to his Sunday school class and left him to attend her own class. He said he was comfortable staying with Mrs. Robins and hugged Hailey before she left. Hailey was sure he was excited about Mrs. Robins' blueberry muffins.

Hayden was a little less enthusiastic but Hailey encouraged him to keep a good attitude and be friendly. "That really nice boy you played with Wednesday night is here," she said quietly to him as they neared the door to his class. "I think you'll be okay."

Hayden shrugged but Hailey thought he was actually looking forward to seeing his new friend.

As Hailey sat with her new friends, a strange sense of belonging washed over her.

"Glad you came back." Wade moved over on the couch to make room for Hailey.

Janie scooted over on the other end and greeted Hailey enthusiastically. "Hi! You look nice today."

"Thanks." Hailey appreciated the encouragement.

The lesson started a few minutes later and they all quieted down and paid attention.

Chad taught the Sunday school lesson with the help of an older man who touched on some deep theological topics.

"Mr. Waters used to teach Bible at a Christian college," Wade whispered an explanation to her. "He helps out with the class quite often."

Hailey listened intently to the Bible lesson, eager to get as much out of it as she could. Never before had Hailey had so much Bible teaching in just one week. This was just what she'd been hungering for.

After Sunday school, Hailey found her brothers and Kyra. They took seats in the sanctuary with the Duncan children and Wade while they listened to Pastor Evans' message. Hailey liked the pastor's teaching. He made the Bible come to life for her. She hoped her brothers and Kyra got something out of it, too.

Once the service ended and the congregation filed out of the building, the children did their part to make it look like they were leaving.

"We'll see you tonight, right?" Janie asked as they neared the door.

"Of course." Hailey watched Janie walk outside with her family and quickly looked around for Kate Evans. She'd not seen her yet today and for some reason Hailey wanted to say goodbye.

Hailey found Lane finishing up a conversation with a few men in the foyer and waited for a moment to talk to him. She'd asked her siblings to wait outside for her.

"Well hello, Hailey. You like to be the last one in the church I'm thinking," he smiled.

*Pastor Evans has no idea how right he is about that…*

"I was looking for Kate," Hailey said.

Lane glanced toward the large, glass doors where he could see Kyra, Hayden and Grant outside talking. "Kate wasn't feeling the best today."

Hailey noticed that the pastor's eyes grew suddenly somber. Was everything okay? Was it serious? "What's wrong? Is she sick?" Hailey knew it wasn't really any of her business, but she liked Kate.

Lane gave a sad kind of smile and shrugged. "I don't guess Kate would mind me telling you this. Most of the church already knows." The pastor blew out a heavy sigh. "About two years ago we had an adorable little foster baby we hoped to adopt. She was with us for over ten months. Everything was ready to go for the adoption but then the birth mother changed her mind and decided she wanted to keep Joy. So… today is the anniversary of when we would have adopted Joy. Kate's having a hard time."

Hailey's eyes misted. "I'm so sorry." She glanced toward the door and tried to ignore Hayden who was pressing his mouth and nose against the glass and making faces.

Lane nodded. "Thanks."

"Can I do anything?"

Hailey's words seemed to catch Lane off guard. He grinned. "You know, maybe you kids could stop by one day this week. Just pop in on Kate. She'd probably love that."

Hailey nodded enthusiastically. "We will."

They said their goodbyes and walked outside. Hailey waited for the pastor to get into his car before leading the children to their hiding place in the woods. They waited patiently for his car to drive away so they could get back into the church.

***

Hailey was somber after Lane drove away. *Poor Kate.* Hailey knew what it felt like to lose someone you love. She'd wondered if Lane and Kate had children of their own. She'd not seen them with any. *Could they not have children?*

After a week of living in Warsaw Chapel, all five children felt at home.

Just after lunch, they heard someone enter the building. Once again a familiar voice called out asking if anyone was there.

Hailey motioned for the boys to hide in the pantry closet with Kyra while she snuck quietly down the hall to investigate. Now that she was officially doing church clean up, if she was caught, Hailey figured she had a good excuse.

Hailey could see a light coming from the church office and ducked into the clothing closet. She could hear his humming echo across the hall. *If only I was hiding in the office… I could see what he's actually doing.*

The man was only in Ruby's office for a few minutes and Hailey watched him intently as he slipped out with something in his hand. Hailey strained her eyes to see if it was money. She was sure it was. Hailey tried to think of a rational reason for him to be taking money from the office. *Maybe he is in charge of depositing the money in the bank.* But, at the pit of her stomach, Hailey wasn't convinced.

She waited until he left to check out Ruby's office.

Hailey didn't have the key to Ruby's office, but she'd already figured out that the door could easily be opened using her school identification card. *At least I can use it for something.*

Once in Ruby's office, Hailey glanced around trying to figure out what the man might have been doing. She saw a large manila envelope on the desk that was labeled offering. *This has to be it...* Hailey was almost afraid to touch the envelope herself for fear that someone might catch her and believe her to be a thief. She patted it a few times and felt that the envelope was full. *Well, if he was here to get the offering to make a deposit then why didn't he take it all?*

*Dear God, is that man stealing from the offering?* Hailey prayed softly. It seemed unreal that anyone would do that. It was like stealing from God.

She hurried out of the office and back to her brothers and Kyra. "It was that man again... and I think I know what he is doing."

*** 

During Sunday night youth group, Hailey was distracted. The man in the church office concerned her. If he was stealing from the offering and anyone ever noticed the money missing, couldn't she and her brothers be accused of it? Especially if it was ever found out that they were living in the church.

She sat with her new friends and tried to focus on the lesson.

Hailey was also distracted thinking about Kate. She wondered if Kate and Lane were still trying to adopt or had they given up after losing the little girl they thought they were going to keep.

No one ever tried to adopt her and her brothers. Hailey sometimes wondered if having an older sister robbed her brothers of the chance of getting adopted. People wanted cute little babies and toddlers. Hayden and Grant were little when their grandmother died, but Hailey was eleven. Who wanted an eleven year old? Her eyes traveled to the ceiling. *And who would ever want a fifteen year old?*

It seemed unfair that there were so many children wanting parents while there were so many adults only wanting babies. *When I grow up, I'm going to adopt older children.*

"That was a pretty good point," Janie whispered to Hailey.

Hailey blushed. She'd missed most of Chad's talk and had no idea what point Janie was referring to. Hailey glanced around the room and saw that most of the teens were listening intently to Chad.

"I just want to remind you all that God wants to be that in your lives," Chad was saying. "I challenge you to allow Him to be… no matter where you're at in your walk with Him, God wants to spend time with you. Are you in His Word every day? Are you talking to Him? Are you asking for His wisdom, His help, His direction? If not, why?"

Chad motioned for Wade to come up front and lead the group in another worship song.

After youth group, Hailey asked Janie about her aunt. "Pastor Evans said she was wasn't feeling the best today. He told me about Joy."

Janie nodded. "It was pretty terrible when they took Joy away. We all thought Aunt Kate and Uncle Lane were going to be able to adopt her." Janie lowered her eyes. "We all took it pretty hard but of course Aunt Kate took it hardest. I still miss little Joy. She was so sweet."

"Does Kate ever get to see her?"

Janie shook her head. "Never. They took her away and she was gone forever."

Paul and Wade walked up while the girls were talking about it and joined in.

"And they took her away from all of us," Paul interjected.

Wade nodded. Hailey figured he knew the story as well.

"I was thinking of going to Kate's house to visit her this week." Hailey leaned back on the sofa, pulled her legs up close and wrapped her arms around her knees. "Do you think she'd mind?"

"I think she'd like that." Paul pulled up a chair and sat across from her. "We went over for lunch this afternoon. I could tell she was down but having company encourages her."

Hailey nodded. She liked the idea of encouraging Kate.

"I guess your little brother has become friends with my little brother." Wade changed the subject.

"Really? Which brother? I have two."

"The little red head."

Hailey nodded. "That would be Hayden. He told me he had a new friend. It's a huge blessing. His first week at church I didn't think he'd be willing to come back." She brushed a long hair away from her face. "What's your brother's name?"

"Caleb."

"I hope Hayden has been… well behaved." Hailey had a sudden moment of panic. What if Wade was telling her this to express disapproval?

Wade laughed. "Well, from what I can tell, your little brother is quite a little character, but Caleb really likes him. He said Hayden isn't a Christian and he's made it his goal to lead Hayden to Christ."

"That suits me fine. I've been working on Hayden for years."

"Does your little brother really know how to hot wire a car?" Wade's grin revealed a dimple.

"Not that I know of." Hailey shrugged. "I think that was his way of making up for not knowing how to find the books of the Bible."

Wade laughed. "And I supposed you really don't have a movie theater in your basement…"

"I can see I'm going to have to talk to my little brother." Hailey shook her head. "I'm sorry."

"Don't apologize. Like I said, Caleb is on a mission. He's been praying for him every night."

Janie and Paul needed to leave and waved goodbye to their friends.

"I'm glad Caleb is praying for him. Hayden really isn't a bad kid. He's just got some issues."

"Don't we all?" Wade moved to the seat across from her where Paul had been sitting. "So, your brother's not a Christian…

how about you?"

Hailey nodded. "I gave my life to Christ when I was nine. My grandmother led me to the Lord."

Wade's blue eyes showed that he was pleased. "I'm glad to hear that."

"How about you?" Hailey wasn't used to asking people questions about their relationship with God, especially really cute high school guys, but since he had she felt it was only fair.

"I got saved when I was about five, but I didn't really start taking my faith seriously until I was about fourteen. Now Jesus is pretty much my life."

Wade's blunt admission of his love for Jesus was unlike anything Hailey had ever heard from a peer. She wasn't sure how to respond. *That's what I want to be like.*

"How did you get to that place in your faith?" she asked softly.

Wade leaned back and took a deep breath. "I started seeing the direction so many of my friends were going. Even my older brother had turned into a partier. He was a mess. I didn't want to be like that. I knew there had to be more to life... more to live for than the social scene, girls, being popular, all that. So I asked God what to do. He showed me Galatians 5:24-25 'Now those who belong to Christ Jesus have crucified the flesh with its passions and desires. If we live by the Spirit, let us also walk by the Spirit.'" Wade's eyes shone as he quoted God's word. "I realized that because I belong to Christ, I needed to live my life walking in the Spirit. Every day I ask Him to help me lay down the flesh and walk in His Spirit."

Hailey's eyes were wide. "That's what I want..."

"Hey Wade," a girl Hailey had seen in the youth group but not met yet interrupted them. "You two look like you're having a deep discussion."

Another girl joined them and smiled admiringly at Wade. "Can we join in?"

Wade's eyes lingered for just a moment on Hailey's, as if he was trying to communicate something to her, and then he greeted the others. "Have you ladies met Hailey Evans?"

The first girl gave Hailey a complacent nod.

The second girl scanned Hailey with a cynical grin. "Hey, I know that shirt. I donated it to the clothing closet." There was a chuckle in her tone that made Hailey feel suddenly insecure. "It even has the same little spot on the back." Clarissa's rosy pink lips curved into a smile and she and motioned toward the spot.

"This is Gina and Clarissa," Wade offered their names since they didn't.

"Nice to meet you." Hailey wondered if that was actually a lie. These two girls didn't seem at all interested in meeting her and Hailey wondered if the one Wade called Clarissa purposely chose this moment to bring attention to the shirt from the clothing closet. If so, that was downright mean.

Clarissa had short blonde hair and daring green eyes. Her name brand blue jeans and trendy blue shirt were spotless and new. Hailey wondered if she ever owned anything so fashionable.

"Do you live in that old trailer down the road?" Clarissa asked.

"No." Hailey felt herself suddenly grow shy.

Clarissa laughed as if she didn't believe Hailey. "Oh. Sorry. I thought I saw you and your brothers walking from there on the way to church this morning."

Hailey lowered her eyes. Had she done something to offend this girl?

"So, Wade," Gina changed the subject. "Did Mrs. Underwood say she was definitely having our class retake that English exam? I totally hope so. I flopped majorly on it."

Wade nodded. "She said she was going to let us take it again on Monday if we needed to."

"Don't you need to?"

"No. I got an A."

"Of course you did," Clarissa blew out a heavy sigh. "You've got Mrs. Underwood wrapped around your finger." Clarissa held out her little finger and made a twirling motion.

"No. I studied the first time."

Hailey still felt the weight of Clarissa's subtle slam and wanted to escape. This seemed like a good time. "See you guys next week." She got up to go.

"Oh, hey…" Wade got up with her. "I'll walk down with you. I have to pick up Caleb and he's probably playing with Hayden."

Hailey appreciated that Wade opted to walk out with her, although she felt Clarissa's eyes burning into her back as they walked from the room.

***

Once they were out of the youth room, Wade slowed down to talk to her. "I'm sorry they acted that way," he said.

Hailey shrugged. She was used to girls acting that way. Just not at church.

"There's nothing wrong with shopping the clothing closet." He watched her curiously.

"I know."

Wade paused awkwardly. "Do you live in the trailer they were talking about?"

"No."

"Because it's no big deal if you do…"

Hailey shook her head. "I know. But no… that's not where we live."

"Where do you live?" he asked.

This was no position to be put in. If she said not far then he'd probably think she was just lying about the trailer. "Not in the trailer," she kept it cryptic and grinned. Who cared what he thought?

"You know," Wade lowered his blue eyes and spoke encouragingly. "When I first made the decision to really walk in the Spirit, the enemy did all kinds of stuff to try to pull me down. He wanted to make me ineffective for the kingdom of God." He glanced up the stairs toward the youth room. "Sometimes things like that are ways that the enemy tries to thwart our efforts."

Hailey blew out a heavy sigh. "Thanks."

He placed a comforting hand on her shoulder. "Don't let them get to you. Pray for them."

Hailey nodded. Wade was unlike any young man she'd ever met.

94

Once they reached the sanctuary, they spotted their brothers running across the chairs.

"Caleb," Wade called out kindly. "We've got to go."

"But we can't get down. The whole church is flooded and there are killer sharks and piranhas!"

"Oh no!" Wade grabbed Hailey's hand and pulled her up onto one of the chairs. "We'd better be careful!"

Hayden and Grant were laughing and Hayden let himself fall off a chair and feigned the sounds of someone being attacked by a killer shark.

"This is quite the scene." Lane walked into the sanctuary and laughed. "You could be heard all the way to my house I'd bet."

Hayden kept up the act and lay on the carpet as one dead. "Well, I guess he's a goner." Hailey stepped down from the chair. "Can you help me drag his corpse to the dumpster?"

"I'll throw him out for you." Lane walked over and picked Hayden up, attempting to throw him over his shoulder but Hayden started laughing and ran away.

"Are there many more teens up in the youth room, Wade?" Lane asked.

"Just a few. Chad is probably going to run them out soon."

"Alright."

"Come on boys," Hailey called her brothers. "Where's Kyra?"

"She's outside. The stars are really bright here. She said she wanted to find Orion."

"Do you want me to drive you guys home?" Wade offered.

"No. We're good." Hailey thanked him for the offer and walked toward the door. She had to make sure they didn't walk in the direction of the trailer. Hailey wasn't sure what trailer Clarissa even meant, but she was sure that it was an insult.

# Chapter 9

Monday afternoon the children worked hard to get the church cleaned up. Hailey wondered when they would get paid. She was anxious to pay off the money she borrowed from Keith.

Lane and Chad worked most of the day in their offices. Chad invited Hailey and Kyra to an upcoming youth retreat for both high school and middle school students. He gave them the permission forms and told them if money was an issue that scholarships were available.

"We'd love to have you come," he encouraged.

Hailey glanced over the information about the trip. It was just two weekends away. "I don't think we'll be able to do this." Hailey offered him the form back.

"Why not?" Chad didn't let it drop.

"Our parents are kind of funny about trips like that," Kyra stepped in. "They already think we practically live at this church."

Hailey wanted to smack Kyra. "We have a lot of responsibilities with our brothers, so… I'm sorry."

Chad tilted his head and studied the girls curiously. "You need to do stuff for you sometimes."

"That's what youth group is for." Hailey gave him a quick grin and shrugged. "But thanks for the offer."

She tugged Kyra's shirt. "We'd better get those bathrooms cleaned."

Chad watched the girls walk away and sighed.

\*\*\*

The children decided they would visit Kate the next day. Hailey hoped Kate would be happy to see them. She worried that they would be a bother.

After the pastors left the building, the children spent a few hours in the church library reading a Bible history book they stumbled on the week before when they met with the homeschool group. The church library was a real gem and they found all kinds of books that interested them. Hailey knew Grant still wanted to know how *The Boxcar Children* ended, though, and hoped she'd be able to find it some day.

For dinner Hailey heated up a couple cans of soup from the food pantry and the children went to bed quite content.

Hailey lay awake for quite some time thinking more about her conversation with Wade. She'd made a point of asking God to help her walk in His spirit Monday morning and felt a strong desire to get to know God even better.

She thought about Clarissa. It put a little damper on how excited she'd felt about the youth group up until that point. She wondered if Clarissa was going on the youth group retreat. Hailey wished she could go. Was Chad disappointed with her that she couldn't? Would Wade be disappointed? She hoped they would not view her not going as a measure of her desire to grow in the Lord. She wanted to grow in Christ, but she really couldn't go. There was no way in the world she was going to leave her two little brothers alone in the church for a weekend.

Hailey didn't know what time it was, but she knew she needed to sleep.

\*\*\*

The children were extra quiet slipping out of the choir room window. They knew it was still early and heard voices in the church all morning.

Hailey wished she could have baked some cookies or something to bring to Kate, but there was no using the kitchen today.

The walk to the Evans' house was an easy one. Hailey glanced up at the quaint farmhouse, taking note of the neatly lined walkway and well-manicured shrubs. This looked like the kind of house Kate would live in. Hailey loved the green metal roof and covered porch. She imagined sitting on the porch swing in the summer time just reading a nice long book.

Kate was noticeably surprised when she opened the door. "Hi you guys," she smiled at the little group and invited them in.

The children stepped through the door into a well-lit hallway. Hailey noticed a vase of fresh flowers on a stand beside the door. The colorful array of carnations, roses, and baby's breath made the bright room feel even more cheerful.

"Should we take off our shoes?" Hailey noticed a few pairs of shoes lined up neatly against the wall.

Kate shook her head. "You're shoes look clean. There's no need to take them off."

Hailey was thankful. She was conscious of the fact that her socks showed great signs of wear.

"I'd like you to meet my mother."

A lovely, older version of Kate walked toward them with a friendly smile.

"Mom," Kate motioned to the children. "This is Hailey, Kyra, Hayden and Grant."

Hailey was impressed that Kate remembered all their names.

"I'm Helen," Kate's mother extended a soft wrinkled hand and shook each of theirs kindly. Her eyes lingered just a moment on Hailey. "You look so familiar. Have we met before?"

Hailey tried to keep her hands still. She wasn't sure. "I... I'm new to the area. Maybe you've seen me at church?"

"I don't attend Warsaw Chapel anymore," Helen explained. "I moved to the other side of Newark so I found a church closer. But you look so familiar."

Hailey swallowed back a nervous lump in her throat.

"You remind me of someone..."

This conversation had to stop. "Hayden, Grant, why don't you take off your coats?" Hailey did her best to change the subject.

"I'm going to have to think about it for a bit." Helen glanced at her daughter. "There's something about her eyes. That dear young lady resembles someone I know. Don't you hate it when you forget things like that?" She smiled at Hailey. "I'll figure it out eventually."

Hailey nodded and hoped she wouldn't.

"Mom brought me some homemade cookies. Why don't you come help me eat them?" Kate motioned for the children to follow her to the kitchen.

"I like cookies!" Grant spoke up.

Hailey let her eyes scan the remodeled farmhouse kitchen. The old maple floors were refurbished but the white kitchen cabinets looked new. She noticed how clean the beige, marble counter tops were. A large island with a stove sat in the middle of the kitchen and the table sat in a windowed alcove with a lovely old-fashioned pulley light hanging over it.

"What brought you guys out?" Kate asked.

"We wanted to come by and visit you," Hailey said. "I missed you Sunday."

Kate smiled. "I'm the one who usually comes to visit someone when they've missed. You sound like me."

"Kate, I'm going to go ahead and leave now, sweetheart," Helen said to her daughter and gave her a hug. "If you need me, just call."

"I will, Mom." Kate returned the hug.

"It was nice meeting you, children." Helen nodded toward them. "I hate to hurry off but I have an afternoon appointment."

"It was nice to meet you too." Hailey said politely.

"And I'll be wracking my brain where I've seen those eyes." Helen winked at Hailey.

After Helen left, Kate set out several napkins, cups, a gallon of milk and a plate of chocolate chip cookies. "Are you hungry?"

"We never turn down food." Kyra reached for the milk and grinned. "Thank you."

The children all accepted cookies and milk and ate them eagerly.

"I'm glad you came to visit me." Kate poured herself a cup of coffee and offered some to the girls.

"I'll take a cup." Hailey's eyebrows went up. "But I like about half milk."

Kate poured Hailey a cup of coffee and topped it generously with milk.

"Pastor Evans told us about Joy." Hailey lowered her eyes. She hoped Kate wouldn't mind that they knew.

Kate nodded. "He told me." Kate did her best to smile. "My emotions kind of snuck up on me." She shrugged. "Sometimes all those feelings just come back. But I'm okay now."

Hailey nodded.

"Can me and Grant rake your leaves?" Hayden looked out Kate's back yard at a huge maple tree whose leaves covered the ground like a bright yellow blanket.

"Grant and I." Hailey corrected his grammar.

"Sure." Kate was more than happy to the let the boys rake. "There are two rakes on the back deck. Be sure to jump in the piles a lot though, they just don't bag right unless they've been jumped in."

"Really?" Grant's eyes were wide.

Kate giggled. "Really you can jump in them, but I guess they bag okay either way."

Grant was pleased with the answer and hurried to rake with Hayden.

"He's always wanted to jump in the leaves," Hailey said without thinking.

Kate stirred her coffee and leaned back on the kitchen chair. "Do you not have any big trees in your yard?"

Kyra glanced at Hailey to see how she was going to answer.

"No. Not really." Hailey wasn't sure how many big trees were around the church. But they sure didn't have any near their house in Cleveland.

"Jumping in the leaves is a part of being a kid." Kate watched the boys raking.

"I've never done it either." Kyra finished her milk.

"Do you want to?" Hailey asked.

Kyra shrugged. "I guess I could go help the boys. Keep them in line, you know."

"Go ahead. We only have two rakes but I'm sure you can share."

Kyra hurried outside and Kate watched her join the boys. "They seem like they're having fun."

Hailey nodded. "Thank you for letting them do that."

"I should be thanking you. You not only came to visit me but they're out there raking for us." Kate turned her kind eyes on Hailey. "So tell me about you."

Hailey quickly stiffened. "Me? Oh... there's not much to tell. I... I'm just me."

Kate laughed lightly. "Where did you live before you moved here?"

"Northern Ohio."

"What part?"

Hailey licked her suddenly dry lips. "Different parts. We moved around a lot." She tried to keep all her answers honest.

Kate tilted her head. "Where do you live now?"

*Please don't ask me that...* Hailey's eyes grew somber. "I'd really rather not answer that."

Kate was noticeably surprised by Hailey's response. "Okay." She nodded supportively. "But you know, there is nothing to be ashamed of…"

Hailey cleared her throat. "I know."

Kate offered Hailey a refill on her coffee and Hailey accepted.

"Are you learning much in youth group?" Kate changed the subject.

"I am. It's amazing. I had a really good talk with Wade… I don't know his last name…"

"Parker," Kate offered.

"Yeah. Anyway, he talked to me about surrendering yourself fully to God and walking in the Holy Spirit." Hailey's eyes showed her enthusiasm. "I'd never really had that kind of conversation with anyone before, but I'm trying to do that… I asked God to help me walk in His Spirit."

"That's awesome, Hailey." Kate couldn't hide her pleasure. "It's important that we as Christians lay down the sin that hinders us and walk in Christ." She reached for her Bible and found a verse. "I love this verse in Hebrews 12. It tells us to lay aside the things that weigh us down, sins that entangle us, and run the race that is set before us." She pointed to the verse and Hailey read Hebrews 12:1 aloud.

"'Therefore, since we have so great a cloud of witnesses surrounding us, let us also lay aside every encumbrance and the sin which so easily entangles us, and let us run with endurance the race that is set before us,'" Hailey glanced up from the Bible. "Who are the witnesses surrounding us?" she asked.

"Everyone. As a Christian, the world is looking at you, other Christians are looking at you, your little brothers and sister are looking at you," Kate explained. "So we need to lay aside the things that are keeping us from running that race for God, or another way of looking at it, things that are keeping us from walking in the Spirit, and walk in Him."

Hailey nodded. "I like that."

Kate smiled. "You seem to have a heart that really wants to grow in Christ. I like that."

Hailey took a sip of her coffee and watched her little brothers dive into the huge pile of leaves they'd created. Kyra was already in the leaves, lying there with her arms stretched out and her face toward the sky. "Pray for Hayden and Kyra. They don't know Him yet."

"We have been."

Hailey wasn't surprised.

"What time do you have to be home?" Kate glanced at the clock.

"Oh… we don't have anything going on tonight. Whenever we get there is fine."

"I was going to grill some chicken. Do you think your parents would care if you ate dinner with us tonight? Lane will be home in about forty-five minutes and I like to have dinner ready for him when he gets here."

The idea of grilled chicken sounded amazing. She knew her brothers and Kyra would never forgive her if she turned Kate down. "I'm sure that would be fine."

"Do you need to call your mom first, maybe?"

"Oh no. She'd be fine."

"I'd feel better if you did." Kate got up and walked to the refrigerator to pull out her package of chicken. "I've got another one in the freezer I'll pull out if she says that's okay. Your parents would be welcome too if they'd like."

Hailey took another sip of her coffee. How should she answer?

"You can use my phone if you need to." Kate laid the cordless on the table.

Hailey picked up the phone and dialed random numbers while she walked toward the living room. "Hi, Mom…" Hailey's mouth went dry as she played out her deception. She knew Kate could hear her. "Kate asked if we'd like to stay at her house for dinner. Is that okay?" She paused long enough for a fake answer while a phone recording told her she'd dialed a number that was no longer in service. "Cool. Thanks. See you later." Hailey pushed the hang up button and closed her eyes against the tears that wanted to escape.

"So, your mom said yes?" Kate called from the kitchen.

*Of course my mom didn't say yes... she's dead...* "Its fine." Hailey squeezed the words out.

"Did you invite them?" Kate peered around the corner into the living room.

"No. They're not much for visiting." *They're in the grave... six feet under.*

"Well I'm so glad! Let me get more meat out of the freezer." Kate hurried to get things together.

After Hailey recovered she offered to help. Kate had Hailey cut potatoes while she thawed the chicken and prepared a glaze to put over it. "This is one of Lane's favorite chicken recipes."

Kate poured ingredients into a bowl. "It was my grandmother's recipe but I adapted it to the grill. Lane and I love grilling. Do your parents grill?"

"No. Never." *Finally, an honest answer.*

Kate made a quick call to her husband to let him know the Evans children would be joining them for dinner when he got home. Hailey was glad she used the phone to dial up her husband. Part of her feared that Kate might hit redial and figure out the hoax.

*I'm such a liar. How can I walk in the Spirit when I'm a liar?* Hailey felt a moment of personal failure and thought that once again the enemy was working to keep her from walking in the Spirit.

Kyra walked in to ask if Kate wanted her and the boys to bag the leaves. Kate was more than happy to give them the job and showed Kyra where the large trash bags were. "Lane is going to be so surprised!"

"Are we eating here tonight?" Kyra asked in a tone that said she was totally excited if they were.

"Yes. Hailey checked with your parents already and they said yes."

103

Kyra raised her eyebrows at Hailey for just a moment and Hailey felt guilty all over again. *Now Kyra knows I lied.*

"Well, the boys will be ecstatic! Thank you, Kate!"

*\*\*\**

When Lane arrived home from church, Kate and Hailey had the table nicely set with six place settings and an arrangement of leaves in the center of the table.

"The boys thought that would make the table look more autumn like," Kate explained to her husband.

"Did I see the back yard all raked up?" Lane walked to the window and glanced outside.

"Yes. Hayden, Grant and Kyra raked and bagged all the leaves from that huge maple."

"Wow. I'll get out there and thank them." Lane opened the back door and called to the children. "Wow! You guys are amazing!"

Grant ran to Lane and began talking endlessly about how many times he'd jumped in the leaves and that they'd buried Kyra and that he and Hayden dove into the leaves at least a hundred times.

Hailey walked to the door and enjoyed her little brother's banter.

"That's wonderful, Grant." Lane smiled. "And I have to thank you guys for doing all this. The yard looks great."

"We'll do it every fall for you if you want," Hayden offered.

"Yeah! Tara never let us rake the leaves." The words rolled off Grant's lips before Hailey could stop him.

"And we don't have any good trees in our yard," Kyra interjected. "But that tree is amazing. How long does it usually take you to rake all those?"

Hailey was relieved that Kyra could think fast on her feet.

"Oh, we spend a couple hours on it usually."

Kate called them in to dinner and Hailey told the boys to wash their hands. "Don't forget to use soap," she reminded them.

"You're quite the little mom," Kate said to Hailey. "Your little brothers really listen to you."

Hailey shrugged. Kate had no idea.

After the boys and Kyra washed up and Lane changed from his dress pants into a pair of jeans, the small group gathered in the dining room.

"This is really nice." Kyra eyed the table with wide eyes. "I like your plates. They're pretty."

"Thank you, Kyra." Kate sat to the right of her husband and motioned for the children to all take a seat.

After Lane asked the Lord's blessing on their food, they all waited for Kate to begin dishing out the meal.

Hailey breathed a sigh of relief that her brothers used enough discretion to not just dig in, as was the norm at the Prescott household.

"Upward Basketball practice sign-ups begin next week," Lane said to the boys. "Are you planning on playing?"

"I want to," Grant said through a mouth full of mashed potatoes.

"Grant, don't talk with your mouth full." Hailey corrected. "What about you, Hayden?"

Hayden shrugged. "If I can be on the same team as Caleb Parker I will. But if I can't then I don't want to."

Lane raised an eyebrow. "Ahh, I see… if you can't have it your way you don't want it."

Hayden took a bite of the grilled chicken and did his best not to smile. "This is good."

"I don't care whose team I'm on," Grant said after chewing the next bite. "I like basketball."

"You've never even played basketball, dumb wit." Hayden scowled at Grant.

"Hayden!" Hailey's tone was a harsh rebuke.

"Whatever."

Hailey wondered why Hayden was suddenly in a sour mood. He'd been having so much fun outside.

"Are you going to tell Mom?" Hayden gave Hailey a challenging stare and topped it off with a sarcastic smirk.

Hailey wasn't sure if it was appropriate to apologize or just crawl under the table. She shoved her amazing grilled chicken around on her plate and wondered if this was her punishment for lying earlier.

"You know, Hayden," Lane spoke up. "It really isn't nice to call people names. Do you like it when others call you names?"

Hayden shrugged. "No. But it doesn't stop them."

"But Jesus tells us to treat others as we would like to be treated. Are you doing that to Grant when you call him a name?"

Hayden rolled his eyes. "I was just kidding."

"Don't try to dismiss it. You really should apologize." Lane's tone was gentle but firm.

Hailey glanced up to see her brother lower his own eyes and take a deep breath. "I'm sorry, Grant."

"I forgive you." Grant's sweet voice was enough to make Hailey smile.

"Thank you, Hayden. You showed yourself to be a real man," Lane said sincerely.

Hailey studied Lane for a moment and wondered at the power he had over her little brother. Hayden seemed genuinely repentant.

"I'm really impressed with how my yard looks." Lane changed the subject. "How much do I owe you for all that raking?"

"You don't have to pay us," Kyra said. "We had a blast."

"But I want to pay you. I also owe you for cleaning the church. You've done a great job. I've actually had a few people at the church remark about how nice things look."

"Really?" Hayden took a long sip of his orange juice and actually smiled. "I'm the one who cleaned the men's bathroom."

"You know, I noticed that the men's bathroom looked very nice. You're doing a great job." Lane gave Hayden an approving nod and put his fist out for a fist bump.

"You fist bump?" Hayden asked before extending his fist.

Lane laughed. "Yes, that and surfing. It's kind of hard to believe isn't it?"

Hayden shrugged and gave the pastor the fist bump. "You're pretty cool, I guess."

"When I grow up I want to be a pastor." Grant spoke up, "I want to be just like you."

Hailey's lips curved into a smile and she glanced from Lane to Kate to gauge their response. They'd only known Lane and Kate for a short time… She'd never seen her brothers take to a man like this before.

Lane didn't seem to know how to respond. "I am truly honored." There was emotion in his voice.

"Why don't you have any children?" Grant asked.

Hailey blushed. She couldn't believe her brother just asked that in light of what she knew about the little girl they tried to adopt. Sometimes Hailey wished she could just write a script for her little brother to follow. She glanced at Kate and saw sadness flash through her eyes.

"Well." Lane gave his wife a comforting nod. "God hasn't given us any children yet. But maybe someday He will."

Kate nodded but Hailey noticed that her eyes were misty.

"I think you would be the best parents in the world." Grant scooped more corn onto his plate and asked for more chicken. "I wish I had parents like you."

*Oh please Grant stop it...* Hailey felt totally out of control of this conversation. Grant was walking a very fine line and Hailey wasn't sure he'd know when to stop.

"Thank you, Grant. That is quite a complement." Lane reached his hand to his wife's and gave it a supporting squeeze. "But, God gave you your parents for a reason."

Grant looked across the table at Hailey. She could see the questions in his eyes. Grant couldn't remember either of his parents.

"My goodness." Kyra licked her lips and reached for another piece of chicken. "This is the best grilled chicken I've had in my entire life!"

Leave it to Kyra to know how to lighten the mood and change the subject. Hailey breathed a sigh of relief. "It is good chicken. Grilling really gives it good flavor."

"And speaking of grilled chicken," Kyra continued. "I was looking for the first book in *The Boxcar Children* series. Do you happen to know where I could find it? It wasn't in the church library which is understandable because its not a Christian book, but Grant has been wanting me to read it to him and I have not been able to find it."

"But I like your Church Mice Children story even better than the Box Car Children," Grant was quick to explain.

"Thanks, Grant." Kyra smiled at the younger boy.

"What is the Church Mice Children?" Kate asked.

*And what in the world did the Box Car Children have to do with chicken?* Hailey tried to avoid another conversation, realizing how close the Church Mice Children were to themselves. *Why is Grant telling Pastor Lane and Kate all this stuff? Is he trying to get us caught?*

"It's a story that Kyra is making up every day..."

"I just threw the chicken in to be random," Kyra interrupted and laughed.

"So you tell stories?" Kate asked Kyra.

*Does she ever... we all do... we're a bunch of liars.* Hailey cleared her throat. "Kyra is amazingly creative. She also reads a lot. I'm always blown away by how much this girl reads." Hailey really wanted to avoid talking about Kyra's story. "Can we help you do the dishes?"

Kate glanced at the table. "No, I don't want to keep you children too late. It's already getting dark outside. Maybe Lane should drive you home."

"No," Hailey and Kyra said in unison.

"Um, our parents are really funny about us driving with people." Kyra continued.

"Yeah. But we really don't mind helping you clean."

Kate appreciated the offer. "Maybe next time. But I don't want you walking in the dark. How far away are you?"

"Not far at all." Hailey rose from the table and motioned for her brothers to do the same. "Boys, get your coats on."

"Well, I'm glad you could stay."

"Thank you so much for this amazing meal, Kate." There was no way Kate could possibly know how deeply they appreciated it.

Kate glanced at the empty serving dishes and chuckled. "I hope I made enough."

"Oh, we're fine. It was great." Kate tousled Grant's hair. "Why don't you go give Kate a big hug?"

It didn't take much convincing. Grant gave both Kate and Lane huge hugs. Kyra and Hailey were next hugging Kate. They both felt a little awkward about hugging the pastor. Hayden was already standing at the door. No hugs from him tonight. But he did thank Kate and Lane for the best meal he'd ever had in his life.

"All these complements are going to go to my head." Kate winked at Hayden as he walked outside with his siblings.

"Good night." Hailey waved and breathed a sigh of relief.

# Chapter 10

"That was so much fun." Kate sat on the sofa after the children left and wrapped her arms around herself.

Lane sat beside her and took Kate's hand. "It was nice, wasn't it?"

"Where are those poor children's parents?" Kate sounded offended. "If I had those children I'd want to be with them all the time."

"They're homeschooled, so maybe their parents get enough of them."

Kate shrugged. "Little Grant is so cute. He wants to be like you." Kate's eyes misted again. "And he hugs so tightly. I didn't want to let him go."

"Hayden is a tough cookie to crack." Lane put his arm around his wife. "He really needs a man to correct him, not his sister."

"I would hope he gets that from his dad."

Lane shrugged. "I hope so." He turned his eyes toward the dark windows. "He really needs the Lord."

"So does Kyra. We need to keep praying." Kate leaned into her husband's arm. "I hope they don't have far to walk. They act so funny about where they live."

Lane agreed. "Chad said Hailey and Kyra left that part blank on their youth group forms.

"Tonight I asked Hailey where she lives and she looked me square in the eyes and said she preferred not to tell me."

"Wow." Lane's eyes expressed his surprise. "That's pretty blunt for a teenager. What do you suppose they are hiding? Do you think they are just entirely ashamed of their house?"

"That has to be it," Kate said. "I can't imagine being so ashamed of my house that I would refuse to tell where I live."

"It must be pretty bad."

"Or else they are afraid we will visit their parents and their parents don't like visitors." Kate blew out a sigh.

"Or they're ashamed of their parents."

"Oh, Lane. That would be terrible. I can't imagine them being ashamed of their parents."

"Let's just keep loving them. Eventually maybe they will open up."

Kate nodded and the couple prayed for their new friends.

***

Hailey was quiet on their walk back to the church. She let Kyra do all the talking and tried to calm the internal storm in her heart.

They slipped into the church and readied themselves to spend the rest of the evening doing schoolwork. Hailey sat with Grant on the sofa in the youth room and let him read to her.

Hailey reflected on how Hayden behaved at the pastor's house that evening. She couldn't ever remember him behaving with such outward disrespect toward her. Why would he listen to Lane more than her?

It was discouraging. Hailey thought about what Wade told her. Was this spiritual attack?

Hayden sat on the other sofa copying the spelling words she and Kyra gave him to learn for the week. So far he hadn't complained about the work they gave him.

She and Kyra found the spelling words in a story from the church library. Every day she and Kyra took turns doing a read aloud to the boys and they tried to find words from the book to use as spelling and vocabulary words.

The church library also proved to be a good resource for science material. They found a book by Answers in Genesis about Dinosaurs, the geological impact of the flood, and birds. Hailey also took the things she was learning from the physical science book she borrowed from the school and did mini lessons with the boys about that.

It was refreshing not to have to get on the bus every morning and face an onslaught of other people every day. Homeschooling fit Hailey's introvert personality.

Hailey wondered about the two girls who interrupted her conversation with Wade on Sunday night. She glanced down at the shirt and jeans she was wearing now. They were from the clothing

111

closet but she liked them. Would Clarissa point out every outfit she recognized from the clothing closet? Surely all the clothes in there weren't hers.

"Did I say that word correctly?" Grant pulled Hailey from her thoughts.

Hailey blinked a couple times. "Can you say it again, I'm sorry, I missed it."

"Aardvark."

"Yes, Grant." Hailey touched the little blonde curls on his head. "You said it just right."

"Hailey," Kyra interrupted. "Would you care if we all went over to the other building? I really want to take a shower and get all these pieces of leaves out of my hair and I also have some clothes that need to be washed."

The children were all too afraid of the old church to go there alone. Especially since the shower, washer and dryer were in the basement. There was no place scarier in Hailey's mind than the basement of that old church building.

The children turned out all the lights in the youth room and made their way outside into the dark. The only light came from the moon, which was partially hidden by the clouds. They walked up the stairs to the old building and Hailey unlocked the old mahogany door.

Hailey noticed a car drive past and hurried the others inside, hoping the person in the car hadn't noticed them. She peered out the window to see the car continue driving passed the church. It was probably nothing to worry about.

\*\*\*

Wednesday night Hailey was excited to see her new friends again. Kyra hurried off with Angela after dinner and Hailey went with Janie, Paul, and Wade to the other building to help with the children's program.

Wade brought his guitar and led the children in some simple praise songs while Paul and Janie taught the little ones the hand motions to go with the songs.

Grant sat next to Hailey through the singing and Hayden sat with Caleb.

Caleb took his brother's worship leading seriously and wouldn't let Hayden distract him in any way. Hailey smiled to herself when she saw Hayden actually do a few of the hand motions.

Grant also had a new friend at the church. It was a sweet little girl named, Leah. After the music, Leah took his hand and led him to a room where the first and second graders would be doing their Wednesday night craft.

"It looks like both your brothers have made friends." Wade watched Grant leave with Leah.

"I'm so glad." She watched Hayden and Caleb go with their group to a room where the fifth and sixth graders would hear the Bible lesson. "Your brother kept Hayden in line during the music."

"I saw that."

The teens dispersed to go help in the different areas where they were needed. Only a handful of teens worked with the Wednesday night program. Many of the other high school students had school activities or attended some of the adult Bible studies going on at the church.

Hailey helped out in the craft room with Janie. Every twenty minutes the children rotated to their next place so that they all got to have a Bible lesson, do a craft, play a game, and have a small group time where they would talk about what they were learning and pray together with their own age groups. Hailey thought it was laid out very nicely. It was the closest thing her brothers were getting to being in school and she figured it was good practice.

After the program, the teens helped clean up the rooms in the old building.

"Are you going on the youth group retreat?" Paul asked Hailey.

Hailey shook her head. "I wish I could, but no. I can't."

"Why?" Janie stopped wiping down a table and glanced up at Hailey.

"I need to stay home and take care of my brothers." She gave an honest answer.

"Do your parents work?" Janie persisted.

Hailey shrugged. "I just need to be here. I'm sorry."

Wade sat down on one of the tables and let his feet hang off the end. "We'll miss you."

Hailey nodded. "I've never been on a youth retreat. You'll have to tell me all about it when you get back."

They promised they would.

***

Meeting with the other homeschoolers to do schoolwork on Thursday morning provided a nice way to get out of their little cave. With her arms loaded with books, Hailey motioned for Kyra and her brothers to follow her out the window and back into the building.

Janie and Paul made room for them at their table and they did their best to do their schoolwork while carrying on small conversations.

Hayden sat at one end of the table and glanced around mischievously. Hailey didn't see that he'd brought a straw with him from the church kitchen.

One by one various children felt themselves lightly popped by a spit wad. Hayden paced himself well, waiting for just the right moment to pop someone else.

Paul figured it out first. He nudged Hailey and wrote her a little note telling her what Hayden was doing.

Hailey got up and asked Hayden to come to the hall with her.

"What is with you, Hayden?" She reached out her hand and demanded the hidden straw.

"I'm just having fun."

"Hayden, it's not fun to have a nasty piece of wet paper in your hair. Give me the straw."

"No."

"You know you're the one who is going to have to vacuum the library."

"I don't care." Hayden shoved a piece of paper into the straw and was about to blow one at Hailey before she snatched the straw from his mouth.

"That's enough."

"You're not my mom!" Hayden tried to get the straw back from his sister.

"Hayden, stop this!"

Footsteps could be heard walking down the hall and Hailey glanced up to see Lane walking toward them. *Oh great, once again the pastor catches me unable to control my little brother.*

"Hi Hayden. Hello Hailey. What's that?" He glanced knowingly at the straw. "Oh, a spit wad machine. Hailey, I didn't know you used those…" His eyes twinkled.

"It's mine and she's trying to take it from me!" Hayden grabbed the straw in his sister's hand and gave it a yank.

"And why is she doing that? Is your sister just trying to be mean and ruin your life?"

Hayden clutched the straw in both of his hands. "No." He glared at Hailey for a moment and Hailey took a step back to allow the pastor a moment with her brother. Lane seemed like the only person who could get through to him.

"Does she just want to rob you of fun?" Lane pressed.

"No."

"Then why?"

"Because she said the other kids don't like it." Hayden admitted. He blew out a heavy sigh and shifted his feet uncomfortably.

"Then why are you doing it and why get mad at your sister?"

"I just wanted to have a little fun. Didn't you ever shoot spit wads?"

Lane's lips curved into a smile. "Of course I did. And I usually got my sister… but I also got in trouble. Because my sister didn't like it and I wasn't showing her respect by doing it."

Hayden reached the straw toward Hailey. "Fine. Here."

Hailey took the straw and carried it to the trashcan in the office. Apparently, Ruby could hear the conversation because she winked at Hailey and told her to keep it up. "You're a very good big sister."

*What must they think of us?*

"I'm sorry, Hailey," Hayden said when she walked back out into the hallway.

115

*Hayden apologized.* More evidence that her brother responded better to Pastor Evans' discipline than hers.

***

"Why can't we just sleep on the couches in the youth room?" Hayden stood outside the entrance to their cubby and crossed his arms.

"It's too risky," Hailey explained.

"No one ever comes on Friday nights or Saturday mornings. I'm tired of sleeping under the stage. The couch is softer." Hayden turned to walk from the choir room.

"Hayden," Hailey called. "You are not sleeping in the youth room."

Kyra slipped out of the cubby and furrowed her eyebrows. "Come on, Hayden. Quit acting like this. You promised Hailey that you'd listen to her."

"But it doesn't make sense." Hayden turned around. "There are four perfectly good sofas in the youth room and we're sleeping on the floor under the stage."

"And what happens if someone shows up unannounced?" Hailey wanted her brother to consider the risk he would be putting them in if he were found in the youth room. "You agreed to obey me, Hayden, and I'm telling you not to go to the youth room."

Hayden blew out a sniff.

"Come on, Hayden." Kyra held the door open for him.

Hailey agreed that the sofas would be far more comfortable, but under the stage they were well hidden. Hailey felt safe under the stage. She wasn't sure she'd be able to sleep on the sofa all night if she tried.

Hayden finally complied and slipped into the cubby. He crawled into his sleeping bag and zipped it up close to his face.

Hailey watched him for a few minutes and prayed that he would begin to show her some of the respect he showed Lane.

It occurred to Hailey as she got ready for bed that Hayden had not been asking for any night pants since their first night at the church. He must be staying dry. Hailey smiled. That was an answer to prayer.

*** 

Streams of sunlight pouring though the church windows Saturday morning drew the children's attention to the outdoors. The sky was clear and blue. Hailey watched a flock of birds cut through the clear blue sky on their way to their southern destination. It was a perfect day to take a hike through the countryside.

Grant had more questions about the Amish and Hailey thought it would be fun to take a nice, autumn afternoon walk and see if they might run across any.

Their walk took the children past a large white farmhouse where an Amish woman was hanging out clothes to dry on long clotheslines that ran from her barn to the house. Grant tugged on Hailey's jacket and pointed at the rows of matching hand made blue pants and plain matching dresses.

"Why doesn't she put her clothes in the dryer?" Grant asked.

Hailey didn't want the woman to hear them talking about her so she spoke softly. "The Amish don't use electricity, remember?"

Grant nodded.

"You have to have electricity to use a dryer."

"Oh." The light bulb went on in Grant's head and he nodded. "How did she wash all those clothes then?" he asked.

"Most likely they have an old fashioned wringer washer," Hailey explained. "It has a round tub filled with water and two or three rollers attached to a hand crank over top so that after they hand wash the clothes in the tub they run them through the rollers to squeeze out the water."

"That sounds like a lot of work." Hayden grabbed a handful of tall grass from the side of the road and skipped ahead.

"It is a lot of work. I remember watching an Amish woman wash her clothes when I was a little girl." Hailey gave one last respectful glance toward the woman hanging up her clothes and continued walking.

"I wish I had a horse." Hayden stopped beside a rickety wooden fence to watch a couple horses graze in their wide-open pasture. The tall brown quarter horses were totally absorbed in eating. "Have you ever ridden one, Hailey?"

Hailey shook her head. "No. I'd love to though." She stood and watched the quiet statuesque creatures silhouetted against the light blue sky. There was something very peaceful about grazing horses. Hailey imagined what it would feel like to ride one of the beautiful creatures through a wide opened field.

Hayden stepped onto the first rung of the wooden fence and called to the horses but they ignored him. "Stupid horses." He hopped down from the fence and threw down his handful of grass.

"Why do you always call things 'stupid' when they don't do what you want them to?" Kyra asked.

Hayden didn't answer.

"To be honest, calling someone 'stupid' shows an individual's stupidity." Kyra didn't let it drop. She turned and continued walking up the road.

Hayden glared at Kyra. "You're stupid!"

"That's enough, Hayden!" Hailey attempted to silence her brother.

"You see?" Kyra stopped, turned around, and put her hands on her hips. "You know I'm not stupid." She did a little head bob. "But because I didn't answer the way you liked, you called me that, showing that ultimately you are the ignorant one." Kyra did her best to use words above that of a fifth grader.

Grant put his feet in the lower rung of the fence and stared out at the horses while the other three argued.

"Hayden, you know Kyra is not stupid and you know the horses are not stupid. Kyra's point is that you need to quit using that word when you're angry with someone or something for not responding the way you want it to."

Hayden kicked the gravel road and said a word Hailey didn't know that he knew. "Just leave me alone." He stormed off ahead of them down the road.

Kyra stood with Hailey for just a moment and put a hand on her shoulder. "Just let him think about what you said for a few minutes."

Hailey sighed. "So much for our peaceful little walk."

"I'm sorry I said anything," Kyra shrugged.

"No, I'm glad you did. Thank you. I couldn't do this without you." Hailey smiled at the younger girl. Kyra was becoming more and more like a real sister every day.

They were both quiet for a moment, watching Grant as he darted ahead of them on their walk and trying to keep Hayden in view as best as they could. Most of the leaves were off the trees, but it was beautiful. Hailey studied the way the trees silhouetted against the sky, like intertwined dark lace.

An Amish buggy wound its way down the road and Grant jumped up and down in rapturous excitement, probably making the Amish wonder if he'd just seen a snake. The steady clip clop of horse hooves echoed through the air as the buggy drew closer.

"Are you still glad we ran away?" Hailey finally asked once Grant quieted down and they could continue walking.

"I grow happier and happier every day." Kyra pulled a dry Queen Anne's Lace from the roadside and twirled it around in her hand. "I love it here. Everything about this place is wonderful."

"But there isn't an adult in your life... do you feel..." Hailey tried to form her thoughts. "The need for a mother?"

Kyra shrugged. "I've always felt the need for a mother, but I haven't had one in so long I wouldn't know what it felt like if I did have one."

"What happened to your parents?" Hailey asked.

"I never knew who my father was. I doubt my mother knew either." Kyra shrugged. "I only lived with my mother for a few years. I don't even remember her quite honestly. She went to jail."

Hailey's mouth went dry. "Is she still in jail?"

"No. But when she got out she resigned custody of me. I haven't seen her since I was five."

"I'm sorry." Hailey's eyes misted.

"Why are you crying?" Kyra grinned. "Stop it."

"I just... you and I have never talked about it." Hailey called to Hayden to slow down. He was almost out of sight. "Have you had any good experiences in your foster homes?"

"Yeah. I lived with a really nice family for almost four years. But the husband got transferred and they moved." Kyra shrugged. "Then there was a really bad family before the Prescotts."

"Worse than Tara and Keith?"

"Oh yeah." Kyra shook her head. "I guess they didn't like black people. They had a word for me that my social worker said was inappropriate."

Hailey shook her head. She guessed what Kyra meant.

"But I love this." Kyra spread her arms out and turned herself around in the middle of the dirt road where they were walking. "This is amazing. And the people at Warsaw Chapel are so nice."

"They are." Hailey couldn't agree more.

"Thank you for taking me here." Kyra bounced a few steps back to Hailey and put her arm around the older girl's arm. "Even if we got caught tomorrow I have at least had these few memories."

"That sounds so poetic."

Kyra chuckled. "I've been doing poetry for my creative writing the past couple days. You should do it. It's fun."

"Maybe I'll try."

A car drove past on the road and Hailey called for Grant to move off the road. She tried to strain her eyes for Hayden but couldn't see him.

"We should probably try to catch up to Hayden."

Kyra nodded and they picked up the pace.

"Hayden!" Hailey called. She tried not to panic as they sped up and she still couldn't see him. "Hayden!"

Kyra held Grant's hand while Hailey ran ahead of them. This was getting frightening.

At the top of the hill Hailey glanced all around and couldn't see her brother anywhere. She grabbed her hair and tried to still the beating of her heart. *Where is he? Dear God, where is he?*

All kinds of fearful thoughts flashed through her mind. What if that car picked him up? What if he ran away? … *because I set that example in his life.*

"I'm hungry." Hailey heard Grant say to Kyra as they approached the top of the hill.

"We'll get some lunch later," Kyra said softly. "Where is he?" Kyra scanned the horizon.

All they could see was miles of farmland and rolling hills.

Over and over they called his name but a lonely rolling echo was their reply.

"Why would he do this?" Hailey sat down on the side of the road and buried her face in her hands. "What made me think I could take care of a ten year old little boy by myself?"

"Stop, Hailey. This isn't your fault."

"Sure it is. I'm the one who brought him here."

Kyra began yelling in earnest now.

"It's no good. Hayden won't be found unless he wants to be found."

Grant walked over to Hailey and curled up in her lap. "Let's just ask God to help Hayden come back."

Hailey nodded. She wiped away her tears and let her little brother pray.

"Dear God," Grant began. "Please help us find Hayden. We don't have a lot of family and we really need him even if he does get mad a lot and call us names."

Hailey smiled at Grant's honesty.

"But he needs you, God, and I think that's the real reason he's mean sometimes. So please help us find him so he can become a Christian and start being nice." Grant paused for a moment. "And please help us get some good food tonight and not soup."

When Hailey opened her eyes they were misty with tears. She pulled Grant into her arms for a hug and kissed the top of his head. "Thank you, Grant."

"Let's think of the things Hayden might possibly do." Kyra sat beside Hailey. "He might be off behind a couple trees beside one of these pastures just laughing at us."

Hailey nodded. That was a viable option.

"Or he may have gone back to the church."

Hailey wasn't sure he would do that.

"Or he may have gone to see Pastor Evans," Grant spoke up. "That's where I would go."

Hailey blew out a sigh. "Why would you go there, Grant?"

"Because today is Pastor Evans' day off and I would want to see what he was doing today. Maybe he is going hunting or something fun like that."

Did Hayden really respect Pastor Evans enough to run away to his house on a Saturday afternoon when he just had temper tantrum? Hailey couldn't see it. "Why don't we go back to the church, get something to eat, and hope he shows up there soon?"

Kyra nodded. "I'm hungry."

Hailey could not imagine eating but she knew that the others needed their food. All the way back to the church Hailey agonized over where Hayden could be.

Once inside, Hailey pulled out a jar of peanut butter and a package of saltines and paced the kitchen floor while Kyra and Grant ate. "We can't just sit here all day waiting for him to show up."

Kyra agreed. "Why don't we try Grant's idea?"

"But if he's not there then Pastor Evans and Kate will be worried too."

"It's worth a try." Kyra spread peanut butter on a cracker and closed the jar. "We've got to find him."

Hailey agreed. At this point anything was worth trying.

\*\*\*

Hailey never felt more like hugging and clobbering someone at the same time. After giving in to Grant's idea, they walked to Pastor Evan's house and there stood Hayden, chopping wood. Lane stood beside Hayden coaching him on how to hold the axe.

Hailey heard Kyra let out a relieved breath.

Hailey's initial reaction was to start scolding him as soon as she saw him, but the look on his face while he learned from Lane was priceless. Hayden's eyes sparkled as he drew the large chopping instrument into the air and brought it down on the small round log, tearing it into two nice sized pieces of firewood.

"That was a perfect cut," Lane said approvingly.

"Hailey, look what I just did!" Hayden carried his logs to Lane's firewood pile with a beam on his face. "I cut a bunch more, too!"

Grant hurried to greet Lane with one of his wonderful hugs.

Lane knelt down to properly greet the boy.

"Can I cut logs too?"

"You know, Grant, I think you'll have to wait a couple years. Its kind of a big boy job," Lane explained softly. "But when you're a little bit older, I'd be happy to teach you."

Was Hayden going to say anything about the fact that he ran off on them and scared her to pieces? Hailey forced herself to smile and pretend that she wasn't about to explode inside.

"Hi you guys!" Kate walked outside carrying her purse. "I didn't know that you all came down. What are you ladies doing this afternoon?"

"Just out enjoying the day," Kyra spoke up.

"I've got to do some shopping in town today. Would you like to come?"

Hailey's heart tightened at the invitation. She would love to come. But there was no way. "I… Kyra and I have to watch the boys."

"I'll take care of the boys," Lane offered.

"Can we?" Kyra whispered to Hailey.

"Um…" Hailey didn't know what to say. "I don't have my money with me."

"Which reminds me, I haven't paid you yet for this week." Lane stood up and pulled his wallet out of his jeans pocket. He handed Hailey eighty dollars. "Now you've got money." He grinned.

Hailey needed to put this money with the rest of the money she was saving to send to the social worker. She was anxious to pay off her debt to Keith Prescott.

"Let us stay with Lane," Hayden used the pastor's first name.

"You mean, Pastor Evans," Hailey corrected him.

"Lane is fine," the pastor spoke up. "Unless your parents don't want you to use first names when addressing adults."

"They don't care what we do." Hayden grinned mischievously at Hailey.

Hailey wasn't sure that it was best to reward her brother's bad behavior by letting him have his way. Hayden had given them all a terrible scare. And what if he or Grant messed up and told Lane that they were living in the church? What if they mentioned their foster parents and running away?

"The children should probably call their parents first to make sure it's okay. I don't feel right about taking the girls into town without their mother knowing."

"I'll call." Hayden ran toward the house.

"Why don't you let your sister do it?" Kate handed Hailey her cell phone.

Hailey held the cell phone in her hands and swallowed. Cell phones kept numbers. If she dialed her made-up parents then Kate could redial and catch them in their lie.

"Um, my mom is at work right now. I'm not sure I should bother her." Hailey hated herself for lying.

"Where does she work?"

"Wal-Mart." Hailey said the first thing that popped out of her mouth. "But I know she won't mind. She trusts you guys."

"Does she work in Zanesville or Newark? We could swing by and let her know…"

Hailey shook her head. "That's not a good idea. Let me just talk to Hayden and Grant real quick before we go and I'm sure it will be fine."

Hailey pulled her brothers aside and stared evenly at Hayden. "I really shouldn't let you stay. I feel like I'm rewarding you for disobeying."

Hayden's eyes softened. "I'm sorry."

He apologized without being told by the pastor. Hailey studied him for a moment.

"I told Lane that I was mad at you. He said I was wrong to run off." Hayden shrugged. "I guess I scared you pretty bad."

"You scared us all," Grant scolded his older brother.

"I won't do it again. Just please let us stay. I want to hang out with Lane."

"Me too!" Grant's big blue eyes pleaded with Hailey.

"Fine. But remember… don't tell Lane anything personal. If we get caught we'll never see Lane again."

The reality hurt Hailey and she hoped her little threat wasn't manipulative. But it was true. The new lives they had here in Warsaw would be taken away just like that if anyone found out the truth.

124

# Chapter 11

It seemed strange to be in a car again. Hailey ran her hand over the soft, tan upholstery and reflected how clean Kate's car was. There was no trash on the floor; no half eaten candy bars or old soda cans. Kate kept things nice.

Hailey leaned her head back and turned to face the window. Kate played contemporary Christian music on the radio while she drove them into town.

"I have to get a few groceries, swing by the mall real quick and stop by my mom's."

"What do you need at the mall?" Kyra perked up at the idea of going to the mall.

"I was having my necklace repaired at a jewelry store there and it's ready for me to pick up. But we can shop a little if you'd like."

Kyra glanced at Hailey for approval. Hailey appreciated that her foster sister seemed to respect her. "I'll give you twenty dollars to spend," she pulled the money out of her pocket. "But remember, we have to be wise with our money.

Kyra didn't know about the borrowed money, and Hailey didn't want the younger girl to feel like she was hoarding all their earnings.

Kyra seemed pleased with the twenty dollars. "Thank you."

Kate watched the interchange curiously.

After getting Kate's necklace, they walked around the mall for a little while.

The Heath Mall wasn't a large mall compared to the ones Hailey remembered in Cleveland. But it was a nice mall. Hailey appreciated how un-crowded it was, although she wondered how these stores could ever do business with so few people.

In one of the stores, Kyra spotted a few outfits she liked and held one of them up to herself. It was a very low-necked short dress with sparkly sequins.

Kate used this moment to talk about modesty.

"You know," she said in her soft, wise voice. "Even though our society says it is okay to wear really short skirts and low necklines, we have to be careful that we are not cheapening ourselves as women."

The girls waited for Kate to continue.

"A skirt that short will get attention, there is no doubt about that. But is it the kind of attention you really want? If a young man is noticing you because of your low-necked shirt and short skirt, he is looking at you for what is on the outside, not what is in the heart. Ultimately, you've cheapened yourself to being an object. Not a precious young woman of value."

Kyra put the dress back on the rack and lowered her eyes.

"I'm not trying to be preachy. But when it comes to modesty, I feel it is important for young ladies to understand that what you wear communicates a lot about you. It can also be a stumbling block to young men who are trying to keep their thoughts pure."

"What does that mean?" Kyra asked.

The three of them walked toward the coffee shop in the mall and Kate offered to buy them something to drink. "When a young man has given his life to Christ, he needs to be careful not to look at a girl lustfully. He should keep his thoughts pure and honoring to God. If he sees a girl dressed immodestly, it makes him think things he shouldn't toward the girl."

The barista handed the three ladies their drinks and Kate paid.

"Thank you," Hailey took a sip of her mocha cappuccino and savored the taste.

"Yes, thank you!" Kyra echoed Hailey's example.

"I want to understand this more," Kyra pressed. "Are you saying that its wrong for me to wear a mini skirt?" Her tone was a little defensive.

"I'm saying that in whatever you are wearing, you need to think to yourself, does the way I am dressing show that I value my purity and want to protect it and does it show that I value the convictions of the young Christian men I know?"

Kyra was quiet for a few minutes, taking long sips of her chocolate coffee drink. "You know I'm not a Christian, right?" She finally spoke up.

Kate motioned for them to take a seat at a small table right outside the coffee shop. "Well, I wasn't sure…"

"This God stuff is new to me. What you're saying about dressing to show that I value myself makes sense to me. I mean, I'll be straight up, we say pretty mean things about girls who dress… bad. But I guess I never thought about a pretty dress like that as bad."

"What is the difference? It was very short and showed more of your chest than you even have." Kate's eyes twinkled.

Kyra giggled at Kate's joke.

"Do you really want to draw attention to your body that way? Or wouldn't you rather be valued for who you are inside the skin?" Kate's eyes grew tender and she placed a loving hand on Kyra's dark arm.

Kyra looked at Hailey. "But you've worn short skirts when we lived with… Aunt Tara."

*Nice cover…* "I know. I guess I never thought about modesty that way either. But, Kyra," Hailey's brown eyes pleaded with Kyra. "You can't look at me as the example of what a Christian should be. I do a lot of things wrong."

"We all do, Hailey," Kate spoke up. "The Bible tells us that while we were still sinners Christ died for us."

"But I remember my Grandmother telling me there was a verse in the Bible that said that we were not to keep sinning so that God's grace would abound."

Kate nodded. "Yes. The Bible does say that. Jesus tells us to go and sin no more. But that doesn't mean we're perfect. We will still make mistakes. Look at David in the Bible. He was a man after God's own heart and yet he took another man's wife and had relations with her and to top it off, when he thought he might get caught because he got the woman pregnant, he had her husband killed.

Hailey shifted nervously. How could she explain it? Hailey was continuing in her lie. She lied every day to cover their story of living in the church. She was teaching it to the others.

"You seem upset." Kate placed her tender hand on Hailey's arm. "Are you okay?"

"I'm not a very good example of a Christian, that's all."

"Yes you are!" Kyra defended. "You're amazing!"

"I'm not, Kyra. You know I'm not."

"You're the real thing, Hailey, and I've always known that. Even though I don't follow it, I respect you because you are different."

Hailey appreciated Kyra's kind words. "You're sweet."

"Why don't you follow Him, Kyra?" Kate asked the younger girl.

"Because I can't believe a God who really cares would let so many bad things happen in this world."

"But it's not God who causes the bad things. It's sin that is in the world. God gives people choices and sometimes their choices have consequences that affect others."

"Hailey has said almost that same thing."

Kate gave Hailey an approving smile.

"I've talked to Angela about it some too. She's really nice."

"She is nice," Kate agreed. "So do you believe that? Do you believe that its other people's wrong choices that cause much of the suffering in the world?"

"I can see that. But what about sickness and people dying?" Kyra asked. "I know some of it is because of our own choices, but not always. Sometimes good people get sick and die."

*Sometimes they get into car accidents or become sick because of grieving or old age.* Hailey thought about her own family.

"And the Bible tells us that God makes all things work together for good to those who love God and are called according to His purpose," Kate paraphrased from memory. "He can use even those bad things that we don't understand."

Kyra lowered her eyes. "I need to think about things. Ask Hailey, I'm an analytical thinker."

"She is," Hailey nodded.

"But I'm glad you talked to me about all of this."

"I'll keep praying for you, Kyra." Kate's kind dark eyes searched Kyra's face. "And you." She patted Hailey tenderly.

Their spiritual conversation shifted to checking out a few more stores before running to the grocery and stopping by Helen's house.

*\*\*\**

On the way to Kate's mother's house, Hailey thought about the pretty sweater she'd tried on in the last store they were in. She really liked it. But it was expensive. Hailey would have spent more than half of the money she'd earned if she bought it.

It was a mental struggle. She thought about wearing that pretty, new, sweater to youth group and showing Clarissa that the clothing closet wasn't her only wardrobe. But Hailey knew she needed to pay off Keith. *And the clothing closet really is my wardrobe.*

Hailey was happy that Kyra bought something for herself. She found a nice pair of jeans that fit her well and got them at a very good price.

Once they pulled into Helen's driveway, Hailey suggested maybe she and Kyra should wait in the car. "I don't want to bother your mother." *... or have her try to figure out who I am.*

"Nonsense. My mom will be happy to see you."

Hailey dreaded that. The two girls followed Kate to the front door where they were greeted like the dearest of friends.

"Come on in. Wait till you see the puppies!" Helen led the way to the back of the house.

Hailey had no idea they were coming to look at puppies.

"This is Molly. She got out a while ago and came back pregnant." Helen seemed happy about it. "Kate, you and Lane have to take one of these. They're so cute.

Helen pulled out a puppy for everyone and sat on a rocking chair holding one of her own. "I've named this one Cupcake." She snuggled the puppy close.

Hailey and Kyra sat on the floor in sudden puppy rapture.

"I've never held a puppy before," Kyra said as she held the squirming animal up in both hands. "It's so cute!"

Hailey smelled the puppy's breath as he licked her face excitedly.

"That one likes you," Kate said.

"Oh my goodness," Hailey rubbed its soft fur against her face. "It's so cute. Can you imagine Hayden and Grant if they could see them?"

"They would be ecstatic."

Both of her brothers always wanted a puppy. They asked Tara once… once was all it took to shoot that dream down. Tara could make you feel like asking for a puppy was a criminal offence.

"You can have one of them if you'd like," Helen offered. "I'll need to find homes for them in a few weeks. They're still nursing, but when they're ready…"

Hailey shook her head. "We can't have a dog where we live." *That was the truest statement I've ever made about where we live.*

"Well if Kate and Lane take one you can come visit it." Helen smiled at her daughter. "You know you want one."

"Of course I want one. I want two. But I'm not sure what Lane will say."

"If Lane knows you want one, you know he'll consent." Helen pulled out the last of the puppies and patted the anxious mother dog on the head. "Look how cute they are." She held two puppies up in her hands. "Who could say no to these."

"What kind are they?" Hailey asked.

"A mix between a Corgi and I'm thinking a Beagle. I don't know for sure who the father is," Helen explained. "Molly is a Corgi. I never had her fixed because I planned to breed her some day."

"Just not to a Beagle," Kate teased.

"I think they're perfect." Hailey held the furry little animal against her heart and wished there was a way to take one. *I can barely keep my brothers quiet in the church; imagine trying to keep this thing quiet…*

Molly was getting anxious about her puppies so Helen suggested they return them to their mother. "She's still very protective of her pups. If I walk through the house with one she follows at my heels and watches me like a hawk."

"She's a good momma." Kate placed the pup she'd been holding in the box.

Hailey and Kyra returned their puppies and thanked Helen for the opportunity to see them.

"They're absolutely adorable." Hailey glanced at Kate. "If you get one then Hayden and Grant will never want to leave your house." She returned her eyes to Helen. "My little brothers adore Lane."

"How sweet," Helen said. "Now see, Kate, another reason for you to get one."

Kate rose to her feet and brushed a bit of dog hair off her shirt. "I hate to hurry off, Mom, but I've got groceries in the car and I need to get these girls home. We didn't even tell their mother they were coming with us."

"Oh," Helen seemed surprised. "Why not?"

"She works at Wal-Mart and the girls have no way of getting through to her." Kate grabbed her coat from the chair and slipped her arms inside.

Hailey and Kyra followed her example. Hailey hoped they could go before Helen asked about it. Telling Kate that her mother worked at Wal-Mart was eating at Hailey. Now Kate was spreading Hailey's lie. *Does that mean I'm making Kate tell a lie?* Hailey wasn't sure, but it bothered her.

"What about your dad?" Helen asked.

Hailey pulled on her gloves and pretended not to hear the older woman.

"He's a truck driver." Kyra pulled the idea from her imagination.

Hailey felt her stomach tighten. *Does Kyra know that my dad was a truck driver?* Hailey was sure Kyra didn't know that.

"We don't see him much," Kyra added.

Hailey hated that she not only lied but she was influencing Kyra and her brothers to lie. Why did her perfect day out with Kate have to end this way?

\*\*\*

Hailey was quiet the rest of the way to the Evans' house. Kyra did a good job keeping the conversation going with Kate, for which Hailey was thankful. For some reason it was difficult to look at Kate just now.

Kate was wonderful. Hailey respected her more than any woman she knew. There was gentleness about Kate that reminded Hailey of of her mother.

Both her mom and her grandma made her feel safe. Hailey figured that was what she liked about Kate. She made Hailey feel safe. She was wise and she listened… *and she likes to be around me.*

Hailey wished she could tell Kate everything and that Kate could rescue her from the situation she was in. But that could never happen. Hailey couldn't risk Kate ever knowing. In order for Kate to know the truth, it would have to come out about their running away from foster care. If that happened, Hailey was sure she would be taken to juvenile detention.

The implications of Hailey's crime stared her right in the face. She'd taken her brothers away from their foster home; she'd stolen three hundred dollars, even if she did intend to return it, not to mention living in a church building. She was sure that was probably against the law too. If they were ever discovered, Hailey was convinced she would be put away until she was eighteen. *Maybe longer.*

She brushed a tear from her eye and turned her face toward the window. *I've messed up my life.*

Hailey considered her future. Once she did turn eighteen, she couldn't simply come out of hiding with her brothers. Social services knew who she was. They would find her and maybe press even harder charges.

*I'm a criminal.*

\*\*\*

All the way back to the church, Hailey listened while her brothers chatted on excitedly about Lane and the fun they had with him.

"Lane said he would teach me to shoot a bow," Hayden said enthusiastically. "He hunts. I saw the buck he shot last fall. It's huge." Hayden extended his arms as far as they could reach. "He has it hanging in his office. Lane told us that Kate preferred not to decorate the rest of the house with deer heads." Hayden laughed.

It was nice to hear Hayden laugh. Her little brother really liked the pastor and Hailey was glad.

Hailey opened the door to their hiding place and they all crawled inside. She glanced around their large cavern and thought about how cramped it was compared to a real house.          Kate's house was beautiful. Hailey loved the stone fireplace in the Evans' living room. Several photographs and an antique clock lined the wooden mantle. Hailey thought it would be wonderful to sit on the cozy, overstuffed chair beside the fireplace and read while a fire burned inside.

"You've been so quiet since we left Kate's mother's house." Kyra interrupted her thoughts. "Are you okay?"

Hailey faked a smile and nodded. "Just tired." *Why not just keep lying... I've become so good at it.*

\*\*\*

Sunday morning Hailey skipped Sunday school to take a walk. She dropped her brothers off in their rooms and hurried away down the road.

The sky was slightly overcast, which fit Hailey's mood perfectly.

She avoided the eyes of the drivers who passed by hoping no one she knew saw her.

This was their third week at Warsaw Chapel. How could so much happen in only three weeks? They'd run away, moved into a church, gotten a job cleaning, and made wonderful new friends. Hailey wondered why life moved so much slower in Cleveland.

Her walk took Hailey in the opposite direction of the pastor's house. She figured they were already at the church, but didn't want to see their home.

A few drops of rain told Hailey it was time to head back. It was close to ten and Sunday school let out in twenty minutes.

Hailey found her siblings and ushered them to the sanctuary to find seats. In spite of her desire to be unsocial, several youth group teens greeted her and she did her best to be friendly.

Lane's message was the worst. He spoke on integrity and Hailey squirmed under the heat of conviction.

"Let's go guys." She motioned for Grant to take her hand after the service.

"But I want to talk to Angela." Kyra didn't wait for Hailey to stop her.

Hayden took Kyra's cue and hurried away to find Caleb.

Hailey sighed when she saw Grant's pleading eyes begging to let him run off with Leah.

"Go ahead." Hailey plopped herself back down on the soft sanctuary chair and crossed her arms. *I'm trapped.*

"Hailey," she heard Wade call her name from a few rows back. He approached her wearing his always-handsome smile and she lowered her eyes to avoid them.

"We missed you in Sunday school. Were you with your little brother?" Wade took the seat next to her and studied her curiously.

"No." Hailey was embarrassed to answer.

"Where were you?"

*Why do some people not just take yes and no answers?* "I went for a walk. I needed some alone time."

Wade nodded. "I understand. I've done that before."

"You have?" Somehow it surprised Hailey to learn that Wade would skip Sunday school to take a walk.

"I don't do it very often. I love Sunday school, but sometimes its good just to get alone with God and your thoughts. This country road is perfect for that."

*But I wasn't talking to God...*

"Is everything okay?" he asked.

"Yeah. Its fine."

Wade's blue eyes twinkled. "You're a terrible liar."

Hailey blinked. "Actually, I'm a very good one." *Wade has no idea how honest I'm being right now.*

Wade chuckled. "Come on. Something's bothering you. Care to share?"

"Not really."

Wade nodded. "I can respect that." He lowered his gaze for a moment. "Have you prayed about walking in the Spirit since we talked?"

"Yes."

Wade seemed to be waiting for a response but Hailey didn't give one.

"I hope this isn't about what happened last week with Clarissa and Gina."

Hailey shook her head. "It has nothing to do with them." She did her best to fight the tears that wanted to surface. Why was this nice young man talking to her? It hurt to have someone care. She wanted people to care. But she couldn't let them. There was too much at risk.

"What are you doing this afternoon?" He watched his brother run around the sanctuary with Hayden.

"Watching my siblings."

"Paul was planning on coming over after lunch," Wade explained. "Maybe you and Janie could come too and your brothers could play with Caleb and your little sister can hang out with us. We'll probably shoot some hoops and stuff."

"I'm sorry. I can't today." Hailey wished she could. She swallowed back a lump in her throat.

"Come on, Hailey. You look like you're about to cry." Wade wasn't going to let it drop. "What's wrong? Are you under spiritual attack?"

"I can't talk about it." Hailey brushed a tear away and hoped that the group of teenagers who were congregating at the back of the sanctuary were not about to approach them.

"So you've given this thing to God?"

"I can't..."

"Why not? There's nothing we can't give to God." Wade said.

"It's complicated."

"So, you've asked God to help you walk in His Spirit and yet you can't give something to Him to handle?"

"I can't walk in His spirit." Hailey finally turned her brown eyes to his blue ones.

"Of course you can," Wade's tone grew soft. "I know it's difficult sometimes but..."

"But in order to walk in the Spirit I have to be able to surrender my sins to the Lord and there are just some things I can't surrender." Hailey got up and walked to the exit at the back of the sanctuary. She'd find Kyra and her brothers later.

Wade wasn't about to let this drop. "Hailey." He caught up and walked outside with her. "I don't understand."

"I want to be close to God. More than anything in the world I do. But there are some things I truly can't surrender." Hailey blew out a heavy breath. She was glad she got that off her chest and scared at the same time.

"There is nothing you can't surrender."

"Okay. True. I could surrender it. But the consequences would destroy my life and probably the lives of three other people. I can't…" Hailey couldn't keep her tears at bay. She buried her face in her hands and Wade gently led them both away from the church where she could cry in private.

Wade seemed to sense the seriousness of Hailey's situation, although he had no idea what it was. "Can you please let me help you?"

"No, Wade. You can't help. I just need to suck it up and go on. But I can't surrender it to God."

Wade's eyes showed concern. "Are you in some kind of trouble?"

"Please don't ask any more questions." Hailey pleaded with him.

"Okay." He placed a tender hand on her shoulder. "But I'm going to be praying every day and I'm here for you… no matter what."

Hailey appreciated his kindness but she was almost afraid of his prayers. God stood for truth. Praying for her would be like praying she gets caught.

\*\*\*

The church had been empty for over an hour. Hailey didn't know exactly what time the mystery man was going to come into the building, but this time she and her siblings decided they would be prepared for it.

The children all hid in the clothing closet while Hailey hid in a large empty box Ruby had in the church office. The box was tucked under a table and Hailey turned it so that she could see out of the cut out handle.

Hailey realized that what she was doing was dangerous. If that man was doing something illegal and he caught her, she had no way of knowing what he might do. He might turn the whole thing around and blame her. He might actually hurt her. But Hailey was willing to take the risk. She had to know who this man was and why he came into Ruby's office each Sunday afternoon.

The children waited for almost an hour. They were about ready to give up. Hailey was cramped and hot in the box. She was tempted to crawl out into Ruby's dark office when she heard the door open.

"Hello?" The man's familiar voice echoed through the empty halls.

The office light switched on and the man came into view.

Hailey could see him very well this time. He was a big man with a good-sized tire around his midsection. He was also bald and wore glasses.

The hair on Hailey's neck stood on end and she tried to quiet her breathing.

The man crept quietly into the office and opened the offering envelope. Hailey watched him count out a portion of the money and close the envelope. He slipped the cash into his pocket and turned the light off in the office before he left.

Hailey let herself breathe. *That man is stealing from the offering.* There was no doubt about it. Hailey couldn't tell how much he took, but she was sure it was significant. How long had he been doing it? How could he?

She heard a knock on the office door signaling that the coast was clear.

"That was insane." Hailey brushed a sweaty hair out of her face. "I need a shower now from being in that box for so long."

"What happened?" Kyra asked.

"He is stealing money. Just like we thought."

"Let's look in the church directory and see if you can identify him," Hayden suggested. "That's what they do in all the cop shows."

"Look in church directories?" Hailey teased him.

"No. Look at mug shots. But this is kind of the same thing."

The children found a church directory on Ruby's desk and carried it out to the hallway. Very slowly Hailey flipped through the pages in search of the man whose face was now burned into her mind.

Her mouth went dry when she found the man. "This is him." She pointed at the picture of him with his wife. Hailey lowered the church directory and licked her dry lips.

"Bill Pierce," Kyra read the name. "He looks like a cabbage."

"He is a cabbage if he's stealing from the church." Hayden spat. "There, I didn't call him stupid."

Kyra grinned and returned her eyes to the directory. "His wife is pretty though. I think I've seen her at church. She has kind of big hair."

"What should we do? We can't tell Lane, then he'll know we've been in the church on Sunday afternoons." Hailey leaned her head against the wall. How could a man steal from the church?

Hailey stood up and carried the directory back to Ruby's office before locking it and closing the door. "We'll think of something. I need to get cleaned up for youth group."

# Chapter 12

Janie, Paul and Wade all arrived together. Hailey remembered that they were going to hang out together after church. *At least I was invited.* That meant something.

"We missed you today," Janie ran to greet Hailey. "I didn't even see you at church."

"I'm sorry. I was kind of anti-social this morning." Hailey shrugged.

"I get it. Are you still?" Her eyes twinkled.

"No. I'm glad to see you." Hailey sat beside Janie on the couch and they talked about the weekend.

Paul and Wade played a quick game of Ping-Pong and then joined the girls while Paul taunted his victory over his best friend.

"We missed you in Sunday school this morning," Chad greeted Hailey as he walked passed her to the stereo.

"I'm feeling the love today," Hailey forced herself to smile. When had she ever been treated with this much friendliness?

The teens chatted until the room filled up and Chad motioned for Wade to lead them in worship. Hailey hoped Chad wasn't going to talk on truth or deception this evening. She didn't think she could handle it.

Hailey noticed Clarissa walking into the room but didn't see Gina with her.

Unconsciously, Hailey glanced at her shirt and hoped it wasn't one of Clarissa's old ones. *I wish I could have bought that sweater.*

Kate carried the left over pizza to the sanctuary so whoever was downstairs waiting could eat it. When she returned, she took a seat behind Hailey and whispered a quiet greeting to both girls.

Wade sat on the other side of Hailey, and Kate complemented him on the worship music.

Chad's talk was on how to share your faith. Hailey appreciated the topic thoroughly until Chad pointed out that you hurt your testimony if you weren't living your faith.

139

*Of course.*

"When your friends see you walking with the Lord you are sending a message about what a Christ follower should look like."

"But we still all mess up sometimes, don't we, Chad?" Wade spoke up with a question Hailey was sure Wade knew the answer to.

*He's asking that question for me.*

"Of course we do. And if we can humbly come to the Lord and confess that sin, God is faithful and righteous to forgive that sin. Sometimes God can even use that area of our lives to help us be an even greater witness."

"Thank you for that," Hailey whispered to Wade.

"What? I was just curious," he whispered back.

"Sure."

After the group closed in prayer, Kate gave the girls hugs and told them she and Lane had to leave so that Lane could drive home an elderly gentleman who he'd brought to the men's prayer group that evening. She took the time to say goodbye to several other girls in the youth group and Clarissa approached the small group of friends. Hailey wished she could leave.

"Still hanging out with the homeschool circle, Wade?" She said it in such a playful tone that anyone who didn't know Clarissa would have thought she was teasing.

"Well, someone's got to help us un-socialized homeschoolers learn how to hang out with other teenagers," Paul spoke up.

Clarissa laughed playfully.

Hailey thought she sounded flirty.

Clarissa completely ignored Hailey, which suited Hailey just fine.

"Its really coming down out there," Clarissa grabbed her jacket off the chair she'd been sitting on. "Hopefully it doesn't rain on the retreat next weekend. Are you all going?"

Everyone nodded except Hailey.

"Oh, you're not going?" Clarissa finally seemed to notice Hailey.

*Just my luck...* "No. But I hope you guys have fun. It sounds like a really nice opportunity."

"Maybe you can come next year." Wade snapped his guitar case shut and picked it up. "Let's go make sure our brothers aren't tearing up the sanctuary too bad."

"Are your parents picking you up or am I driving you?" Wade asked Janie and Paul.

"Dad's here for the men's prayer meeting." Paul and Janie grabbed their Bibles and said their goodbyes.

Clarissa lost interest in the boring little circle of friends. Hailey figured the girl didn't recognize the tan sweater she was wearing tonight.

"That wasn't so bad tonight now was it?" Wade held the door for Hailey. "And by the way, I thought your reply was very nice."

"It wasn't easy, trust me."

"But I'd say you were letting the Holy Spirit help you."

Hailey walked down the youth room stairs quietly. "I want to."

"It's pouring out there. Why don't you let me drive you home tonight?"

"No. We're okay."

"Seriously, Hailey. It's torrential."

Hailey contemplated telling him that her parents didn't let her drive with high school drivers, but decided not to lie.

"Come on, Caleb. Mom said you needed to finish up a little homework tonight." Wade called to his little brother.

"Does your dad attend the men's prayer group?" Hailey wondered if Wade only brought Caleb for Hayden.

"Some weeks he does. But my dad has to go into work at three in the morning, so he's gone to bed."

"Does he do that very often?" Hailey asked.

"No. Just twice a month." Wade walked with his brother toward the door and glanced around the sanctuary at Hailey's siblings. "Are you sure I can't drive you home?"

"I'm sure. We don't have far to walk."

Wade nodded and waved.

\*\*\*

Hailey did her best to keep to herself the rest of the week. The children did their chores on Monday, attended the Wednesday night service, and hung out with the other homeschooled kids during women's Bible study on Thursday, but Hailey put up some protective walls to prevent herself from getting too close to these new friends.

She wished she could say the same for her siblings and Kyra.

Never in all her life did Hailey remember her little brothers taking to a man as well as they took to Lane. It was like they saw him as a father figure.

Before the homeschool kids left Thursday morning, Lane stopped by to say hello to them all and Grant ran into Lane's arms.

Lane seemed to love the attention he was receiving from this adorable little seven-year-old who treated him like a hero. Hailey couldn't blame him. Grant was precious.

"I wish you could go on the youth trip this weekend." Janie gathered her books together.

"Yeah. Me too." Hailey paused for a moment. "Where is the trip?"

"It's close to Xenia."

Hailey wasn't sure where that was, but it wasn't Warsaw and she had an idea. "Can you do me a favor?" Hailey chewed on her lip for just a moment trying to think if this would work.

Janie shrugged. "I can try. What?"

"There's this person I sometimes send letters to and I wanted to send her a letter from some random city just for fun." Hailey hoped this wasn't too far of a stretch to make it a lie.

She didn't quite have the whole three hundred dollars yet, but if she could send out part of it at least that would be a start. Hailey knew that she'd need to send it from somewhere else so her social worker couldn't track the postmark.

Janie laughed. "Sure, I'll do it. Do you have the letter?"

"No. Let me get it."

Hailey hurried from the room hoping not to be followed. She slipped into the choir room and pulled two hundred dollars out of her purse along with her social worker's business card.

Hiding the money in her pocket, Hailey hurried to the office and asked Ruby if she could have a thick envelope and buy a couple stamps.

"Sure, honey. How many stamps?" Ruby pulled a padded manila envelope out of a drawer.

"How about four?" Hailey wanted to make sure she had enough.

Ruby gave Hailey the four stamps and told her not to worry about paying her back. "You do so much around here, just call it a tip."

*You have no idea how much this church already tips me...* Hailey tried to hide her guilty feelings. She stepped into the hall and stuffed her money into the envelope just as Chad walked out of his office.

"Stashing some big bucks in there," he grinned.

Hailey let out an embarrassed laughed and carried the envelope into the homeschool room where she could address it.

Leaving off the name 'Social Services', Hailey addressed the envelope to Dahlia Cooper, S.S.

For a return address, Hailey wrote, "Somewhere in the U.S.A."

"That's cryptic." Janie glanced over Hailey's shoulder.

Hailey quickly hid Dahlia's business card in her pocket. She scribbled a short note saying she'd enclosed a portion of the money she owed to Keith and Tara and planned to send the rest as soon as she could. "This is it," she handed the envelope to Janie. "Just make sure that you don't mail it from anywhere around here." She licked her dry lips. "Other wise I lose the game."
*That's the truth.*

"I promise." Janie took the envelope. "What's in here?" She squeezed it a few times.

"Hundreds of dollars." Hailey winked at her and zipped her backpack closed. "Have fun this weekend."

\*\*\*

Hailey sat in the church office with Kyra on Saturday evening wondering what to do about their offering thief. Hayden had the idea of hiding a camera in the office and video taping him, but Hailey didn't know where they could get a camera.

"Why don't we get into the offering money before him and write a note like, 'I'm watching you?'" Kyra suggested.

Hailey's eyes lit up. "Or 'Thou Shalt Not Steal,' which is one of the Ten Commandments." Hailey grinned. "I like it. If that doesn't freak him out and stop him I don't know what would."

"And then you could remind him that God is watching."

"Let's do that!" Hailey pulled a sheet of paper out of Ruby's copier and using a dark marker she wrote the note.

*Thou Shalt Not Steal.*
*- God*
*Ps. God is watching you, Bill Pierce*

"Tomorrow afternoon we'll slip in here and add our message." Hailey showed the note to Kyra.

"Wow. Using his name is excellent. He's going to wet his pants!"

Hailey hoped so.

***

Very few students showed up for high school Sunday school. Most of the youth group had gone on the trip. Because Chad was gone, his wife taught the class.

Hailey only briefly met Laura the week before, but she liked the petite blonde. Laura was an introvert like Hailey.

Laura brought her baby into the class and Hailey peaked into the car seat carrier at the slumbering infant. "She's beautiful," Hailey said softly.

"Thank you."

"What's her name?"

"Caroline Grace." Laura smiled proudly at her sleeping one month old. "We named her after my mother."

Hailey reached out her hand and touched the baby's soft fingers. "She's a miracle."

Laura nodded. "In more ways than one."

Hailey waited for Laura to explain.

"Chad and I were told we couldn't have children. But what's impossible for man is possible for God." Laura leaned back in on the sofa and smiled at the few other teens in the room.

Those words gave Hailey something to think about. She was in a difficult situation. It seemed like an impossible one. Could God help them? *Why would He want to? I'm a deceptive liar who pulled Kyra and my brothers out of foster care to hide out in a church. The only way out of this for me is juvenile detention.*

The thought made Hailey's stomach hurt. What good could come of this?

Laura started the lesson and Hailey did her best to listen. It was a thought-provoking lesson on prayer. Laura talked about the many distractions in life that keep us from taking time to spend with God.

"Some times I go through my whole day and realize I haven't spend any quality time talking to God," Laura confessed. "I'll get phone calls and texts and respond to them, but I give God the busy signal."

Hailey appreciated the phone analogy.

"When we talk to Him we get to know Him better. We can take our burdens to Him and ask for His help." Laura glanced around the room with her kind, sensitive eyes. "We have ten minutes left of class. I thought this would be a good time to just be still and talk to God."

Hailey glanced around and noticed a couple of the teens getting up to find a more private place in the room. Laura knelt beside her baby and closed her eyes to pray.

There seemed to be no way out of it. God wanted to talk to her. Hailey bowed her head and faced her Creator with a heavy heart. *I do want to walk in Your Spirit, Lord. But I don't want to give away our secret. I don't want to leave Warsaw Chapel… I love it here.*

\*\*\*

After Sunday school, Hailey and her siblings sat together near the back of the sanctuary. Hailey glanced around at the many faces wondering if she'd see the offering thief. She smiled at a few friendly people she recognized and felt a warm sense of welcome.

Hailey reached for her Bible and realized she left it in the youth room. She quietly slipped out to retrieve it. She found the Bible on the sofa where she'd sat during Sunday school. She ran her hand over the worn leather and wondered how many times her grandmother brought this very same Bible to this same church week after week. *We both belong here.*

On her way back to the sanctuary, Hailey was caught up in her thoughts. When was the last time anyplace felt like home? She clutched the Book against her heart and almost bumped into a man.

"Oh, excuse me," she apologized quickly before glancing up into his face. Suddenly, Hailey's eyes grew wide. She was staring at Bill Pierce, the man who'd been stealing from the church.

Bill hardly seemed to notice her. He moved out of the way and opened the sanctuary door to sit by his wife.

Hailey watched him nervously. He was bigger face to face than he appeared from her hiding places. How would he react to the note she planned to put in with the offering money? What if he didn't try to steal it today and Ruby found the note when she made the actual deposit?

The praise band began leading worship and Hailey forced back her fears and slipped back into the sanctuary.

\*\*\*

"I saw the man face to face today," Hailey told Kyra as they broke into Ruby's office using Hailey's school ID.

"Mr. Pierce?" Kyra asked.

Hailey nodded. "I almost walked right into him."

"What's he like?"

"He's big… and he's intimidating." Hailey pulled the note she'd written out of her pocket and reread it. "Maybe he was just scarier because of what I know."

Kyra flipped on the light and they found the large, gray offering envelope. "I wish I could watch his face when he reads the note."

Hailey placed the note inside the envelope and blew out a trembling breath. "Are you sure we should do this?"

"Of course. Why wouldn't we? He needs to stop stealing from the church."

Hailey agreed. "I guess seeing him in person just really scared me."

"He'll have no idea who wrote the note. That's what makes it even more fun. We know who he is but he doesn't know who we are."

"He could take that as a threat."

"Well, isn't it?" Kyra and Hailey turned the lock on Ruby's door, switched off the light and pulled the door closed.

"Should we hide in the clothing closet to watch him?" Kyra wanted to know.

"I'd like to. But I think the boys should be under the stage. I seriously don't want to risk getting caught now that we're putting that note in there."

"Why are you so scared?" Kyra and Hailey headed toward the kitchen to tell the boys to hide under the stage. "You sat in a computer box last week and watched him steal the money. That was even scarier."

Hailey nodded. But somehow this felt worse.

*** 

*Right on time.* Hailey glanced at her grandmother's watch when she heard the church door open. As usual, the man called out to anyone in the church, making sure he'd not get caught.

Hailey and Kyra buried themselves as deep into the clothing racks as they could and watched him open the office door. He walked in and the girls waited.

Hailey's heartbeat quickened as she thought about what his expression must be at that very moment. He had to be reading the note. He was taking far longer than he usually did. Or did it just feel that way?

Bill walked around the office for a few minutes as if he was inspecting something. Was he looking for a camera?

When he passed the door, Hailey could see the white sheet of paper with her cryptic note written on it, in his hand. "Hello?" he called out.

Bill never called out after he got the money. "Who are you?" Bill's footsteps moved to the hall and he seemed to be going into each room.

*This can't be good. He assumes someone is here.*

"Is this some kind of joke?" His voice called through the hallway. "Don't think I won't figure out who wrote this." He returned to the office and turned out the light.

Bill walked around the entire church before Hailey and Kyra heard him leave the building. They were both too scared to come out of hiding for at least ten more minutes.

"He seemed upset," Kyra confessed.

"That didn't sound like a man who was repentant and scared of God's wrath."

"What do you think he would have done with us if he'd have found us?"

"I don't plan on ever finding out." Hailey tried to still her breathing. "Let's check the boys."

# Chapter 13

The youth group returned to the church at close to five. Lane greeted his wife upon their arrival and invited Chad and Laura to have dinner with them after the teens left. There was no youth group this night, so the youth pastor was free to relax the rest of the evening.

"We can order pizza, that way Kate won't feel pressure to make anything." Lane placed his arm around his wife and kissed her. "I missed you."

"I missed you too." She wrapped her arms around her husband and hugged him.

"I'll be excited to hear how the trip went."

"It was excellent." Kate waved goodbye to some of the girls she'd just spent the weekend with and gave Lane the go ahead to order pizza.

"Are you sure you're not too tired for company?" Laura asked Kate.

"I'm fine. How was Caroline this weekend?"

Laura's eyes shone. "She was an angel. But the house felt empty without Chad."

"Thanks for going with us, Aunt Kate." Janie gave her aunt a hug. "I had such a great time. The speaker was amazing and the praise and worship was awesome."

Kate walked her niece to Anne's car and said good-bye to Paul as well.

"Did my children wear you out?" Anne asked.

"Not at all. We were blessed by the whole weekend." Kate waved to her sister as they pulled out of the parking lot.

"Are we ready?" Lane asked Chad.

Chad nodded. "I'm starved. I hope you ordered ham and pineapple."

Lane grinned. "Of course."

The two couples arrived at Lane and Kate's house just before the pizza arrived. Kate quickly smoothed a brown and white checked tablecloth over the round oak kitchen table and set out four stoneware plates.

"Caroline is fast asleep." Laura wrapped a blanket around her sleeping daughter's legs and made sure the baby was comfortable in her portable crib. "Can I help you do anything?"

"If you'd like to pour the iced tea that would be great."

Laura knew her way around Kate's kitchen well enough to find the glasses and pour the tea.

"Lane, can you cut up a lemon?" Kate asked her husband.

"Already done." Lane pulled a saucer out of the refrigerator with freshly cut lemons and set them on the table. "I was all ready for you."

Kate leaned over the table and kissed her husband. "You're too sweet."

The two couples sat down at the table and Chad asked the Lord's blessing on the meal.

"So tell me about the weekend." Lane opened one of the pizza boxes and pulled out a thick, cheesy slice of pizza.

Chad and Kate shared bits and pieces of their retreat experiences, including some of the trouble a few of the teens got into for toilet papering their cabin.

"Overall, I think this was a very successful retreat. I wish all the teens could have gone," Chad said.

"It's amazing how empty the church feels with seventy-five percent of the youth group gone." Lane took a bite of his pizza.

"The teens do add a lot of energy on a Sunday morning." Kate smiled. "I know I enjoyed the energy of this morning's worship with all those high school students on the retreat. "How was Sunday school?" she asked Laura. "Did very many students show up?"

"We had a handful. Hailey was there," Laura offered.

Kate smiled with her eyes. "Hailey is precious, isn't she?"

"Very. She's quiet, but she's a deep thinker. I was impressed by how well she got the things we talked about. It's like she internalized everything I taught her."

"Speaking of Hailey." Chad cleared his throat. "I just thought this was kind of strange."

The others waited for him to continue.

"Last week I saw Hailey stuff a large amount of money into a medium sized manila envelope. I made a joke about it when I saw her. She was being all sneaky and I think I embarrassed her. Then on our way down to Xenia, Janie asked me to pull up to a roadside mailbox. Before I could ask her about it, she mailed what looked like the same envelope." Chad finished his iced tea. "I asked Janie about it and she said Hailey asked her to mail it for her."

"And you're sure it was the same envelope?" Lane asked.

"I can't be positive." Chad got up to refill his glass. "But, get this... I asked Janie what was in the envelope and she said Hailey joked that there was hundreds of dollars in it." Chad sat back down and raised his eyebrows.

"Maybe she wasn't joking."

"That's what I think."

"Where was she sending it?" Kate asked.

"I don't know. Janie mailed it before I had a chance to get a look at it. She said she didn't really pay attention to where it was going."

"Why would she mail cash?" Lane questioned. "You're never supposed to mail cash."

"Maybe I should ask her about it," Kate suggested.

"It wouldn't hurt." Chad squeezed a lemon into his tea and took a long sip. "I really wish she could have gone with us on this trip."

Kate agreed.

"Why couldn't she go?" Laura asked.

"Hailey seems to carry a lot of the responsibility for the children," Kate explained. "From what I understand she needed to be there for them this weekend."

"Have you ever talked to their parents?" Laura got up to get Caroline. "Chad told me that Hailey and Kyra left their address blank on the student information forms." She sat back down with the baby and rocked her gently.

Lane shook his head. "Kate and my theory is that the children are somehow ashamed of where they live." He leaned back on the dining room chair. "But I've never heard them say anything bad about their parents."

"They don't really say much about their parents," Kate added. "The only thing Hailey ever told me about her mom is that she works at Wal-Mart."

"The boys have never mentioned their dad," Lane added. "But they are hungry for male companionship."

"They're great kids." Laura spoke up.

"Do you have any idea where they live?" Chad asked.

Lane shook his head. "That's another weird thing. I have no idea where they live."

"I asked Hailey recently and she flat out told me that she preferred not to say." Kate reached for the pizza box and pulled out a slice of ham and pineapple. "She wasn't rude about it. Hailey is never rude. But I don't understand."

"She left her address and phone number blank on the youth group information form." Chad leaned back in his chair. "It's the strangest thing. So neither of you have ever met their parents?"

"No. They don't go to church and I don't know how to get a hold of them." Lane polished off his last bite of pizza and took a sip of tea.

Chad shook his head. "I haven't met them either. I don't even know their names." He chewed on his lip for a moment. "I mean, there are other teens in the youth group whose parents don't come to church. But I at least have an address or phone number."

Lane shrugged. "I'll just ask Hailey what her parents names are. We can always look them up if we need to talk to them."

"That's a good idea." Kate nodded at her husband. "I'd feel better if we at least knew their names."

\*\*\*

Hailey woke up in a cold sweat. She glanced at her grandmother's watch and saw that it was the middle of the night. It was dark under the stage, but Hailey could hear the steady breathing of the other children and it gave her comfort.

She'd had a bad dream. Ever since she met Bill Pierce face to face, Hailey was struggling. The conversation she'd overheard between Bill and Ruby on Monday didn't help either.

On Monday Bill came by the church to ask Ruby a few questions about a security system. Hailey overheard part of the conversation while she was cleaning in the hallway.

"Who all has a key to your office?" she heard him ask the secretary.

"Hardly anyone," Ruby answered. "Only you, Pastor and Kate Evans, Nancy Troyer and Ned. Why?"

"We need to keep track of the keys. Do you have a list of everyone who has a key to the actual building?"

"No. Those we've given out more liberally."

"It would be a good idea if you did. If we do install a security system, everyone who has a key will need to know how to turn off the alarm."

"I don't see why we need a security system." Ruby's tone was unconvinced. "We've never had a break in."

"You don't wait until you have a problem before coming up with a solution," Bill said.

Later, Hailey found out from Ruby that Bill was one of the church trustees. She guessed that was why he had a key to the church and Ruby's office.

It troubled Hailey that Bill was obviously trying to hunt down everyone who had a key to the church. She would be on that list. How easy would it be for him to figure out that it was her who knew he was stealing? What would he do if he figured it out? Hailey needed to keep herself discreet.

*You could just go to Kate and Lane and tell them…* The thought popped into Hailey's mind a couple of times, but she quickly dismissed it knowing that to tell them was a huge risk. Lane would want to know why they were in the church on a Sunday afternoon. Lane told them he didn't want them cleaning on Sundays, so she couldn't just tell him that they saw him while they were cleaning. Even if he didn't figure out that they were living there, he would think she was misusing the key he'd entrusted her with. Hailey didn't want to lose Lane's trust.

The whole thing weighed heavy on her shoulders. She hated having this secret. A church trustee was stealing offering money and she knew about it. Hailey had to find a way to expose him without exposing herself.

She closed her eyes and tried to go back to sleep.

153

***

Tuesday morning it was a little chilly under the stage. Hailey found herself snuggling deeper into her sleeping bag in an attempt to get warm. As the temperatures outside were dropping, it occurred to Hailey that there were no heating vents in the cubby.

Hailey's bad dream was still fresh in her mind. In the dream Bill Pierce was running after her in the church. The hallway seemed to go on and on forever and Hailey couldn't get away from him.

She glanced at her grandmother's watch and saw that it was after eleven. She needed to wake up Kyra and the boys so they could sneak outside and make their afternoon entrance into the front door of the church.

Kyra was already awake and reading quietly in her corner using a flashlight they found in the cleaning closet for added light.

"Good morning." Hailey crawled to Kyra and spoke softly. "What are you reading?"

"A book I found in the church library." Kyra turned the book over in her hand and read the title. "It's a true story about a woman named Elizabeth Elliott."

Hailey nodded. She'd heard of Elizabeth Elliott. "Wasn't she a missionary?"

"Yes." Kyra closed the book and slipped it under her pillow. "Time to wake up the boys I guess."

Hailey nodded. Kyra didn't seem to want to talk about it.

Quietly, they woke up Hayden and Grant. There was enough food under the stage for them all to have a quick bite to eat.

Hayden tore open a granola bar and mumbled something about being tired of granola bars. "I want scrambled eggs and toast," he said with his mouth full. "I bet Kate makes scrambled eggs for Lane."

"We don't live with Kate," Hailey reminded him. "And granola bars are better than the nasty food Tara gave us."

"I'm tired of living under this stage." Hayden crossed his arms.

154

Hailey understood. She was growing tired of it too. "Well for now it's all we have." She picked up Hayden's wrapper and threw it into their cubby garbage can. "Let's get out there so we can walk around."

No one needed to be reminded to wear a coat. One by one they slipped out the window with one eye on the choir room door to make sure no one walked in. Hailey wondered what would happen if Lane or Ruby walked in while they were climbing out the window.

Together they scrambled around to the other side of the church and walked in through the front doors. Lane greeted them as soon as they walked in.

Grant ran into Lane's arms for a hug. The look in Lane's eyes told Hailey that Lane appreciated the hug as much as Grant did.

"Hey there big fella." Lane reached out to give Hayden a fist bump.

Grant reached out his fist and returned the bump. "It's getting really cold outside."

Lane nodded. "It is." He walked to the church thermostat and turned it up a couple degrees. "That should help us in here I guess."

Hailey and Kyra got right to work gathering their cleaning supplies while Grant and Hayden asked Lane all kinds of questions about hunting.

"Can you teach me to fire a shotgun?" Hayden asked.

"Now, I think I'd have to ask your parents before letting you shoot a gun." Lane leaned against the welcome counter and watched Hailey unwind the vacuum cord.

"They don't care," Hayden spat.

Lane cleared his throat. "I was actually thinking that since you are here so much, I should get your parent's names in case there was ever an emergency." He was clearly addressing Hailey.

"Shawn and Beth," Hailey said as she plugged in the vacuum.

Hayden glanced at Hailey curiously. Hailey wondered if he remembered their parent's names. *Shawn and Beth Goodman.* She wasn't sure why she gave Lane their real first names. Of course, he would assume it was Shawn and Beth Evans and she wasn't about to correct his assumption.

Lane grabbed a church pen from the welcome counter and wrote the names on a scrap piece of paper. "Can I get a phone number?"

"Um… right now they don't have a phone." She shifted nervously.

Lane glanced at the names on his piece of paper. "Okay. Well, let me know when they do."

Hailey nodded. She turned on the vacuum and hoped Lane wouldn't press for their address.

***

Lane sat at his desk in the pastor's study. It was a comfortable room down the hall from Ruby's office. The room was painted rich, warm beige and trimmed with a dark burgundy border. The large, oak desk was a gift from one of the church members. It was hand crafted with dovetailed drawers and hand carved acorns for drawer handles.

He leaned back in his leather chair and crossed his arms behind his head. The list of people named Evans in the community was still on his computer screen. He and Kate's name was part of the list. He could not find a Shawn Evans in the area. There were two Elizabeth Evans listed, but both of them were at least twenty minutes away. Lane considered the Internet might not have up to date information yet. Perhaps they only used cell phones.

Lane knew Hailey called her mother from their house once. Did she call Elizabeth's cell phone or work? Lane studied what information he could find and narrowed the list when he saw that one of the women was only twenty-two years old. *That can't be her.* Lane shook his head. *And I don't know if this one is either.*

He didn't want Hailey to know he was snooping on her. But Lane felt like he should at least know who their parents were in case he ever needed to get in touch with them.

They were great kids. But they acted so strange when it came to their parents.

***

Wednesday night Hailey got to hear all about the youth retreat from Janie, Paul and Wade.

"The speaker could quote entire chapters of the Bible," Wade said enthusiastically. "I've never seen anything like it in my life. I asked him how he got to that point. I mean, how in the world do you memorize that many verses?" Wade took a sip of his drink. "The man told me that he reads through the entire Bible at least nine times a year."

"That's convicting." Hailey shoved a French fry around on her plate.

"It is. It really challenged me. I need to be in the Word more. The guy said that he didn't know the Lord until later in life so he realized how much he'd been missing. I think I take God for granted sometimes because I've always gone to church." Wade's eyes showed the intensity of his feelings.

"I don't think you take God for granted, Wade," Paul said in his logical tone. "You're more passionate about God than anyone I know."

"But I need to put that passion into action and really delve into God's Word. The Bible is one of the greatest ways God communicates with us. I need to listen more."

Hailey listened intently. "I wish I could have gone on that retreat."

"Just listen to Wade." Paul grinned. "He's just about as good as the speaker at retelling it all."

"There are books of the Bible that I've never even read all the way through," Hailey confessed.

"That's probably true of a lot of Christians." Janie dipped a fry in ketchup and popped it into her mouth. "Oh, hey, I mailed that letter for you."

"Thanks!" Hailey was relieved to hear it.

"Did you really have money in that envelope?"

Hailey glanced around for a moment. *Walk in the Spirit… don't lie…* "Yes." She noticed Hayden running with his plate of food. "Hayden, don't run. You're going to spill your food." Hailey was thankful for the distraction. "So about the Bible thing… I want to hear the rest. Did the speaker give any ideas for how to get into God's Word more?"

157

Wade let out a dry chuckle. "He said that the average person spends several hours a week watching television. His challenge to us was to cut out a television show every day and use that time to read God's Word."

Hailey nodded. Since moving to the church, she and her brothers never watched television anymore. *What could I cut out to give myself more time?*

Janie glanced at the clock. "We're going to need to get to the lower building to help set up for the kiddies."

Hailey nodded. She liked helping out with the children's program. It gave her a chance to help out with her brothers and it gave her time with Janie.

As the teens walked toward the lower building, Kate stopped Hailey in the hall. "How was your weekend?" Kate asked. "We missed you so much!"

"Wade gave her the whole talk," Paul teased.

Hailey appreciated that Kate missed her. Hailey missed seeing Kate as well. "I definitely missed you guys. It sounds like you had an awesome weekend."

"We did. I'm glad Wade gave you a recap." She smiled at Wade. "He's good at that."

Hailey agreed.

"Hey, Lane promised Hayden and Grant that he would teach them how to use a bow. Friday is Lane's day off and we thought if you and your siblings didn't have anything going on you could come over and have dinner with us."

"I'm jealous," Wade teased.

Hailey tried to come up with a good reason to decline, but Hayden and Grant would be disappointed if she did. "That's fine. What time?"

"Come around three and we'll eat at five thirty. That will give the boys time to play and us girls time to talk."

Hailey nodded. "We'll see you then."

# Chapter 14

Hailey sat with her Bible in her lap thinking about how much there really was to learn about God. She'd spent the past half hour reading to Kyra and her brothers from the Old Testament. The chapters she read were not new to her, but Hailey marveled at how every time you read the Bible something new popped out at you.

Kyra's response to the Bible was fun as well. Hailey loved that Kyra wanted to learn about God. Even though she hadn't yet put her faith in Christ, Kyra's heart seemed to be slowly opening.

Hailey couldn't tell about Hayden.

At two-forty Hailey told the kids they needed to leave if they wanted to get to Lane and Kate's on time.

Hayden crawled across the cubby floor carrying a camouflage jacket. "I found this in the clothing closet yesterday." He slipped his arms through it. "I always wanted a camo jacket."

"Always, Hayden?" Hailey grinned at her little brother. Just little over a month ago, Hailey couldn't be sure her brother knew what a camouflage jacket was. Moving to the country had its influences.

The children donned hats and gloves and slipped quietly out the back window to begin their short trek to the pastor's house. The weather was growing much cooler and Hailey pulled her scarf close to her face to ward off the wind.

The walk seemed to take longer because of the cold, but there was a spring in the boys' step that said seeing Lane was worth the trek through the cold.

"You children look about frozen." Kate grabbed Kyra's cold fingers and pulled her into the house. "Let me make you some hot cocoa."

Kyra's eyes twinkled. "Do you have marshmallows?"

Kate held up a bag of jumbo marshmallows. "Do these work?"

"Yes!" Kyra did a little dance.

The boys went out back to find Lane all ready with his bow and a bull's-eye.

"Lane actually bought a couple smaller bows for the boys. He wasn't sure they'd have the physical strength to pull back on his." Kate poured milk into a pan and began adding ingredients. "He's been looking forward to this for days."

"Can I stir?" Kyra asked.

"Absolutely." Kate resigned her place at the stove and sat down next to Hailey at the kitchen table.

Hailey's eyes were on the boys in the backyard with Lane. "They love him so much." Hailey tried to keep her emotions at bay.

Kate was quiet for a moment as if trying to gear up to speak her thoughts. "Are they close to their dad?"

Hailey wouldn't allow herself to look at Kate. "No. Not at all."

"It's about to boil." Kyra inhaled the smell of the hot cocoa and licked her lips. "This smells a hundred times better than the packaged stuff."

Kate poured in a teaspoon of vanilla. "Just wait until you taste it." She grabbed three large mugs and filled them with the warm liquid.

"This is really good!" Kyra took a taste and smiled. She breathed in the warm chocolaty smell and took a long sip.

"Thank you for doing all this." Hailey's eyes followed Kate as she wiped up the cocoa drips from the counter and carried her mug to the kitchen table where the girls sat.

"I love hot cocoa. Its good to have an excuse to make some."

"Can I ask you a kind of personal question, Kyra?" Kate asked.

Kyra nodded. "Sure."

"How old were you when you were adopted?"

Hailey's eyes moved quickly to Kyra's. How was the younger girl going to answer?

"You see," Kate continued. "Lane and I have been trying to adopt a baby for a few years but we keep hitting a brick wall. We talked last night about whether we really had to have a baby and quite honestly, we both feel peace about adopting an older child. That's why I wanted to know. I thought you might have a genuine perspective."

Hailey glanced out the window and watched her little brothers learn to shoot a bow with Lane while Kyra answered Kate's question.

"I'll be honest with you," Kyra began.

Hailey hoped Kyra's honestly wasn't about to be some long made up lie.

"When I was little I used to hear about all these people wanting babies and I resented it. I thought about how there were so many little kids like me who wanted a mom and dad so bad while everyone was competing for the babies. It doesn't seem fair." Kyra paused for a moment. "I know people think that older children have all these problems and stuff, but everybody does, right? I mean, come on - is anyone perfect? And if some good parents like you and Lane came along and loved them, maybe they could work through their problems…"

Hailey felt her eyes fill up with tears. Kyra was speaking the truth. It was the truth for all four of them.

Kyra took a long sip of her hot chocolate and set down the empty mug. "There are lots of really nice older kids who would love you and Lane." She stood up. "Would you mind if I went outside and watched them shoot the arrows? It looks like so much fun."

Hailey wondered if Kyra was just looking for an excuse to get out of the conversation. She'd done a great job avoiding the original question and Hailey was glad the younger girl didn't lie.

"That's fine." Kate carried Kyra's mug to the sink and rinsed it out. "Thank you for your perspective. I really appreciate it."

Kyra nodded, put on her coat and hurried outside into the cold, leaving Hailey alone with Kate.

"I really appreciate Kyra's honesty," Kate said. "I wasn't sure if it was difficult for her to talk about her adoption but I really wanted her perspective."

Hailey glanced into her hot cocoa mug and she swirled it around. She appreciated Kyra's honesty too. "I don't think she minded."

Kate brushed a stray hair from her face and sat across from Hailey with her mug in hand. "You've been quiet the last few times I've seen you."

Hailey hoped this wasn't about to get personal.

"Is everything okay?"

"I'm fine."

"That's such a convenient answer." Kate rested her arm on the table. "Lane and I have decided that there must be multiple definitions for fine. I like, 'Faking It, Need Encouragement.'"

Hailey grinned at Kate's acronym.

"Okay, well, at least let me ask you a question that's been on my mind the past few days," Kate said. "Chad said that Janie mailed a letter for you this weekend."

Hailey's hands grew suddenly sweaty. "Yes."

"He was a little concerned," Kate continued. "He said you put money into an identical envelope earlier in the week. Were you mailing money?"

Hailey lowered her eyes. Kate was asking her a direct question. *I can't lie...* "Yes." She turned her face toward the window.

"I'm not trying to be nosy, but they tell people not to put cash in the mail because it can easily be stolen."

"I know."

"I would have written a check for you and allowed you to give me the cash."

Hailey shook her head. "No. That wouldn't have worked."

"Why?" Kate pushed.

"Because I don't want this person to know where I live." Hailey was painfully honest.

Kate studied Hailey curiously. "That's troubling. Does your mother know about this?"

"No." Hailey answered honestly. She rose and walked to the window where she watched Hayden shoot the target with his new bow and arrow. He jumped up and down and gave Lane a high five. *He's so happy. They love Lane.* Hailey couldn't bear to watch it anymore. She turned back around and faced Kate. "Can we not talk about this anymore? I just can't..." Hailey felt herself coming unglued. "I honestly can't talk to you about it. I'm sorry.

Kate didn't push. She nodded with understanding and asked if Hailey wanted to go outside and watch the boys learn to use their bows. "We can cheer them on."

Hailey nodded. She appreciated that Kate was willing to let it drop. They joined the others outside and Hailey did her best to feign a smile.

***

Dinner was wonderful. The boys chatted incessantly though the meal about how they learned to shoot a bow and that Lane was going to take them hunting some day.

Kyra seemed entertained, but Hailey was distracted. Try as she may, it was difficult to hide her emotions.

After the meal, Kate suggested that they play a game together, so they all played a few board games, ate desert and had lots of laughs. It was almost dark before Hailey realized it was past time to leave. She didn't want to give Lane and Kate any reason to insist on driving them home.

"I hate to run off." She glanced at the clock. "But we are going to need to get home."

"Why don't I drive you?" Lane offered. "It's getting dark out there."

"No. We're good."

"But I hate to have you walking home in the dark."

"We don't live that far. We'll hurry." Hailey got up from the table and motioned for the others to follow.

"We'll see you on Sunday." Grant hugged Kate. "Thank you for my bow and arrow!" he turned to Lane.

"You're welcome, little man." Lane tussled the hair on Grant's curly blonde head.

"I love you!" Grant gave Lane a hug so full of emotion that Hailey could almost feel it.

"Come on, Grant. Time to go." Hailey waved her farewell and they all slipped out the door into the cool evening air.

***

"I had such a great time with the boys," Lane said after the children left. "They were so excited about the bow and arrows." Lane sat on the sofa with a contented grin.

"They're so sweet and grateful for everything."

163

'They are." Lane accepted a cup of peppermint tea from his
ınd breathed in the fresh minty scent. "They both did really
ıl hitting the target. I think that was the most excited I've ever
:en Hayden." He dunked the tea bag a few times and cleared his
throat. "Grant said something kind of strange tonight," he began.

Kate listened curiously and sat beside her husband on the
couch with her own cup of tea.

"The boys were so excited about the bow and arrows. I
asked them if they'd ever been to the hunting store in Newark.
Hayden said they didn't have a car." Lane took a sip of his tea. "I
asked him how his mother got to work without a car and Grant said
the Amish drive her."

"To Wal-Mart?" Kate asked.

"That's what I said. Hayden told Grant to be quiet and just
changed the subject."

"Maybe Grant is confused."

Lane shrugged. "I don't know."

Kate sighed. "Well, I did talk to Hailey about the money."

"What did she say?" Lane wanted to know.

"She was mailing cash. She said she sent cash because she
doesn't want the person to know where she lives."

"That's strange."

"It is. I asked her if her mother knew and she said no. That
concerns me."

Lane agreed.

"The whole thing has me confused. Does it seem like we
should find out who their parents are and let them know their
daughter is going through something?"

Lane leaned back on the sofa. "Let's pray about it. God is
in control. He has brought those children into our lives for a reason
and I believe He has a plan."

Kate nodded and the couple joined hands to pray for the
children.

\*\*\*

"Hailey," Kyra snuggled close to the older girl in their
hiding place under the stage. "You seem really sad."

Hailey's lips curved into a smile. "I'll be okay. I'm just struggling with some stuff."

"Please tell me."

Hailey blew out a heavy sigh. She wanted to tell someone. But what would Kyra think of her taking the money? Even though she planned to return it – it was borrowing without permission. "I want to tell you, but I don't want you to think I'm terrible."

"I could never think you're terrible, Hailey. You're my big sister, remember?"

Hailey blinked in the dark and tried to make out Kyra's sweet dark eyes. "I borrowed money from Keith in order to pay for our bus tickets." *There… I said it. It's off my chest.* But I'm paying it back. I already sent money to Ms. Cooper this week to give to them."

"How did you send money? Won't she know where we are now?"

"No. I had Janie mail the envelope while they were on their trip. I told her I didn't want the person to know where I mailed it. I made it sound like a game… Janie had no idea. But I guess Chad recognized the envelope and told Kate. Tonight, Kate asked me about it."

"So what did you tell her?"

"That I mailed someone money." Hailey massaged her temples. "I'm so tired of the lies, Kyra. I can't stand it anymore. I can't live this way."

"But we have to, Hailey. We're all together; we have plenty of food, a nice place to live… I'm happier than I've ever been before."

Hailey reached for Kyra's hand in the dark and gave it a little squeeze. "I'm glad you're happy, Kyra. But there is more to this than just being happy. What kind of a witness am I being for the kingdom of God when I am leading you in lies?"

Kyra was quiet for a moment.

"I want you to know and love my Savior, Jesus Christ, but I'm not living in a way that brings Him honor while I'm making up stories to cover up where I live and who I am."

"But you are a witness, Hailey," Kyra said. "You really are. I can see that you love Jesus and I know that you want to obey Him. I respect that about you more than anything."

165

Hailey wiped away a tear. "But the lying is wrong. Jesus . t want me to keep sinning just because He has forgiven me."

"So let's stop lying. I can do that. Did you like how I got .ound her question tonight?" Kyra asked.

Hailey grinned in the darkness. "Yes. You did well. But it's not about doing well. It's about surrendering your life to Jesus and allowing Him to guide you, not trying to do it yourself. The Bible tells us that our good deeds are still like filthy rags compared to His righteousness."

"I get it."

"You do?"

"Yes," Kyra said. "Even me trying not to lie does not omit the fact that I am a sinner."

Hailey could hear her brothers' soft breathing in the little stage shelter but wished she could see Kyra's face. She turned on her flashlight and set it upright. "You recognize that you are a sinner?"

"Yes." Kyra nodded. "I never really understood it before."

"And I sure haven't been a good example."

"That's not true. You see... I've been able to see for a while how you agonize over the lies you've told. I never thought much of it. When I made up those stories for that lady on the bus the lies just rolled off my tongue like butter on a warm breakfast roll. But you... you cringed at every lie you told. I figured there must be something bad about lying if it caused you so much grief to do it. Then I started thinking about it and realized that lying really is wrong. Chad talked about the Bible verse that said that Jesus is the truth and that satan is the father of lies."

"John 14:6," Hailey reflected. "Jesus said to him, I am the way, and the truth, and the life; no one comes to the Father but through me."

"You've only shown me that you're human, Hailey. I know that you've been feeling guilty about it. If you didn't love God it wouldn't have bothered you."

Hailey appreciated Kyra's kind words.

"I want the truth, Hailey. Can you help me find it?" Kyra's tone was soft.

"It's in Jesus Christ. When we give our hearts to Him, surrender our lives to Him and ask Him to forgive us of our sins, He gives us eternal life."

Kyra was quiet for a few minutes and Hailey wondered if she was crying. "Are you okay?" she asked.

"I want that, Hailey. I really do."

Hailey tightened her hold on Kyra's hand. Hailey found it hard to believe that God would have used her to point Kyra to Jesus. "All you have to do is pray and ask God to save you," Hailey said. "You confess that you are a sinner and need His forgiveness and ask Him to come into your life and be your Lord and Savior."

Before Hailey could say another word, Kyra grabbed Hailey's other hand and began praying. Kyra's sweet, vulnerable heart came out in every word she spoke to God.

After she was done she looked up at Hailey in the dimly lit cubby. "Is that all I have to do?" she whispered almost reverently.

Hailey nodded and wiped away a tear. "Now you begin to walk in your relationship with Him. My grandma used to say it was like being married. You spend time with Him, get to know Him better by reading the Bible and praying, and you obey Him."

"I want to do that."

Hailey hugged Kyra. "I'm so glad, Kyra. You're so precious!"

"I love you, Hailey."

Hailey choked back a sob. "I love you too, Kyra."

Now Hailey was doubly determined. She could no longer lie. She had to walk in the Spirit and show this new sister in Christ what it really meant to be a Christ follower.

# Chapter 15

Sunday morning dawned with a new hope. Kyra was more excited than ever about church and Hailey could feel the girl's enthusiasm.

"I can't wait to tell Angie that I'm a Christian now," Kyra said.

All day Saturday, Kyra asked Hailey questions about the Bible and what certain things meant. Hayden told the girls he was tired of all their religious talk, but Grant loved it.

Hailey also took the time to apologize to the boys for lying. "It was sin and I should never have done it. I plan to set a better example to you now."

"So what happens if someone asks you about us? Are you going to tell them the truth?" Hayden tested her.

"I can honestly tell them that I prefer not to answer, can't I?"

Hayden shrugged.

Hailey still had to pray about the fact that they were living in the church building. She knew that the food they ate and the clothes they wore were all for the needy, to which she could honestly say they were. But Hailey knew that it was wrong to run away.

\*\*\*

"So I hear that we have some praising to do," Kate greeted Kyra Sunday morning before the service.

Kyra stood beside Hailey and smiled. "Did Angela tell you?"

"No, your Sunday school teacher did."

Kyra nodded. "I announced it in Sunday school this morning."

Hailey was impressed. It showed boldness for Kyra to announce to the whole Sunday school class that she was now a Christian.

"They all prayed for me," Kyra said.

Kate reached for Kyra and gave her a huge hug. "I am so happy!"

"Me too. Hailey really helped me." Kyra glanced at Hailey and nodded.

"Hailey is pretty wonderful, isn't she?" Kate reached an arm out to hug Hailey. "You both are." She smiled. "When did this happen?"

"Friday night after we left your house," Kyra explained. "Neither Hailey or I could sleep so we stayed up talking about what it meant to be a Christian and prayed together."

"That's wonderful. Lane will rejoice too, I'm sure."

"Now we just need to pray for Hayden," Hailey said. Her little brother was at the other end of the church with Caleb and she watched him laughing and playing with his new friend.

"By the way," Kate held up a gift bag. "This is for Grant. It's the first Box Car Children book."

"Thank you!" she smiled. "Let me call Grant over. He will be so excited."

Grant and Leah were walking through the church chairs greeting all the people Leah knew and Hailey called them over.

"Grant," she placed a tender hand on her brother's back. "Kate has something for you."

Kate handed Grant the bag and his eyes lit it up when he pulled out the book. "Now we can finish reading it!" He hugged Kate.

\*\*\*

After the service, the children enjoyed a quick lunch and hid under the stage. They weren't entirely sure what to expect from the offering thief. Hailey saw him at church that morning and did her best to avoid looking at him. She noticed that he glanced around a lot, as if he was watching people. She wondered if he was trying to figure out who wrote the note. The children weren't sure what they would do if he showed up today. They were all a little nervous.

169

At the time of his usual arrival, the children all sat quietly in the dark under the stage. They strained their ears to listen for his voice but couldn't hear him.

By four thirty the children decided the man had either come and left or wasn't going to come. Chad usually got there by five, so they children hurried to get ready and slip out of the building.

At six, the youth room was full of teenagers and Hailey left her siblings with a few pieces of pizza to join her youth group. She was eager to talk to Janie, Paul and Wade about Kyra and also wanted to tell Wade that she was sincerely moving toward surrendering in order to walk in the Spirit.

"Angela is so happy." Janie sat next to Hailey with her pizza. "She has been praying for Kyra since she met her. My little sister loves Kyra."

"We've just got to keep working on Hayden," Wade interjected.

"Pastor Evans has been doing a great job with that. Hayden simply adores him."

"I noticed that." Wade took a bite of his pizza. "He shadows the pastor everywhere."

"When he's not with your brother," Hailey added.

"True." Wade nodded. "And speaking of Caleb, my brother is having a birthday party next Saturday. He has an invitation for Hayden, but I figured it might be good for me to talk to you. It's from three to six."

Hailey knew that Hayden would love to come. But how would he get there? "Where do you live?"

"About fifteen minutes from the church. It's real easy, I can give you directions."

Hailey shook her head. "We don't have any transportation," she said honestly.

"That's no problem. I can pick him up." Wade studied Hailey for a moment.

She felt nervous under his observation. Her mind raced with how to answer. Hayden would love to go to Caleb's party. Had he ever been to a birthday party before? She wasn't sure. "I have an idea. I could do a few things at the church on Saturday, why don't you pick him up here?"

"I can do that. But you'll need to tell me where to drive him home."

"Just bring him here. It's easier." Hailey finished her slice of pizza and carried her plate to the trash.

A rumble of thunder echoed through the walls of the church and Hailey glanced toward the door with concern.

"That was a pretty good one." Paul smiled. "We're supposed to get a thunder storm tonight. I guess the weather man was right."

Chad encouraged all the teens to wrap up their conversations so they could begin youth group.

"Its good to have Laura back to help us." Chad smiled at his wife.

"Can I hold Caroline?" one of the girls asked.

"She's sleeping right now." Laura peeked into the baby's car seat carrier. "I think I'll just keep her close to me."

As usual, Wade led the youth in a few praise songs and Chad opened their time up in prayer.

"Tonight, I'd like for some of you to share ways you've applied what you learned at camp last week to your life."

Several teens raised their hands and took turns sharing what they learned and how it influenced their lives.

"I've made it my goal to read through the entire Bible in a year," Janie said. "I know it's not nine times like the speaker from camp, but I don't want to make my goal so big that I get discouraged if I don't meet it."

One of the other teens raised his hand and Chad called on him.

"I decided to take my television out of my bedroom," the young man said. "I realized that ever since I've had one in my room I spend more time watching T.V. than I should. I put it in the basement and haven't even missed it."

It was interesting to hear the various teens share their experiences and goals. Hailey appreciated how vulnerable some of the teens were. She glanced across the room and noticed Clarissa whispering indifferently with Gina. *Who am I to judge them? I'm a sinner just like them.*

Hailey's ears piqued when Wade spoke up to share his experience.

"It was a good motivator for me. Even though I love leading praise and worship and I do seek to grow in my faith, I know that I've been lacking in my Bible reading. I guess hearing the speaker share how much he longs for the Word of God made me take a look at myself and ask if I hunger that way. I've asked God to help me to hunger for the Bible, to want to read it so bad that nothing else will satisfy me."

Chad nodded appreciatively. "That's kind of where I'm at with it," he agreed. "I get so busy with day to day life, even good things like youth group, but more importantly than all those things is the need to be in God's Word."

The youth group closed their time with a few more worship songs and prayer. Hailey felt blessed by hearing the many teens share their testimonies.

Even Kate shared that she was challenged by the weekend.

Hailey admired Kate's willingness to be so open with the teens. *I want to be like her some day.*

***

After youth group, Hailey and Wade went to find their brothers in the sanctuary.

"Here." Hayden handed his sister a note card. "I told him I probably couldn't go," he said in a sour tone.

Hailey knew right away that this was the invitation. She glanced at Wade and back to her brother. "Actually, you are going. Wade is picking you up at the church Saturday while I'm here getting some things done."

Hailey hoped her brother understood that 'getting some things done' was just a front.

"You're picking me up?" Hayden's face beamed at Wade. "Really? I can go?" He looked like he might jump out of his skin with joy.

"Yes."

Hayden gave Caleb a high five. "I can go!"

The boys did a quick race back and forth down the hallway and Hailey thanked Wade. "You've made his day."

"No problem." He glanced toward the window where the rain was coming down hard. "Why don't you let me drive you guys home?"

Hailey shook her head. "No. We're fine."

"It's raining cats and dogs out there."

Hailey shrugged. "We're used to it. See you Wednesday night." She nodded and motioned for her brothers and Kyra to come. "We'd better go."

Her siblings followed Hailey out the door and into the storm. Hailey hoped the people in the church would hurry up and leave.

\*\*\*

The children were soaked by the time they climbed through the choir room window.

Grant chattered his teeth and hurried out of his dripping coat.

"That was crazy," Kyra said. It seemed to take extra long for the men to finish up their prayer time tonight and the children were in the rain far too long.

"Get out of your wet clothes. We need to warm up," Hailey spoke just as much to herself as the others. She hoped none of them would get sick from their time in the storm.

"I thought the lightening was cool though." Hayden was still on his happy high and didn't seem to mind that he was wet to the skin.

"What am I going to do on Saturday if Hayden is at a birthday party?" Grant asked.

Hailey used her towel to dry her little brother's hair. "We'll find something fun to do."

"Can we make cookies?" Grant's big blue eyes pleaded.

"I don't know. It depends what food is here." Hailey liked to be careful not to make their food consumption obvious. There were plenty of canned goods in the pantry, but butter and milk were harder to use without making it obvious.

"A hot chocolate chip cookie would be wonderful." Kyra licked her lips and leaned back on her sleeping bag. "I think I'll lay here and dream about one."

"Do you think Caleb will have cake at his birthday?"

Hailey nodded. "I'm sure there will be lots of food."

Grant's eyes grew somber. "I want cake."

Hayden threw himself down beside Grant and rolled onto his stomach. "I'll bring you a slice. I'm sure Mrs. Parker will let me."

"Really?" Grant's eyes lit up.

Hailey appreciated Hayden's sudden tenderness. "Thank you, Hayden."

***

Monday morning the children were busy with their cleaning chores. Lane told Hailey that Ned was supposed to be coming home next week, but that maybe they could be his helpers.

She had enough money now to pay off the remaining debt, so she wasn't worried about a cut in pay, but she was worried about a janitor hanging around. Did he ever go far under the stage? What if he showed up while they were roaming around the building?

A voice in the office drew Hailey's attention after she turned off the vacuum cleaner. It was Bill Pierce.

"And you're sure this is everyone?" Bill said.

"As far as I can remember," Ruby replied. "I've racked my brain for the past week trying to think who all I've given a church key to. But if we do get this alarm system, is it going to cost the church very much? We run a pretty tight budget as it is."

"I understand. I still need to present the idea to the other trustees, so this may all be a mute point. But I wanted to have all my ducks in a row if we do decide to get a security system."

Hailey's mouth was dry and her hands shook nervously. Bill Pierce had a list of everyone with a key. She heard him walking toward the door.

"Thanks, Ruby…"

Hailey hurriedly pushed the vacuum down the hallway, hoping to avoid his notice. She could hear his footsteps behind her walking toward the exit.

She brushed a stray hair out of her eyes and prayed that the man would not find them out.

***

Dahlia Cooper sat across from Tara and Keith Prescott while the couple finished reading Hailey's short note asking that her social worker make sure Tara and Keith got the money.

Keith accepted the wad of bills and sniffed. "She still owes us a hundred dollars. Let's see her turn in the rest."

"I truly believe she will," Dahlia defended. "Why would she bother giving this much if she doesn't plan to return it all?"

"The little girl is a thief and a runaway." Tara crossed her arms angrily. "I'm thoroughly offended that you and your people have even felt the need to investigate us. Keith and I feel like we've been under a microscope ever since the children left."

"You withheld information from us," Dahlia reminded them. "You never told us about Hailey's note."

"It slipped my mind."

"I've known Hailey Goodman for four years," Dahlia said. "In those years I have never known her to be a bad kid. But she wrote in her letter to me that she was afraid you would separate her from her brothers. What was the point in making those threats to her?"

Keith scratched his head and glanced at his wife. "Hailey is a bad influence on them."

"And on Kyra apparently," Tara added. "She's a criminal. She was violent with me, she's a liar, she stole money and she dragged the younger children away."

Dahlia tapped her pen lightly on the table. "And you just can't see how your threats might have driven her to the crime?"

"I believe this meeting has gone on long enough," Keith said curtly. "Come on, Tara."

The couple walked from the office in a huff and Dahlia let out an exasperated sigh. Keith and Tara's bad attitudes were the least of her worries. All four children were still missing and every day that passed made finding them seem more hopeless.

She turned the envelope over in her hand and read Hailey's cryptic return address. Dahlia shook her head. *This clever girl doesn't want to be found...* The Xenia, Ohio, postmark was a small

175

lead. Police in the area had been notified to be on the look out for the four children. But Dahlia had her doubts.

***

On Tuesday, Hailey found herself on edge. She and the children hid most of the day and did their school work under the stage, but after Lane and Ruby left, she was cautious about walking freely in the church.

The children all wanted to take showers, so they gathered their towels and clean clothes and hurried across the parking lot to the lower building. Hailey's imagination went wild with thoughts of Mr. Pierce coming in to the lower building while they were there and catching them.

The old building always seemed to bring out Hailey's darkest fears.

"Can we take an evening walk?" Hayden asked. "I haven't been outside all day."

Hailey sighed. All four of them were stir crazy.

"I could use a walk too," Kyra confessed. "Why don't we head over to Lane and Kate's to say hi?"

Hailey shook her head. "I don't want to drop in on them all the time. They need their privacy."

"Let's just go look at the horses," Grant suggested.

Hailey liked that idea. She made Hayden promise that he wouldn't run off. They all used Hailey's hairdryer because Hailey insisted that they weren't allowed outside with wet heads. "We've already had one night wet to the bone. I don't want to risk anyone getting sick."

They were all eager to get some fresh air. Hayden led the way as they walked down the country road away from the church.

Hailey noticed a car driving slowly behind them, but decided she was just being paranoid and tried to ignore it until it passed.

"That car was behind us for a while," Kyra said.

The younger girl had no idea that she was feeding Hailey's fears. Hailey hadn't told Kyra about Mr. Pierce having a list of all the people with keys to the church building.

They walked to the farm with the horses and stood on the wood rail fence to watch the large, beautiful animals in the soft light of dusk. A low fog settled on the countryside and the horses seemed almost ghosted on the horizon.

"Do you think if I tell God that I want to ride a horse that He will make it happen?" Grant asked in the quiet evening air.

"God does tell us to make our requests known to Him, Grant," Hailey said. "So I would try."

"But why would God care about things like horseback riding?" Hayden asked.

Hayden didn't ask many questions about God, so Hailey prayed for wisdom in her answer. "I think God cares about everything about us, Hayden," she said softly. "The Bible says that He notices even a sparrow when it falls, so how much more do you think He would notice us who He created in His image?"

A slight scowl on Hayden's face said the boy wasn't convinced. "I asked God for something yesterday and I don't think He is going to answer it."

Kyra glanced quickly at Hailey and raised her eyebrows. Hailey wasn't sure when Hayden had ever admitted to asking God for anything.

"What did you ask Him for?"

"A present for Caleb."

Hailey studied Hayden's face curiously.

"I wanted to give him something special for his birthday, but I don't think we have anything I can give him."

"Why don't you make a gift?" Grant suggested.

Hayden gave Grant a superior glare. "Because Caleb is going to be eleven. Home made gifts when you're eleven aren't cool."

Hailey gave Grant a comforting rub on his back. "That's not true. I love when you guys make me gifts and I'm fifteen."

"Fine. But you're a girl," Hayden huffed.

"Well, God could still answer your prayer you know," Kyra said. "It's only Tuesday."

"Yeah, well I don't think He's going to."

One of the horses approached from the far field and Hailey reached her hand out to allow him to smell her. He snorted and sniffed from one of his large nostril holes and then Hailey rubbed the white hair on his muzzle. "Hey there, buddy."

"Well I just prayed that one of the horses would come to us and it did," Grant spoke up. He reached over the fence and petted the large animal's face. "He's so big."

Hailey nodded. "Look at his eyes though. They're so sweet and kind looking."

Kyra stood back a few feet and watched from a distance. "Yeah. I think I like them better in books."

Hailey chuckled. She glanced at Hayden who allowed himself the pleasure of petting the horse.

"I wouldn't give up, Hayden. Do you know what Caleb wants?"

Hayden shrugged.

"Let's keep praying that God would show you the best gift you can give your friend."

\*\*\*

The children were tired when they slipped back into the building. Hailey make them a quick supper from the food pantry and they all cuddled into their sleeping bags to sleep. Hailey took time to pray for her siblings and for the fear that seemed to have crept into her life since she first learned who the offering thief was.

Hailey realized she was carrying a lot of things around in her heart and letting them weigh her down.

She glanced at her money jar and realized she could at least get that weight off of her chest.

Quietly slipping out of their cubby place and to Ruby's office, Hailey found another thick envelope and sat down with it at Ruby's desk. Using a black marker, Hailey wrote her social worker's name and address as the return address. With a grin on her lips, Hailey then addressed the letter to her social worker, stuffed one hundred dollars inside, and sealed it closed. Hailey remembered once mailing a letter without a stamp. It came back to her saying 'return to sender' without a postmark. If her social worker's name and address was the only option and there wasn't a stamp, wouldn't the post office simply send the letter back to the social worker? It seemed sneaky, but Hailey hoped it would work. She needed to get the weight off her chest.

Finding a mailbox to use would be another problem. She couldn't ask Janie to do it again because Janie might tell Kate. She couldn't ask Kate because she would only worry more.

Hailey slipped back into the cubby with her letter and tried to come up with a plan.

# Chapter 16


Wednesday night, Hailey enjoyed spending time with her new friends, helping out with the children's program.

It was encouraging to see her little brothers fitting in with new friends and having fun.

"Is your family doing anything special for Thanksgiving?" Janie asked Hailey.

Hailey hadn't really thought about Thanksgiving. It was still a few weeks away, but celebrating it never occurred to her. "We'll probably just have a nice meal." Hailey hoped that was true.

"My parents were talking about our family helping serve Thanksgiving meals at a Christian homeless shelter in Zanesville before we have our Thanksgiving meal with our grandma, Aunt Kate and Uncle Lane," Janie said.

"That sounds really cool."

"It is. We did it last year too. My parents feel like we should understand how thankful we really should be." Janie folded up the tissue paper the children used for crafts and placed it on the craft shelf. "Sometimes I think we take for granted all that we have, you know?"

Hailey did know. When her little brother gets excited on the days when there is milk in the church refrigerator to drink, one really begins to appreciate things.

"Do you have grandparents and aunts and uncles who join you?" Janie asked.

"No." Hailey wiped down the craft table and hoped Janie would stop asking personal questions.

\*\*\*

After the Wednesday night activities ended, Hailey and her siblings left the church until the coast was clear. Hailey noticed a car lingering in the parking lot so she urged Kyra and her brothers to stay still until the car drove away.

"You seem edgy," Kyra said as they finally climbed through the window. "What's going on?"

Hailey didn't want to talk about it with her brothers around. She shrugged and said they'd talk later.

Kyra seemed content with that answer and waited until the boys were asleep to drag Hailey into the choir room where they could talk.

"Are we being watched?" Kyra asked outright.

"I don't know." Hailey hated giving such a cryptic answer. "Bill Pierce got a list of names from Ruby. He knows who has a key to the church."

"But there's a lot of people, right?"

Hailey shrugged. "That's what Ruby said, but I don't really know. I only heard them talking about the list, I've never seen it. I'm sure Mr. Pierce is trying to figure out who knows. It's a threat to him. We're a threat to him. Kyra, I'm scared."

Kyra watched Hailey pace the room. "There's no reason he needs to figure it out. We'll just stay out of his way and make sure he never sees us coming in or out of the building."

"What if we're too late? What if he's already seen us?"

Kyra blew out a heavy sigh. "Then I don't know... then I guess we'll just have to watch our backs."

Hailey nodded. "And pray."

\*\*\*

Hayden was very quiet on Thursday. Hailey wondered if he was feeling well. He had been out in the rain that one day... what if he was sick?

"Are you okay, Hayden?" Hailey pulled her little brother aside after the homeschool study hall in the library.

Several of the teens were still lingering in the building, but Janie and Paul already left.

Hayden sat at the table and shook his head no.

Hailey closed her physical science book and crossed her arms on the table. "What is it?"

"I know what Caleb wants for his birthday."

Hailey wondered why this would have her brother so down.

"Can we go to the sanctuary alone?" Hayden asked.

"Sure." She glanced at Kyra. "Can you keep an eye on Grant?"

Kyra was happy to. She and Grant sat on a giant beanbag chair in the library for Kyra to read to him.

Hayden and Hailey walked to the sanctuary and turned on one of the huge rows of lights. The voices in the building seemed to disappear as her little brother's eyes filled up with tears and ran his hands over his curly red head. "I asked Caleb what he wanted for his birthday and he told me that more than anything in the whole world he wanted me to become a Christian."

Hailey's eyes grew wide. *Wow*... She didn't know what to say. What a beautiful thing for this dear friend to want for his birthday. "That's really sweet of Caleb," she finally said.

"I know." Hayden sniffed. "He said I'm his best friend."

"That's special."

Hayden nodded. "Why does he care so much if I become a Christian?"

Hailey prayed for the right words. "Because he cares about you, Hayden. Just like I do. He wants you to know Jesus and have the joy that only Jesus can give you."

Hayden buried his face in his hands and sobs shook his young form. "But I can't, Hailey... I can't be a Christian."

"Why?" Hailey placed a comforting hand on her brother. Her heart ached for his sorrow.

"Because I told God that I hated Him and that I never wanted to talk to Him again," Hayden sobbed. "About a year ago, I asked Him for a family, I told Him I wanted us three to be adopted and that if He would give me a family I would become a Christian. When it never happened I told Him I was done with Him forever."

"But you've talked to Him since then... just the other day, you asked God to help you find something to give to Caleb."

"I know," Hayden sniffed. "I forgot. But then I remembered and I know God would never answer my prayer, just like He never answered my prayer for a family, and I already told Him I hate Him so He will never forgive me. It's too late." Sorrow seemed to engulf her little brother's heart. He buried his face on her lap and cried while Hailey ran her hand over his soft red curls.

182

"It is never to late. Saying that you hate Him is sin, but so is lying, stealing, being mean… it's all sin. The Bible tells us that we are sinful and separated from God but that through Jesus there is forgiveness of sins."

"But I said I hate Him." Frightened green eyes flashed at Hailey.

"Do you hate Him?"

"No. I was just mad."

Hailey tenderly brushed a tear away from Hayden's face. "Don't you think God knows that?" She hugged her little brother. "Hayden, you've told me that you hate me when you've been really mad and I knew you didn't mean it. Don't you think God, who is way smarter than your older sister, knows?"

Hayden leaned back in the chair. "What should I do?"

"What do you do when you say mean things to me?"

"Apologize."

Hailey nodded. "Tell Him you're sorry."

Hayden lowered his eyes. "What about being a Christian?"

"God is waiting, Hayden. He loves you and wants you to give Him your heart."

Hayden nodded. "I want to, Hailey. I want to be a Christian. You really think He'll let me?"

"Sweetie, the Bible says it is not God's will that any should perish but that all should come to repentance. He loves you. He's been waiting for you to give Him your life."

Without another word, Hayden knelt beside the chair and folded his hands. "Dear God," he prayed through tears. "Please forgive me. I'm so sorry. I don't hate You. I didn't mean it."

Hailey lowered herself on the ground beside her brother and prayed quietly with him.

"I do believe that Jesus died for me and rose from the dead. Please take my heart, Jesus. Please be my Lord and Savior and live inside of me."

Tears rolled down Hailey's face as she heard her brother's tender plea to God.

They sat like that for a while. Hailey finally glanced up when she felt a hand on her back. It was Lane. His eyes were misty and he smiled tenderly at Hailey and Hayden and knelt beside them.

For a brief moment, Hailey wondered if Lane heard Hayden talk about wanting to be adopted. How long had the pastor been there?

"I'm sorry," he interrupted. "I just walked passed and saw Hayden and you in here praying." He rubbed Hayden's back. "Did you just give your heart to Jesus, Hayden?" Lane's voice choked.

Hayden nodded. He moved to Lane and wrapped his arms around the older man. "I was so scared that God wouldn't love me because I'd said mean things to Him. But Hailey said that God would forgive me."

"For I am convinced that neither death, nor life, nor angels, nor principalities, nor things present, nor things to come, nor powers, nor height, nor depth, nor any other created thing, will be able to separate us from the love of God, which is in Christ Jesus our Lord,'" Lane quoted from Romans 8:38-39. "Hayden, nothing can separate you from God's love. He has been waiting for you, and there is rejoicing in heaven right now."

Hayden cried.

"See Hayden, you prayed that God would give you a birthday present for Caleb," Hailey said. "He gave you one."

Hayden nodded. "Caleb said more than anything in the world what he wanted for his birthday was for me to be a Christian," Hayden explained to Lane. His eyes twinkled. "I guess he's getting his wish."

"A lot of us are." Lane tussled the hair on Hayden's head.

"What are you kids doing this weekend?" Lane asked. "Kate wanted me to ask if you can come over Saturday."

"I have Caleb's birthday party."

"What time?" Lane asked.

"Three to six."

"Why don't you come over in the afternoon and we'll hang out together. You can have lunch with us. We can have you back home early enough to leave for the party."

Hailey liked the idea. "Wade is picking up Hayden at the church at two-forty five."

"Well then, we'll have you there at two-forty five."

\*\*\*

Hayden could hardly wait to tell Caleb. He made a card that said, 'you and me, brothers in Christ,' knowing that Caleb would understand. "He's going to be so happy!"

Hailey nodded.

The children curled up on the sofas in the youth room and did their school work all day on Friday. Hailey used the time to give her brothers both spelling tests and math quizzes. She'd found websites with worksheets that the boys could work on and printed them off.

Hayden and Grant never gave her trouble about doing their schoolwork. She figured they must like being homeschooled.

When they were all done with their bookwork, Kyra told another one of her Church Mice stories and they all listened eagerly.

"You really need to be writing these down," Hailey encouraged her.

"I kind of do. But I could do a better job if I had a computer."

Hailey wondered if they could secretly use Ruby's computer and hide Kyra's file under a secret name. But she figured it would be too risky.

Kyra's stories were intriguing. Hailey liked that all the adventures ended happily for the children. Kyra's most recent story ended with a really nice young man from the youth group having a crush on one of the church mice kids. "She's the beautiful church mouse high school student," Kyra teased.

"Is that supposed to be me?" Hailey threw a pillow at Kyra and blushed.

Kyra shrugged. "Is that a problem?

"Can you make one of the stories where they get adopted?" Grant asked.

Kyra considered this idea for a moment. "But then they wouldn't be the church mice kids anymore."

"But wait," Hailey reminded Kyra. "In *The Boxcar Children* books they don't live in the box car anymore and yet they still have adventures." She smiled at Grant.

"Are there more books after the one you read me?" he asked.

"There's a whole series," Kyra explained. "Maybe we can find them some day."

"I like your stories better." Grant moved to Kyra's couch and snuggled closer to her. "You're the best story teller in the world."

Kyra didn't quite seem to know how to take Grant's sudden display of affection.

Hailey noticed it and felt her lips curve into a smile. Kyra was one of them. She was their sister and they all felt it.

"Can we just sleep up here tonight?" Kyra leaned against the cushions of the couch. "There's nothing going on at the church tomorrow and it feels so nice to be on a couch."

"Yeah, can we?" Hayden asked.

Hailey wasn't sure. It seemed risky. Especially with Mr. Pierce looking for the spies who knew his secret. "I don't think we should. What if Mr. Pierce showed up… or someone else? Sometimes Chad comes to the youth room unannounced."

The other kids agreed and reluctantly followed Hailey to their hiding place under the stage.

\*\*\*

Saturday morning the children all took showers, did laundry and got ready for their special plans.

Hayden brought his card to Lane and Kate's house to show them.

"This is a great way to tell him," Kate said. "I'm sure Caleb will cherish this card."

Lane grilled hamburgers while Kate made sweet potato fries.

"I've never had sweet potato fries before," Kyra watched Kate pour the bag onto a pan. "You make the coolest food!"

Kate grinned. "Thank you."

"Can we make some homemade cookies today?" Grant climbed up onto the stool beside Kate's counter. "Me and Kyra were talking about making home made cookies and I've been thinking about it all week."

"I think that's a possibility." Kate smoothed a blonde hair out of Grant's eyes. "You're hair is getting long, Grant." she grinned.

Grant shrugged. "I know."

Hailey hadn't thought about the fact that her brothers hadn't had a haircut in over a month. "Can you cut hair?" she asked Kate.

Kate chuckled. "Believe it or not, I cut Lane's hair."

"You do?" Grant leaned forward on the kitchen counter and reached for the bowl of candy across from him.

"Yes."

"Would you cut Grant and Hayden's hair?" Hailey asked.

Kate poured a glass of milk for Grant and shrugged. "I'd be happy to, but would your mother mind?"

"I'm sure no one would mind." Hailey lowered her eyes shyly.

Kate glanced around the corner to the living room where Hayden was playing checkers with Lane. "Would you like some milk?"

Hayden gave an eager yes and hurried away from the checker game with Lane just a few steps behind him.

"I didn't mean to interrupt your game." She poured the milk. She glanced at Hayden and ran her hand through his long curls. "Would you boys like me to trim your hair?"

"She cuts Lane's hair," Grant told Hayden.

Hayden gave Lane a quick assessment. "Yeah. You can cut mine."

"Want me to get the barber scissors?" Lane offered.

Kate nodded and got a stool ready in the kitchen for a hair trimming. "Where do you usually get your hair cut?"

"A place near the grocery store," Grant said.

That was the truth. Good thing Grant didn't know what it was actually called or what city it was in. Hailey didn't want him accidentally telling too much."

Kate cut Grant's hair first and did a great job. Hayden eagerly climbed in the chair next and let her trim his red locks. "Was I starting to look like a girl?" he asked.

"No, Hayden, you couldn't look like a girl." Kate chuckled. "And it wasn't that long. When did you cut you hair last?"

"Before we moved." Hayden glanced quickly at Hailey to make sure he'd answered appropriately.

"How long have you lived here?" Lane poured himself a cup of coffee and sat on the chair across from Hayden.

All four children grew awkward. Hayden glanced at Hailey and shifted nervously. He closed his eyes while Kate trimmed the hair over his eyes.

"It's been little over a month now," Hailey finally spoke up. It was a true statement. Hailey was sure Lane and Kate were curious about the children's strange response. The husband and wife glanced at one another with question in their eyes.

Lane took a sip of his coffee and offered Hailey a cup.

"Yes, please. I just need lots of milk."

"Would you like me to trim your hair too?" Kate asked Hailey.

Hailey glanced down at her hair. She knew she had some split ends and could use a trim. She also wanted a few layers in her long hair. "Sure."

Kate did a lovely job trimming Hailey's hair and added just a few soft layers, which added body to Hailey's thick long hair.

Kyra declined a haircut saying that hers grew so slow that she couldn't risk taking any off.

"Have you ever considered extensions?" Kate asked.

"I'd love extensions. But they're so expensive."

Kate tilted her head and studied Kyra for a moment. "When is your birthday? Maybe I can take you to the mall and get you some extensions."

"Not till March. But I would love that!" Kyra showed enthusiasm.

After they cleaned up the hair, Kate and the children began making cookies. Grant was in his glory because Kate let him eat some of the dough before she added the egg.

Hailey realized it was growing close to two-forty-five and she would need to take Hayden to the church to meet Wade, but she hated to run Grant and Kyra off while they were having so much fun.

"Why don't I take Hayden to the church to meet Wade and leave Grant and Kyra here. I'll come right back."

"I can drive you." Kate offered.

"No, you stay and make cookies. I like the walk."

Hayden hurried into his coat and grabbed his special card. As much as he loved being with Lane, he was very excited to attend Caleb's birthday party.

*** 

Wade was already at the church when Hayden and Hailey showed up. He honked the horn on his Chevy pick up and waved.

"Hi, Wade. Thanks for doing this." Hailey watched her brother climb up into Wade's truck and put on a seatbelt. "Hayden has been so excited about this all week."

"No problem," Wade's blue eyes flashed warmly. Hailey tried not to think of Kyra's Church Mice Children story.

"We'll be back at six."

"If you wouldn't mind dropping him off at Kate and Lane's, we're hanging out there the rest of the afternoon."

"That's fine. Do you need me to drive you there now?"

"No, you guys just head over to the party. Have fun, Hayden." She winked at her brother and waved them off.

Hailey was about to head back to Lane and Kate's house when she noticed someone walking out of the church toward her. Panic gripped her heart as the man's face came into view. It was Bill Pierce. Hailey froze.

"Well hello, Hailey." Bill's tone was icy cold.

He approached quickly and Hailey took an unconscious step back.

"It's Hailey Goodman, am I right?" He held up what Hailey recognized as her school identification card.

Hailey felt suddenly sick.

"I believe this is yours…" He handed Hailey the note she'd written to him and gave her a sinister smile.

Hailey wanted to run but felt like her knees were about to give out.

"We need to talk, Miss Goodman."

Hailey took a few steps back but Bill followed. "There's nowhere to go," he chuckled. "I know everything about you."

Hailey glanced down at the crumpled note in her hand.

"Did you think that your little cryptic message would send me running?" his chuckled turned into a full-blown laugh. "You little fool. I took this as a challenge. You were pretty easy to find. Ruby gave me a list of all the people who had a key to the church and you were at the bottom of the list. She said you'd just started cleaning at the church." Bill crossed his arms over his large chest. "I started at the bottom of the list and there you were. A family of little punks living in Warsaw Chapel."

Hailey did her best to fight tears. When had she ever been this afraid?

"I'd say we are both in a bit of a conundrum here." Bill narrowed his eyes on hers. "You know my secret and I know yours." He blew out a heavy sigh. "But the way I see it, we can make this work for both of us. You see, I could easily turn you in and accuse you of stealing. I did find this envelope with a hundred dollars cash in it, right in your little hiding place."

Hailey watched Bill pull her envelope out of his coat pocket.

"Not to mention that you are runaways." He cleared his throat. "So here's my proposal." A slimy smile crossed his lips. "It is quite an inconvenience to my Sunday afternoon nap to have to show up every week and get my money. But you're already here. So you're going to be my collection agent. Every Sunday afternoon you'll take out two thousand dollars and give it to me on Wednesdays. I don't usually come to the Wednesday night services but it wouldn't hurt me." There was sarcasm in his tone. "And in exchange for your services, I will give you my silence."

Hailey's mouth was so dry she wasn't sure she could talk. She shook her head. "No way. I could never steal from the church."

"Oh really?" Bill glanced down at his fingernails and flicked out a bit of dirt. "What about the water you steal from the church every day? What about the soap you steal and the food you steal and the fact that every day that you are here you put this church in danger of liability by its unknowing harboring of fugitives?"

Hailey shook her head. This was a nightmare. She couldn't steal from the offering… *no*.

"But in case you need any more convincing." Bill pulled something else out of his pocket and held it up for Hailey to see. "Maybe you would rather me call Ms. Cooper and tell her what you've been doing?"

"No!" Hailey reached for her social worker's business card but Bill kept it out of reach.

"This is my liability, Hailey. I'm not about to surrender her card." He narrowed his eyes through his wire rim glasses and glared at Hailey. "I will call her and I will tell her that I caught you stealing from the offering and trust me little brat, they will lock you up and it won't be pretty."

Hailey's eyes filled up with tears.

"So, you work for me... and you'll be fine. Who knows, I may even reward you. I'm sure you'd like some pillows, maybe a few new outfits, better food. I can do that."

Hailey closed her eyes. She was trapped. There was no hope, no getting out of this... *What can I do?*

"Tomorrow afternoon, you'll collect my money, you will hold it until Wednesday night and I'll find you... but make sure you have the money on you."

He handed Hailey her identification card. "You can keep this. But I'll hang on to your money and Ms. Cooper's card, just in case."

\*\*\*

Hailey watched Bill drive away and sat down on the church steps to cry. Hopelessness washed over her like a dark veil.

If she didn't steal the money for Bill, he would turn her in. He would accuse her of stealing from the church. She would be caught. She would lose her brothers, lose Kyra, and lose the only real friends she had in the world.

An overwhelming sense of defeat pressed itself against her heart and Hailey stared blankly at the woods across from the church.

Should they run away? She could take the boys and Kyra and they could find another church to live in. Start over again. Surely not every church had an offering thief.

*But he should be caught!* Hailey felt a flood of indignation. *There is a church rat at Warsaw Chapel… and he's trapped the church mice kids.* Unconsciously, Hailey wrote a sad ending of the Church Mice Children in her mind. *…and the church mice children never knew happiness again.*

Great tears fell down her face.

Bill Pierce offered her perks for her contributions to his crime. *New pillows, clothes and food… is that supposed to be the balm for robbing the church? I can't rob Warsaw Chapel. These are my friends. This is my family.*

Hailey glanced at her watch and realized that Kate and Lane were going to wonder where she was. How could she face them? How could she go back to their house and pretend that everything was all right? Everything was not all right. Everything was wrong.

Her legs were shaky as she began the mile long walk to their house. Her mind raced with morose thoughts. If she stole from the offering she'd never be able to face Lane and Kate. But, if she didn't steal from the offering, she, Kyra and the boys would never see Lane and Kate again. Which was worse?

Hailey thought about her relationship with God. How could she face God if she stole from the offering? But Bill's words pierced her heart. Wasn't she already stealing from the church… she used the water, she ate the food… Hailey tried to justify it all with thoughts that people in the church wanted to help the needy. But was she really needy? Hailey knew that as a foster child there was government money sitting right there, ready to care for her physical needs.

When Hailey reached Kate's house she forced herself to smile. Grant was overjoyed about the chocolate chip cookies he'd made and surprisingly, Kyra was almost as excited.

"These are the best chocolate chip cookies I've ever had!" Kyra shoved a warm cookie into Hailey's hand.

As good as it smelled, Hailey didn't think she could force it down. Her stomach ached and her mouth was dry. She wanted to go back to the church. She needed to be alone. Tomorrow was Sunday.

"Is everything alright?" Kate asked.

"I'm just tired I think," Hailey said what seemed most believable. "Maybe I should have let you drive." *I could have postponed my run in with Mr. Pierce...* Oh to go back in time. An hour ago this nightmare was not real.

"We should probably go soon," Hailey said to Kyra.

"Why? Hayden isn't going to be back until six."

Hailey couldn't tell her. No. Kyra and the boys didn't need to carry this stress. This was her cross to bear. She brought this upon them.

Lane suggested a quick game of cards and Hailey sat, dreamlike, going through the motions while there was a horror film running though her mind.

When it finally drew close to six, Hailey insisted they go home. "We've been away almost all day. We really should go."

She refused a ride and left Lane and Kate wondering what happened to Hailey in the hour she was gone.

# Chapter 17

Sunday morning Hailey went through the motions. She greeted her friends with the best smile she could muster. Her stomach ached and she wished she would have stayed under the stage and had her brothers and Kyra tell everyone she was sick. That wouldn't be a lie would it?

After Sunday school, Hailey sat at the back and scanned the congregation for the bully that now ran her life. She spotted his shiny, bald, head toward the middle of the sanctuary.

What if she stood up and just told everyone what she knew? Hailey shook her head. She had no proof. She was the mouse in the trap. He was the rat with all the cheese.

Hailey wasn't surprised when Wade approached her after the service. She was quiet during Sunday school and caught him giving her concerned glances throughout the pastor's message.

"Are you okay, Hailey?" Wade pulled her aside after her siblings disappeared with their buddies.

Hailey's eyes welled up with tears. "No, Wade. I'm not. Please pray for me."

"What is it?"

"I can't tell you."

Wade blew out a frustrated sigh. Hailey wasn't sure if she'd ever seen him frustrated before.

"Why?" he asked.

"Just pray for me."

Wade brushed one of Hailey's layers of hair away from her shoulder. "You look very pretty today." He complemented her. "In spite of your pale face and sad eyes."

Hailey's hands trembled.

"Listen." Wade tore of a piece of the church bulletin and wrote down his cell phone number. "If anything changes and you decide you can talk to me, call me. I want to be here for you."

Hailey nodded and accepted the piece of paper. "Maybe."

Wade raised one eyebrow. "Hey, that's a start."

Hailey tucked the piece of paper in her pocket.

"Hayden's testimony was the highlight of Caleb's birthday by the way." Wade changed the subject.

"Really?" Hailey's eyes shimmered with fresh tears.

"Yes." Wade glanced out at the empty church chairs at the few people still standing around talking as they were. "Caleb's actual birthday was Thursday, so that means your brother's born again day is the same day as Caleb's born day."

"That's cool." Hailey couldn't hide the genuine joy she felt about that.

Wade's parents approached their son with a friendly smile and greeted Hailey. "We've got to head out, Wade," his dad said. "Grandma and Grandpa are coming over to celebrate Caleb's birthday with us."

Wade nodded. "Alright. More cake." He winked. "I'm not sure I'll be at youth group tonight," he said. "My grandparents are here from Cincinnati so they kind of expect me to be there to hang out with them this evening."

"I understand. Grandparents are great. Enjoy them."

His parents began to walk away and Wade turned and pointed to his phone. "Don't forget."

Hailey nodded. Maybe.

*** 

Near the usual time of Bill's arrival, Hailey asked Kyra and the boys to hide under the stage. None of them questioned her. Even though they had no idea of the weight Hailey was carrying around with her, they knew she was worried about something.

Hailey sat in the hallway across from Ruby's locked door for over an hour. She knew what she had to do. *Just go in there and take the money. Then you're safe.* Her hands were wet with sweat and her stomach hurt like never before. *Then he owns you.* Leaning her head back on the wall behind her, Hailey felt nauseous. She couldn't hold it in any longer; she ran to the bathroom and threw up what little food was in her stomach.

"I can't!" she sobbed with her hands on the edge of the toilet.

Terror gripped her heart. What would happen if she didn't have the money? What would he do to her? How long till he turned her in? Couldn't she plead her innocence?

It seemed a moot point. She had no proof. He had all the evidence he needed to make it look like Hailey was the criminal.

Hailey washed her face and hands and walked to the hallway where she paced the floor. A moan escaped her lips and she slipped into the sanctuary.

The lights were out in the large room, but Hailey could make out the silhouette of the cross over the stage. Her little brothers and Kyra were under that stage. They were under the cross.

Hailey's heartbeat quickened and she knelt at the foot of the stage and let her eyes rest on the cross.

"Jesus," she whispered. "Please help me." Great tears rolled down her face. "I'm trapped and I can't do this on my own. I don't want to lose my brothers or Kyra. I don't want to lose Kate or Lane… or any of my friends here at Warsaw Chapel. But more than anything, I don't want to lose my closeness to You. I know if I steal that money I won't be able to face You. Please work this whole thing out, Lord. Thy will be done…"

***

Kate came by the church on Monday to see the children. They were just finishing up their cleaning when she arrived with a loaf of fresh baked bread and fresh milk.

"Can we have it now?" Grant smelled the loaf in Kate's hand.

"Absolutely. That's why I brought it." She pulled a jar out of her purse. "And this is home made strawberry jam."

Kyra reached for the jar and beamed. "You made this?"

"My mom and I made it this summer. We do a lot of canning together." Kate seemed to appreciate Kyra's enthusiasm. "Maybe you kids can help us next summer."

"I'd love to!" Kyra walked beside Kate and the boys as they headed to the kitchen.

Hailey left to put away the vacuum. She blew out a heavy sigh.

Her time in prayer the night before was good for Hailey. She knew that it was all in God's hands now. But she wasn't sure how He was going to work it all out. Hailey knew that there were consequences to people's sins and she was willing to accept whatever God thought was best for her.

In the kitchen, she smelled the warm bread and sat down beside Kate.

"Are you ready for a piece?" Kate held the knife to the bread.

"No thank you. I'm not hungry. But it looks good."

Kate nodded. "Lane told me that Ned and his wife decided to stay an extra week with their daughter. Ned wouldn't have felt that freedom if you weren't here. You have been such a blessing at this church."

"Thank you." Hailey did her best to smile.

"I was wondering if you guys were free this afternoon to go see the puppies with me."

"Puppies!" Grant just about jumped out of his skin.

"My mom wants me to decide which one I want because she has some friends from her church who want one."

"And she wants to give you first pick," Kyra completed Kate's sentence.

"She does."

"Can we go, Hailey?" Hayden pleaded with his sister. "I'll do my schoolwork later."

Kate observed the interaction between Kate and her brothers. "Do you need to check with your parents?"

Hailey shook her head. "We can go."

The boys bounced up and down forgetting all about the homemade bread and jam. They were going to see puppies.

"Finish your food first," Hailey advised. "Grant, you've not finished your milk."

Grant downed the whole glass and shoved the bread into his mouth.

"That wasn't exactly what I had in mind." Hailey found herself smiling in spite of her raw emotions.

The children walked down the hall with Kate to tell Lane where they were going.

"I wish we had a mini-van. Then you could go with us." Kate kissed her husband.

"I have too much to do anyway. Just pick out the one you like best. I'm sure I'll like it too."

Grant was still jumping up and down and Lane knelt down to smile into his eyes. "You seem excited. Are you getting a puppy too?"

"No. But if you have one I'll get to see it every week!" Grant said enthusiastically.

Hailey lowered her eyes. *Probably not*

"Well, have fun and be safe." Lane stood up. "I love you, honey," he gave his wife another kiss and watched as they walked away.

***

In spite of her trembling heart, Hailey loved holding the furry little puppies. There was something comforting in holding a little life so close to her heart. Hailey wondered if they ever let the teens hold puppies in juvie.

"What do you think, kids?" Kate sat on the floor while the puppies scampered around her playfully. "They're all so cute. How do I choose one?"

"Pick two!" Grant suggested.

Kate laughed. "I can't get two. But which one do you like the best?"

Hailey glanced into the dark brown eyes of the little female she held and kissed its black nose tenderly. "This one."

Kate extended her arms and took the puppy from Hailey. It squirmed excitedly and relaxed once Kate held it close to her heart.

"That's one of my favorites too," Helen confessed.

The boys drew closer and petted it in Kate's arms.

"She is a pretty one," Kyra said.

"What would you name her?" Hayden asked.

"I don't know."

"How about Blaze?" Grant suggested.

Kate's lips curved into a smile. "Blaze is a nice name, but I think I'll consider that for a future horse."

Grant nodded. "Blaze would be a cool horse name."

"What about Francesca?" Kyra proposed. It's kind of sophisticated and yet unique."

"It is unique and sophisticated." Kate glanced into the pup's dark brown eyes. "But I'm not sure she is a Francesca."

"Well you can't choose Cupcake because that's what I'm naming the little one I'm keeping," Helen said.

Kate extended her arms with the puppy in her hands and studied the little dog carefully. "What about Maggie?"

Hailey nodded. "I like it. Her momma's name is Molly and she'd be Maggie."

"Molly and Maggie." Hayden repeated happily. "I like it too."

"Then Maggie it is." Kate kissed her new pup and handed it to Hayden to cuddle. "When do I get to bring her home?"

"I'd say in another week." Helen petted Cupcake. "They just started nibbling the puppy food."

"I can't wait!" Grant exploded.

"I think you're going to have regular visitors." Helen stood up from the floor, still carrying Cupcake. "I made some gingersnaps. Would anyone like one?"

Hayden handed Maggie to Kate and the boys followed Helen into the kitchen. Kyra laid down among the puppies so they could climb all over her.

"This is like puppy heaven."

Kate agreed. "My mom was not such a puppy nut when I was a child though. It's funny to see her this way."

The girls listened while Kate told them some of her childhood animal experiences. "We were never allowed to keep a dog in our beds growing up," she began. "But my sister, Anne, loved our dog, Pepper, so much and she was determined that he wanted to sleep with her. So she started letting him under her covers at night. It was all good until he got fleas."

"Oh no!" Kyra gasped.

"Yeah. Anne had flea bites all over her legs and we had to fumigate her mattress."

It was late afternoon when they all piled into Kate's car. The children insisted that they needed dropped off at the church.

"We have stuff in there," Hailey said honestly.

As the others walked toward the building, Hailey turned and leaned into Kate's opened window. "Thank you for today." Her eyes misted.

Kate placed a tender hand on Hailey's face. "I should thank you," Kate said. "You and your siblings have brought so much joy to Lane and I."

"The feeling is mutual." Hailey swallowed back a lump in her throat. She wanted to tell Kate that she loved her... that Kate was the closest thing she'd had to a mother since her grandmother died. But she wasn't sure she could get the words out without crying. "Good night."

*** 

Hailey was beside herself with stress by Wednesday evening. This was it. Judgment day.

She took her meal with the other teens and glanced around anxiously. Was Mr. Pierce waiting for her? Where was he?

After they went to the other building for the children's program she relaxed a little. Wade led the children in a few praise songs that touched Hailey as much as they touched the kids.

"The craft involves beans and sand this week," Janie warned her as they walked to the craft room. "We're going to have a mess to clean up."

For the first time Hailey was thankful for the possibility of a mess. *Maybe Mr. Pierce will leave.* She figured that was unlikely.

Grant and Leah were delighted to glue sand and beans to individual stain glassed windows, creating the pattern of a lion and a lamb. Hayden and his friends seemed more interested in putting sand in one another's hair, but Hailey let it go.

*Who knows when Hayden will have a chance to play with Caleb like this again?*

While Janie and Hailey cleaned up Janie asked if Hailey might be able to spend the night some Saturday night. "We could go to church together in the morning."

Hailey loved the idea but told Janie she wasn't sure. "I really would like to." She shoveled a small pile of sand from the table to a trash can. "I just… I'm the one who watches my brothers most of the time."

"But don't you ever get time for you?" Janie asked. She sat on the table and studied her friend.

"Not very much," Hailey answered honestly. "But I'm okay… I love my little brothers and Kyra."

"I love Angela too, but I don't want to watch over her day and night." Janie giggled.

Hailey wiped the table down for the third time, trying to stall for time. She dreaded going to the other building and meeting Mr. Pierce.

Paul and Wade found the girls in the craft room still cleaning up.

"Are you ready, Janie?" Paul glanced around the clean room. "Mom and Dad want to go."

Janie shrugged. "Gotta go." She hugged Hailey. "See you Sunday."

Hailey hoped so.

***

She closed the craft cabinet and walked out of the building with Wade while Janie and Paul hurried ahead.

"How are you doing?" Wade asked. "Since we last talked I mean."

Hailey took a steadying breath. "I'm doing okay. I laid it all at the cross." She grinned softly. "Literally. I knelt at the alter and just gave it to Him."

"That's good. Is it taken care of?" Wade opened the door for her and waved goodbye to the other children's ministry workers.

"Not really, Wade." She scanned the parking lot nervously. "It could get ugly." She let him open the door to the other building and walked inside. "But I know God is in control."

"If you need anything, please call me."

"I will." Hailey had Wade's phone number hidden in her Bible. She decided she would call him if things did get ugly.

Most of the congregation had left the building. There were still a few people standing around talking and Hailey glanced around wondering where Mr. Pierce was hanging out.

The few children left in the building were running around the sanctuary while their parents talked. Hailey and Wade spotted Hayden and Grant.

"Where's Caleb?" Hailey noticed that Wade's little brother wasn't a part of the group of noisemakers.

"I had a special school activity today so I drove separately from my parents. They took Caleb home."

"What did you do?" Hailey asked.

"My journalism class took a field trip to the newspaper in Columbus."

"That sounds cool."

Hayden and Grant found Hailey and asked if it was time to go.

"Yes. Where is Kyra?"

"She's in the kitchen helping Kate," Hayden said. "I'll go get her." Hayden ran off with Grant at his heels.

Wade seemed to be lingering. "Do you want me to drive you home?"

Hailey shook her head. "No. I'm okay."

"But it's dark outside." He lowered his eyes. "Its not safe for you to walk home in the dark. I don't like it."

Hailey nodded. "I know."

Her reply didn't satisfy him. "Where do you live, Hailey?"

"I can't tell you."

"You had me pick up Hayden at the church last week. Why? Why couldn't I pick him up at your house?"

"Wade…" Hailey shook her head. She wasn't sure how to answer him. She glanced around the sanctuary and noticed Bill Pierce standing on the other side of the room. Her face turned white and she gasped.

"What's wrong?" Wade turned to look at what put the look of fear on Hailey's face.

"I have to go." She gave Wade a sad smile. "Thanks for praying and stuff. You've been a great friend." She felt like she was saying good-bye.

Hailey motioned for Kyra and the boys to come with her and she nodded in Mr. Pierce's direction. "You guys go on up to our hiding place," she whispered to Kyra. "I have to take care of something."

"You look like you've seen a ghost." Kyra reached for Hailey's hand.

"Just go." Hailey couldn't handle tenderness at this time. It would push her over the edge.

# Chapter 18

Bill met Hailey in just outside the church doors and motioned for her to follow him to a dark place behind the church dumpsters. Hailey thought it was fitting to meet this rat near the dumpsters. She wasn't sure if the smell was from the trash or from him.

"Do you have it?" Bill reached out his hand.

"No."

Bill stared at her for a moment. "What do you mean 'no'?"

"I don't have it." Hailey geared up for Bill's reaction. There's no way in the world I can do what you've asked me to do."

A word fitting of the dumpster escaped his lips. "You didn't take it?"

"No. I got sick. Physically sick, Mr. Pierce," Hailey confessed. "I couldn't do it."

Bill grabbed Hailey's wrist. "You cost me two thousand dollars you worthless piece of trash," he said under his breath. "I swear it's going to get ugly for you."

"Turn me in. I don't care."

Bill tightened his hand on her wrist. "You don't seem to understand. I'll ruin your life. I'll take from you everything you care about."

"For two thousand dollars?" Hailey pitied the man.

"For eight thousand dollars a month and you just cost me four."

Hailey pulled her wrist free.

"I'll tell your social worker all kinds of things, Hailey. I'll tell her things about Hayden and Grant and Kyra... I'm pretty sure it's going to be Kyra who breaks into my house next week... In fact, I think we can even find some stolen merchandise around the church. Maybe Kyra hid it there after she stole it."

"Next week?" Hailey was trying to understand what Bill was talking about.

"You'll probably hear about it next week. It hasn't happened yet." Bill's evil eyes glared in the light of the parking lot. "But I'm pretty sure this will be found on the scene." He held out a small beaded bracelet with Kyra's name spelled out in beads.

Hailey tried to snatch the bracelet from him but he pushed her away. "Don't mess with me kid, I make over a hundred thousand dollars a year off this church and I don't mean to stop. If you refuse to help, I'll make sure you and your little team of runaways are all placed in juvie and I'll never have to worry about you watching me again. I promise, you'll wish you were never born."

Hailey shook her head while tears ran down her face. She wanted to run, or scream, or have a bolt of lightning hit the dumpster. She let out a silent prayer for help and for strength.

"You either take that money for me this week, or Kyra gets busted for robbery." Bill put the bracelet in his pocket. "I'll be here Monday night at eight sharp. That way I don't have to listen to all these overzealous religious nuts on Wednesday night and wait for them all to leave." He pointed his finger at her face. "You'd better have that money or I'll frame you and your siblings for a few other things."

Hailey watched him walk away in the dark and leaned against the dumpster, the smell of rotting trash didn't even phase her.

*What should I do now, God?*

\*\*\*

"Hailey," she heard Wade's voice in the dark. He approached her quietly. "What was that about?"

Hailey buried her face in her hands and finally let a rush of tears overtake her. "There's nothing you can do."

"What was Mr. Pierce talking to you about? Why did he grab your wrist?"

Hailey drew in a strained breath and considered her options. Everything seemed to be spinning out of control. Should she tell Wade? He was her friend. But would he understand? "Follow me."

Wade followed Hailey along the side of the building and watched her stop beside the choir room window. She opened it and motioned for him to follow her inside the building. After she turned on the light, Kyra, Hayden and Grant slipped out of their secret room not expecting to see Wade.

"Hailey?" Kyra's eyes were wide.

"We need help," Hailey sat on a chair and sighed.

Wade glanced toward the secret door. "You guys live here?"

Hailey nodded.

"How? Why?" Wade sat across from Hailey and watched Grant climb onto her lap.

Hailey started from the beginning and Wade listened to every word of their story. His eyes were intent on Hailey. There was no judgment in his eyes, only compassion. He paused to text his mother that he would be home a little late and not to worry.

"When we figured out that Mr. Pierce was robbing the church we wanted to make him stop but we didn't want to get caught," Kyra added to Hailey's story.

The girls told Wade about the note they'd put in the offering money on Ruby's desk.

"But what I haven't told any of you," Hailey glanced around the room. "Is that Mr. Pierced figured it out."

Kyra's eyes grew wide.

"He was here Saturday after Wade picked up Hayden." Hailey explained. "He told me that I had to steal two thousand dollars every Sunday from the offering and give it to him on Wednesdays. He told me if I didn't do it he would turn me in and accuse me of being the thief."

"What did you do?" Wade leaned forward and asked softly.

"I didn't do it. I prayed and surrendered the whole thing to God. When I met Mr. Pierce today, I told him I could never steal that money."

"So that's what was going on in the parking lot?" Wade clarified.

"Yes. But it gets worse. He has Kyra's bracelet. The one that Angela made her."

"I've been missing that."

"Because he stole it when he figured out we were living here and went through our things. He has the hundred dollars I still owe Keith, he has Ms. Cooper's business card, and who knows what else. He promised me that if I didn't steal the money this week we would all be in so much trouble we would wish we were never born."

Wade ran his fingers through his hair and sighed. "When he grabbed your wrist I wanted to let his face meet my fist. I knew something was wrong."

"I've wanted to tell someone for a while, but it would be his word against mine. He has what he calls proof. I only have my word... the word of a teen runaway."

"Why didn't you tell me this sooner?"

"What can you do, Wade?" Hailey wiped away a tear. "You could go to your parents and they could call the police and then Mr. Pierce will show them the evidence he has and we get busted while he goes free."

"Will we ever get to see Kate and Lane again?" Grant finally spoke up with a quivering voice.

Hailey wrapped her arms around her little brother. "I'm so sorry, Grant."

"But I love them." Tears filled her little brother's eyes.

Hayden had been sitting quietly for several minutes. Hailey glanced at him and noticed his eyes were red with unshed tears. "No!" Hayden stood to his feet and made angry fists. "No!" Hayden ran from the room in an angry rage.

Grant's little arms engulfed Hailey's neck and little quiet sobs escaped his lips.

"I'll go get him." Wade followed Hayden.

Wade returned with Hayden a few minutes later. Hailey thought there were tears in both of their eyes.

"Come on, big guy," Wade motioned for Hayden to climb up into the chair next to him. "Sit next to me."

"What should we do?" Hailey turned her ashen face on Kyra. "I can't let him frame you for robbery."

"We can't steal that money. No matter what kind of punishment we suffer."

"Bill Pierce needs to get caught." Wade spoke up.

"But how?" Hailey leaned back and licked her dry lips.

Wade sighed. "I have an idea." He glanced around the room. "But it will mean your identity is found out and... you won't be able to live in the church anymore."

Hayden buried his face in his hands.

Wade placed a comforting hand on his back. "I'm sorry."

"Let's get this guy." Hayden lifted his head and wiped his face.

"Let's pray." Wade wrapped his arm around Hayden.

\*\*\*

Wade invited Hailey, Kyra and the boys to his house to hang out Saturday afternoon. He picked them up in his mother's SUV. When they arrived at the house, he suggested the boys go play with Caleb.

"We're going to come up with a plan," Wade said softly to Hayden and Grant. "But don't talk to my brother about it, okay?"

The boys nodded and hurried out of the SUV to find their friend.

"Paul and Janie will be here soon. Mom ordered us pizza for lunch. I hope that's okay."

"When is pizza not okay?" Kyra asked.

Upon Paul and Janie's arrival, the teens took their pizza to the basement where Wade's family had a nice sized game room with a pool table, ping-pong table and two nice sofas with a large game table between them. It was just the spot for a meeting.

Wade looked at Hailey. "Do you want to start?"

Hailey nodded.

Paul and Janie sensed this was serious, but had no idea why Wade and Hailey called this important meeting.

"I need to tell you the truth about myself and my family," Hailey began. "We're runaway foster kids."

Paul and Janie listened with wide eyes as Hailey explained the whole story. It felt good to get it off her chest with these friends, but it was painful too. When she got to the part about Bill Pierce she let Wade help her explain.

"Mr. Pierce has been stealing money every week?" Janie shook her head sadly. "How could he?"

"Greed." Wade got up and paced the room.

"No wonder Aunt Kate said the church was struggling financially. That creep has been stealing eight thousand dollars a month from the offering."

"I didn't know the church was struggling." Hailey felt guilty for all the food they'd eaten.

"Not terribly, but she said the offerings had dropped off significantly over the past couple years. This year has been the worst."

"Maybe he's taking more and more."

"Can you imagine him taking over a hundred thousand dollars from our church every year?" Paul shook his head. "Why does he bother having a job?"

"Where does Mr. Pierce work?" Hailey was curious.

"I have no idea," Janie confessed. "I hardly know him. Its just him and his wife."

"She used to come by herself. Mr. Pierce started coming several years ago," Paul added.

"So, what's your plan, Wade?" Hailey finally asked.

"It's going to take a little work on all our parts," Wade began. "He's meeting you Monday night, right?"

Hailey nodded.

Wade glanced at Janie. "You're mom's phone has a good camera on it, doesn't it?"

"Yes."

"And texting?"

Janie nodded.

"We're going to need to borrow it Monday night."

Janie thought they could do that.

"My mom's got one too. We've got to make sure we get this thing on film."

Wade shared the plan and the teens took a moment to pray. Hailey took a deep breath and thanked God for these special friends. *I know it's going to be okay God... I trust You.*

*** 

Kate invited the children to their house for lunch after church on Sunday. "We've got a surprise for you." Her eyes twinkled.

"Does it bark?" Grant asked excitedly.

"Yes and it wags its tail." Kate's eyes twinkled back.

"Can we go… can we go?" Grant pleaded with Hailey.

Hailey nodded. It would be difficult, but she knew her brothers would cherish the memory forever. This would probably be their last lunch with Lane and Kate.

Kyra seemed to sense the specialness of this last lunch with Kate and Lane before the truth came out. She clung to Kate like Hailey had never seen. "Can we drive home with you guys? Then we can just come back for youth group."

Kate glanced at Lane. "We'll have to squeeze together."

"We don't mind." Kyra's eyes were misty.

Hailey knew Kyra was struggling. Her foster sister was usually so full of spark and fun.

"Can we shoot our bows?" Hayden asked.

"Sure. Do you have them here?" Lane asked.

Hayden realized their bows were under the stage. He couldn't go get them. "No. Maybe we can just play games."

After the last person left the building, Lane and Kate led the children to their car. They all squeezed in and rode the mile down the road to the pastor's house.

"I'm going to have to take Maggie out as soon as we walk in the door. Be prepared, she might start peeing."

Hayden laughed.

"She's in a little kennel and she's doing very well."

"I can't wait to see her again." Grant bounded to the house after they opened the door. "I'll help you take her outside. Will she remember me? Do you think she likes me?"

Hailey smiled as her little brother chatted non-stop.

Kate put together a quick lunch of Sloppy Joe sandwiches, baked beans and corn pudding while the children played with Maggie.

Hailey and Kyra were extra quiet, but the boys seemed to be able to forget their worries long enough to play with the puppy.

When lunch was served, the children were not their talkative selves. Hailey felt a strange sentimental feeling wash over her as she glanced at Kate and Lane.

"I really liked your sermon today." Hailey turned to Lane. "I wrote down the one thing you said that stuck with me most."

"What was that?" Lane asked. He loaded a large scoop of meat on his bread.

"You're as close to the Lord as you want to be." Hailey quoted him seriously.

Lane nodded. "I'm glad you liked it." His expression grew thoughtful. "He loves us and He desires to be close to us."

"It's true. I've learned that since I've lived here."

Kyra nodded and set her sandwich down. "Me too."

The boys stopped eating long enough to glance from Kyra to Lane.

"I've learned that too," Hayden added.

Grant put a big bite of beans in his mouth. "You're our best friends."

Kate's eyes grew misty. "You are four of the most remarkable children we've ever met." She dotted her eyes with her napkin.

Lane reached for his wife's hand and gave it a tender clasp.

Hailey admired their obvious love for one another.

"Does your family have plans for Thanksgiving?" Kate ventured to ask.

Hailey's eyes traveled to each of the children. "I don't know what we're doing for Thanksgiving."

"Well, if your family doesn't have plans, we'd like you to invite you and your parents to have Thanksgiving with us," Lane said.

Hailey lowered her face.

"My mother will be here and so will Anne and her family. They all said they would love to have you come." Kate looked hopeful.

"Thank you for the invitation." Hailey made no promises either way.

"I wish we could." Grant moved his chair closer to Lane.

After lunch, the children played a few games with Lane and Kate, but it took effort to show enthusiasm. Hailey wondered if Lane and Kate sensed it.

"I guess we should get you to youth group." Kate looked at the clock. "I'm so glad you got to come over today."

The children put on their coats and crammed into the pastor's car. Grant held Kate's hand all the way into the church.

"I'm going to miss you," he gave her an emotional hug before he wandered off to play with Leah.

Kate pondered his words curiously.

***

Monday morning Kate poured her husband a cup of coffee and topped it off with sweet cream. She set it beside his plate of bacon and eggs and sat down to pray with him.

After asking the Lord's blessing on their food, Kate took a long sip of her orange juice and studied her husband for a moment. "I had a rough night's sleep last night," Kate began.

"I thought you were tossing and turning a lot."

"I'm sorry."

Lane grinned. "I'm only teasing. You know I could sleep through an earthquake."

"You have." Kate took a bite of eggs. "Remember living in California."

Lane chuckled.

"I wish we would have had time to talk last night but I was so tired when we got home and you got a phone call from that pastor in Canada."

"I'm sorry, hon. Vernon needed some encouragement."

"I understand. You're a good friend to him." Kate nodded. "But I have to admit, this has been on my heart since last night."

"What?"

"Was it my imagination or did the children all seem depressed?"

"It wasn't your imagination." Lane took a sip of his coffee. "I've never seen Hayden and Grant so somber."

"Or Kyra," Kate added. "She's usually doing some little dance or making a joke. I don't know what to make of it."

Lane nodded. "It bothered me too."

"Then, before Grant went off to play with Leah he told me he was going to miss me." Kate tried to keep the emotion out of her voice.

"Maybe he's just getting attached. He had a good day with us and he knew that after he went home he would miss you."

"But he shouldn't miss me that way," Kate said. "That love should be for his mother." She shook her head. "Is it natural for children to be that attached to people they've only known a month and a half?"

"Is it normal for us to be that attached to them?" Lane asked.

"I don't know." Kate brushed away a tear. "I'm so jealous of their parents, Lane," she confessed. "Jealous and angry."

"Angry that they never seem to be around?"

"Yes." Kate shoved her plate aside. "They have those four wonderful children whose lives they should be building into and they're not. We don't have any children and… and…"

"And God has given us the opportunity to build into their lives. What a blessing." Lane reached for his wife's hand.

"But what if their parents just up and decide to leave? What if we lose them… like Joy?" Kate buried her face in her hands. "I don't want to lose them, Lane."

Lane left his chair to comfort his wife.

*** 

Hailey wrapped her arms around her stomach to ward off the nervous fear she'd been fighting the past few days. Ned was scheduled to show up in the early afternoon and Hailey aimed to make sure the church was so clean he wouldn't need to stay. She couldn't have some janitor ruining their plan.

Lane was late coming into the office, but Hailey saw Chad and did her best to greet him naturally.

The boys cleaned the men's bathroom sinks and Hailey mopped the floor. Kyra worked on the ladies' bathroom sinks until Hailey was ready to finish things up.

By the time Ned showed up, the children were putting the vacuum cleaner away.

"Well," a tall man in his early seventies walked into the church and sized everything up. Hailey noticed his thick gray mustache and mischievous gray eyes and smiled as soon as he introduced himself. "I guess I'm not needed here any longer."

Hailey reached out her hand and introduced herself. "I guess you could say we wanted to leave on good terms."

"If anything, I think you're leaving a legacy. How in the world am I going to keep the church looking this nice?"

Hailey could tell the man was teasing, but she appreciated it. He obviously approved of their work.

"Lane told me the building was ship shape with you kids in charge. I'm mighty grateful that you volunteered your time this way."

Hailey tilted her head ever so slightly. *Volunteered?*

"You're real gems and that's no joke."

"Thank you, sir. I'd like you to meet the rest of my crew." Hailey called Kyra and her brothers and gave introductions.

"Thank you kids for all your hard work. I was able to spend a nice time out west with my daughter and her husband and my wife. I wouldn't have been able to relax nearly as much if I'd have been worried that the church wasn't being kept up."

"We had fun," Grant spoke up.

"Can you show me what all you've been doing?" Ned asked. "I just got here and it seems like I should at least inspect before I leave."

The children walked around the church with Ned and he continued to express his approval. It was almost three when he said his goodbyes to Lane and Chad and gave the children a few more words of appreciation.

Quietly, the children slipped away into their cubby and waited for Lane and Chad to leave for the day.

# Chapter 19

Hailey heard Wade, Janie and Paul enter the choir room through the window. She climbed out of her hiding place and greeted them with Kyra, Hayden and Grant right behind.

"So this has been your home for the past month and a half?" Janie peaked inside.

Hailey nodded. The other teens crawled inside with them, amazed at the amount of space there was under the stage.

Wade reminded them that they needed to get to business. "Hayden and Grant," he spoke to them like men. "I know you want to be out there, but it could be risky. What we need from you more than anything in the world is for you to be in this cubby praying with all your heart that everything goes according to plan and that God protects us all."

The younger boys didn't argue.

"We will call you when it's time to come out. Until that time, don't stop praying."

"Even if you hear yelling," Hailey added. She hated to cause her brothers fear, but she wanted them to understand the seriousness of the situation.

The teens left the younger boys alone and hurried to the foyer. This was where they planned to bring down Mr. Pierce.

Wade brought a pile of attached empty boxes into the church and slid the contraption into the foyer closet. The foyer closet did not have doors, but was a place where coats could be hung on Sunday morning and where boxes were often stored when delivered through the week.

The boxes were opened on the inside and glued together, making them appear to be several boxes stacked on top of one another. From the back, someone could climb inside and watch out of one of the hand holes.

"Janie will be in the box blind." Wade called it. "She has her mother's phone and will video tape from inside." He motioned for her to try out the box. "Can you see out the hole well enough to catch it digitally?" he asked.

"I can." Janie gave a thumbs up through the hole.

"Paul and I will be on the stairwell to the youth room," Wade continued. "I'll have Paul use my mom's phone to video tape from this angle."

"What about me?" Kyra asked.

"You get to use this." Wade handed Kyra a small tape recorder. "This belongs to my journalism teacher. He let me borrow it, so be very careful with it. Mr. Pierce will know that you are here, so you don't really have to hide. In fact, if you can be with your sister initially and then maybe sit behind the welcome center booth as if you're scared of him. That would be great. You can turn on the recorder and get everything he says on tape."

"This is so cool." Kyra held the recorder in her hand as if she was holding some new kind of spyware.

Wade took a few minutes to show her how to use it. "You don't want to hit the wrong button or the little thing will start talking not recording."

Kyra nodded.

"It's getting close to time." Hailey glanced at her watch.

"Let's pray," Paul suggested.

There was anxiety in the air and the teens sought their Lord for help.

\*\*\*

Hailey and Kyra sat behind the welcome center booth waiting for the door to open. It was just eight o'clock.

"Well, glad to see you waiting for me." Bill said as he walked into the dimly lit foyer.

Hailey turned up the light, walked from behind the counter and stood in line with the box blind.

"Do you have it?" Bill asked.

Hailey took a deep steadying breath. "No. I don't have the money."

Bill took a few steps closer to Hailey.

"I couldn't do it. I can't steal money for you. It's wrong." Every nerve in Hailey's body was on edge. She had to say the right things; she had to get Bill to confess to his crime. But she could see the anger in his eyes. "Just because you have no problem

216

stealing money from the church offering, doesn't mean you can blackmail me into doing it."

"I told you this was your last chance."

"It's wrong to steal, Mr. Pierce. God says, 'Thou shalt not steal…'"

"Don't get preachy with me young lady. This is two weeks now, that's four thousand dollars you've robbed me of."

"No, that's four thousand dollars you haven't robbed from the church." Hailey stepped back slightly. Even knowing that Wade and Paul were hiding in the shadows, she feared this man's anger.

He grabbed Hailey's arm and twisted it. "You little punk! I ought to break your skinny little arm."

Hailey clenched her teeth to fight the pain.

"I'm going to make your life miserable. Just wait," he said. "I told you I'll frame Kyra. I'll also make sure Hayden and Grant get thrown into the mix. The whole rotten lot of you foster brats will go to juvenile detention."

"I don't care!" Hailey pulled her arm free. "You've been stealing from this church long enough. Do what you want to me; I'm going to report the whole thing to the police! You deserve to go to jail!"

"And you think the police are going to believe a bunch of run away little orphans who have been hiding out in a church? Ha!"

Before she could back away, Bill smacked Hailey hard across the mouth.

Kyra jumped and dropped the tape recorder. Suddenly it went into play mode.

"You deserve to go to jail!" It played back.

"What the?" Bill stormed behind the counter and pulled Kyra out of the way by her braid. He grabbed the tape recorder and started to laugh.

"You stupid little idiots. You were trying to record me?" Bill slapped the miniature recorder on the counter and smashed it with a nearby stapler.

"No!" Kyra tried to stop him but he shoved her to the floor.

"I'm going home now and I'm calling the police," Bill walked back around the counter and pointed an angry finger in Hailey's face. "I've got everything ready to report my robbery."

He raised his hand, once again, to slap her when Wade yelled from the top of the stairs.

"That's enough!" Wade turned on the upstairs light. "Send it Janie!"

Bill's eyes flashed angrily and he shoved Hailey out of his way to confront Wade.

"You're caught!" Wade stood to his full height and faced the man.

"Why? Because a couple high school teenagers have a broken tape recorder to prove something?"

"Actually, that was my teacher's and you now owe him a new recorder. But it's the videos that are sure to condemn you."

Paul waited for the video to finally send before standing up from behind the stairway and holding up the phone. "Wade's mom should be getting the video right about now."

Bill took a few steps toward Paul and turned around when he heard his voice being replayed from another device.

"Don't get preachy with me young lady. This is two weeks now, that's four thousand dollars you've robbed me of." Janie stepped out from behind her box with a smug grin on her lips. "And now Aunt Kate and Uncle Lane has the video too."

"Give me that phone!" Bill moved toward Janie but she ran toward her brother.

The phone made a quick swishing sound. "That one went to my mom… But Aunt Kate and Uncle Wade should be here soon. I texted them what was going on."

"I just sent one to Chad," Paul called out.

Bill began to walk toward the door. He was clearly out of sorts.

A car pulling up to the doors of the church took him back.

Lane hurried out of the car carrying his shotgun with his wife right behind him.

"I saw the whole thing," Lane aimed his gun at Bill. "Take a seat. The cops are on their way."

"What kind of preacher are you? Coming in here holding me at gunpoint."

218

"Don't talk." Lane narrowed his eyes.

Kate's face was ashen and she ran to Hailey and Kyra. "Are you girls okay? Did he hurt you? I couldn't see much on my phone, but I heard him slap you."

Hailey found herself in Kate's arms while great sobs overtook her. Kate extended an arm to Kyra and the younger girl let herself cry too.

Within minutes, Wade's parents and Paul and Janie's parents showed up, followed by two police cars and the youth pastor.

Wade went to get Hayden and Grant out from under the stage and commended them royally for staying put in the mist of all the action. "I'm so proud of you guys."

***

It was one of the longest nights Hailey could remember, but it wasn't a terrible night.

The children all gave detailed accounts of the evening's events, presented the police with both videos and the broken tape recorder.

Hailey, Kyra and the boys confessed to the police who they were and how they came to be living in Warsaw Chapel for the past month and a half.

Lane and Kate took everything in with total amazement.

"Our social worker's name is Dahlia Cooper. I had her business card but Mr. Pierce stole it. She works in Cleveland."

One of the officers went to the car where Bill was being held to retrieve the business card.

"Do you wish to press charges against the children?" one of the officers asked Lane.

"No… never, of course not." Lane pulled Grant onto his lap. "We love these children. We just had no idea they… they were living here."

"I'm sorry, Lane," Grant apologized.

"Me too." Hayden fidgeted nervously with his sleeve.

Hailey sat beside Kate and Kyra, still shaken with the events of the evening.

"We never meant to deceive you," Hailey turned to Kate and her sister, Anne. "We wanted a place to live… and then we fell in love with you all."

Kyra nodded in agreement.

Wade's mother placed a tender hand on Kyra's shoulder. "Why did you try to catch this man on your own? Why didn't you come to us?"

"Because Bill planned to pin the whole thing on them," Wade explained. "He had enough false evidence to make himself look innocent and them look guilty."

"How was this man a trustee?" Lane shook his head.

Chad placed a reassuring hand on Lane's shoulder. "For what it's worth, I never would have expected it either."

"We've notified your social worker and she will be down tomorrow." One of the officers told Hailey. "Would you like us to keep them at the station?" he asked Lane.

"No!" Kate and Lane said almost in unison.

"You're not worried about them running away?"

Grant clung to Lane. "I'll never leave Lane."

"We do have foster clearance," Kate added.

"We promise not to leave," Hailey said. "We turned ourselves in didn't we?"

The officer gave Hailey an appreciative grin. "And caught a criminal. That took some guts. Let me verify with your social worker that she is okay with it," the policeman dialed Dahlia's number again and explained the situation.

"She approved it."

***

Hailey knew from the position of the sun in the sky that it was late when she finally pulled herself from the comfortable bed in Lane and Kate's guestroom. Kyra was still sound asleep and Hailey decided not to bother her. She fixed her hair quickly in the mirror and said a quick prayer that God would help her with the events of the day.

The boys were already out of bed. Hailey glanced out the window and saw them outside with the puppy. *Poor Hayden and Grant…*

She heard Dahlia's voice before she actually saw the woman. From the sounds echoing through the hallway, her social worker appeared to be having coffee with Kate and Lane.

Hailey's eyes were puffy from tears and lack of sleep, but she sucked in a deep breath and walked into the kitchen.

"Hello, Ms. Cooper."

Dahlia turned from her coffee cup and smiled at Hailey. "My goodness." She stood up and pulled Hailey to her for a hug. "You have had me searching all over Ohio for you."

Hailey couldn't tell if her social worker was angry or happy to see her. Ms. Cooper was not in the habit of hugging her, although it wasn't entirely out of character for her.

"I'm sorry."

"Come, sit down," Kate reached her hand out and lead Hailey to the kitchen table. "I bet you're hungry."

"Not really." Hailey was rarely hungry when she was stressed. How could one eat when their whole world was about to come crashing down on her?

"How about a glass of milk?" Kate walked to the cabinet to pull out a glass.

Hailey accepted the milk and glanced out the window at her brothers.

"Ms. Cooper would like to talk to you alone. Lane and I are going to go outside with the boys."

Hailey nodded. This was it. She would receive her sentence.

Kate wrapped her arms around Hailey's shoulders and gave her a small hug. "If you want a muffin, I made some for the boys earlier."

"Thank you. Maybe later."

Lane and Kate put on their coats and slipped outside to play with the boys.

Dahlia cleared her throat and moved to the chair across from Hailey. "The police gave me the rest of the money for Keith and Tara this morning. They found your envelope in Mr. Pierce's car."

Hailey was glad they'd found it.

"I'm sorry you were so afraid that you would be separated from your brothers that you felt your only option was to run away," Dahlia said. "Tara and Keith should never have made such threats to you."

Hailey tried to swallow back the lump in her throat. "But I'm sure now I'll be taken to juvenile detention."

Dahlia reached her hand across the table and touched Hailey's hand. "You shouldn't have run away, but Sweetie, I see no reason to put you into juvie."

Tears filled Hailey's eyes. She was glad to hear that, but she still hated the thought of returning to Tara and Keith. "What is going to happen to us then?"

Dahlia's full pink lips curved into a smile and her dark eyes twinkled. "Lane and Kate have asked to adopt you, your brothers, and Kyra."

Hailey blinked a few times. Did she hear right?

"Would that suit you?"

Hailey covered her mouth with her hands and the tears spilled out across her face.

Dahlia moved closer and placed a hand on Hailey's shoulder. "That couple loves you children as their own. If you children are comfortable with it, we will begin the paper work immediately."

"I love them. Oh, Ms. Cooper, I love them so much! Of course I want them to adopt us… I just never dared to hope."

Dahlia nodded. "That's what I figured." She leaned back. "They've already gone through everything they need to move forward with an adoption, so I don't think any of this will take very long."

"Do we get to stay with them until its final?" Hailey couldn't bear leaving.

"Absolutely." She smiled. "I still need to talk to Kyra and the boys, and then we can move forward."

"Do you want me to go get Kyra?" Hailey was ready to start this thing moving right away.

"Sure. It's almost noon, I'd say she's slept in long enough."

\*\*\*

Kyra's response was much the same as Hailey's with a bit more jumping up and down. Hayden and Grant were so excited Dahlia could almost not contain them.

With all four children at the table, Dahlia called Lane and Kate into the house to give them the news.

"Well, it looks like these four children love you as much as you love them," she said.

Kate's eyes filled with tears and Lane knelt down to scoop up the two very excited little boys.

In only moments, Hailey and Kyra were wrapped up in a family hug as Lane and Kate embraced all four of the children in a circle.

Dahlia stood back with tears in her own eyes amazed at this miraculous turn of events.

***

## Thanksgiving Day:

Hailey couldn't remember so much excitement on Thanksgiving. Their adoption was final and Hailey, Hayden, Grant and Kyra now honestly bore the last name Evans. She was convinced that choosing that last name when they'd run away was more than a coincidence. God seemed to have His hand on things all along.

Wade and his family stopped by earlier in the day to drop off two homemade apple pies and offer their congratulations. Hailey appreciated Wade's friendship and was glad to finally be able to speak freely with him about her life.

As Hailey prepared to enjoy her first Thanksgiving meal with her adoptive parents, she sat beside her cousin, Janie. Hailey smiled while her brothers told their new grandmother that she should just go ahead and give them the rest of the puppies who hadn't found homes yet.

Helen laughed. "You'd have to talk your parents into that, not me."

Grant leaned over on Kate and smiled up at her.

"Let's stick with one puppy for now." She tussled his hair.

Lane asked the Lord's blessing on their meal and for blessing them with their four new children and one new puppy, emphasizing the word one.

"Just wait till Christmas, you'll get to meet the rest of the cousins," Paul said as he reached for the corn.

Lane passed Hailey the turkey platter. "You children have lots more family to meet. My parents can hardly wait to come up from North Carolina."

"Prepare to be spoiled." Janie patted Hailey's shoulder.

"I already am." Hailey beamed. "I am so blessed."

Kyra grabbed Kate's hand. "We all are."

"Guess the Church Mice Kids will have to have new adventures with their parents now." Hailey glanced at Kyra.

Kyra agreed. "I was thinking about an adventure where God uses them and their new friends and family to start telling others about Jesus and all He did for them."

Hailey liked that idea. Her brown eyes sparkled joyfully and her smile lit up her entire face. "And that adventure will never end."

Made in the USA
Charleston, SC
17 July 2013